Guy Slater is a writer, theatre and TV director, and producer of many long-running TV drama series, including *Miss Marple*, starring Joan Hickson, and *Love Hurts*, starring Zoe Wanamaker and Adam Faith. He founded and ran the Horseshoe Theatre Company at the Haymarket Theatre in Basingstoke and on tour, and has written over twenty TV dramas, seven radio dramas, four stage plays and has published five books. He knows Cuba – the setting for *Hurricane Maggie* – well, having first visited it when his father was the British Ambassador in Havana.

D1386460

To the memory of my parents, Dick and Barbara, who introduced me to Cuba. Also, to the many friends I made there over the years, I wish them well as they struggle to bring their beautiful country forward.

Guy Slater

HURRICANE MAGGIE

AUSTIN MACAULEY PUBLISHERS™

LONDON · CAMBRIDGE · NEW YORK · SHARJAH

A CIP catalogue record for this title is available from the British Library.

ISBN 9781528985772 (Paperback)
ISBN 9781528985789 (ePub e-book)

www.austinmacauley.com

First Published (2021)
Austin Macauley Publishers Ltd
25 Canada Square
Canary Wharf
London
E14 5LQ

Grateful thanks for advice and encouragement in the long development of *Hurricane Maggie* to Professor Liz Carlin, Dr Luis Sacerio, Atiha Sengupta, Caroline Courtauld and my agent, Diana Tyler.

<u>Gloria</u>

She was a silhouette only ... The sun, hot, bright through the bars. A yacht, I thought. A tall elegant yacht, mysterious, sailing past us little pirates. Then out of the sun and I could see her face. Beautiful and sad. No, not beautiful maybe, but strong. Like a man. But woman. Yes. And, yes, sad. I thought – Russian?

Why Russian?

Eyes deep in her head? Dressed in black. Anna Karenina. How I think of Anna Karenina. I don't know why.

This was the first time you had seen her?

The first time. In her hand her plate of rice and beans, her spoon, her glass of water. A beautiful yacht, sailing past us ... sailing to some other country.

Did you speak to her?

She looked for an empty table. She found it. She sat. The plate – so. The spoon – so. The glass – so. She looked at nobody.

I watched her, all the time I watched her. Who is this woman? Proud, secret, looking at her food only. One little spoon of rice. One more little spoon. So. An obligation.

I must know her, I thought.

I picked up my plate, my spoon, my glass. The women at my table laughed. They had been watching me, watching her. They thought they knew me. They didn't.

I walked over to her. I was nervous, my heart beating fast, fast. I stood by her. She did not look up, but she knew I was there.

I am not a polite person. With her I was polite.

"Podria sentarme con usted?"

Now she looked at me. Had she understood? Did she speak Spanish? I pointed to the chair beside her. Now she smiled. She looked tired, her skin pale. But her smile so beautiful.

She moved her plate, her chair, to make space.

"I am sorry, I don't speak much Spanish." North American.

Not Anna Karenina?

Not. I sat. My heart was still beating in my chest. I was frightened that maybe I was blushing. I never blush. I felt small beside her.

Now I spoke in English.

"My name is Gloria."

"Maggie Barrington."

9

"Why are you in here?"

She look away. Then she look at me again, her eyes into my eyes, and she told me.

[TRANSLATED FROM GLORIA VARGAS WITNESS STATEMENT]

Chapter 1

I've been staring for I don't know how long at the pad Gloria brought me. The paper is yellowy and rough and crumbly looking. I have no idea how she got hold of it and I don't ask. Paper AND pencils. Gloria is from Venezuela and has become my friend. Very important. I'm not sure how I would cope without her. But with her I am fine. Being here, as I am sure you will understand, is not quite what I had expected from my life. It should all be terrifying but just at the moment I sort of don't believe in it, although it is real enough. All part of this journey I seem to have set out on. What I am trying to say is – don't worry about me. The awful thing is I don't know what you are thinking or feeling. You may not be worrying at all. It is very strange and I cannot say I like it.

Gloria has been pushing me to write to you. She marched in, an hour, two hours ago, slammed the pad and pencils down and said, "Do it! Write to them. Now. Tell your boys the truth." She is definitely bossy.

So I have been staring at the paper and wondering how. Can I? Should I? I stare some more. So hard. The problem with us, the family we were, with this whole *mess* may just be this. Communicating. I have sometimes been told that I am 'cold'. Or 'reserved'. The cold heart that goes with the cool legal brain. All nonsense, really. Wasn't always good at showing my emotions, that I accept. Being born British? A cliché but perhaps true for me. Oh, and childhood, I guess. Of course childhood, always childhood. But if I ever seemed cold to you, I regret it deeply. I was never 'cold' on the inside. And certainly not now, writing to you.

The fact is, whatever I try to tell myself, I am very frightened. Not so much because of this place but because of us. I don't know who you are now, what I am to you. Am I to be your mother? In which case I should keep it light, not load too much on to you both. Or am I your supplicant begging forgiveness and understanding? Either way, please remember, both of you, that whatever I say in this – if I ever finish it – I am doing it because I love you and am so desperately sad about how I have failed you, and I want more than anything – more even than leaving here – to put it right.

"Tell the truth," she says. Tough one. Do sons want to know the truth about their mothers? Particularly this mother. Assuming, of course, she is clear what the 'truth' really is.

If anyone had ever asked me, I would have said with some confidence that we were – mostly – a happy family and that I was a good mother. Well, an OK mother. Obviously, I wasn't, and I am sad about that. More than sad. Ashamed, angry with myself. When your father and I broke up and you decided to live with him I was hurt. I tried not to show you, of course. I guess I thought most of it – maybe all of it – was my fault. I know I had become more and more grumpy. And impatient. I was working long hours, keeping the show on the road. I got tired. I was used to moving much faster than any of you and if I thought you were all sitting on your asses, I let you know. I dare say you deserved it but I wish I hadn't now.

Anyway there was a lot of hurt flying around at that time and I told myself that it was perhaps a 'guy thing' and that boys, young men as you are now, would prefer to be with their father, that you three had always hung out while I was at work so this was probably a good thing, a sensible thing. So I dug in.

You know, I am sure, what I am accused of. And I am sure you know I don't deny it. As the words gather at the end of my pencil, they're so ugly I can't write them down. It's a bizarre experience. I have been trying and my hand just won't make the letters. Not to my sons. But what I need you to understand is that what actually happened, the truth, *my* truth, doesn't feel ugly. It would have a few months ago. It would have been literally unimaginable. But that was on the other planet and it doesn't now. Now I think if I am going to earn your love, I need to tell you the whole truth. And risk the consequences.

Okay. The beginning of my journey to the truth must be to confess to having lied to you all your lives.

I have always told you that my father, your grandfather, was a British businessman who died when I was 15 and still at school in England. I told your father the same thing. I had almost come to believe it myself. Granny, Auntie Poppy and I were all quite happy to believe he was dead so it wasn't hard. And Rupert wasn't his name – it seems so bizarre all this now! – but he was actually quite famous and some news clipping might have come up or you might have wanted to google him or something. But, hey, he was British and dead and you never seemed interested.

Your grandfather didn't die when I was 15. He defected to Cuba. He wasn't Rupert Harris, businessman, he was Bernard Harris international concert pianist. And a Communist. Cuba under Castro was apparently his idea of Shangri-La. Oh yes, and he took a large chunk of the money my mother had inherited with him. Perhaps you can see why I didn't mind killing him off when I came to America.

In fact, I dreamed for years of literally killing him – strangling, poisoning, shooting, dousing in gasoline and carefully lighting the match while he screamed in terror. That didn't happen at once, of course. The initial response was the usual bewilderment and utter disbelief. But then – and I can't remember how quickly this happened – a great granite block of unmoveable, undiluted hatred took hold of me, becoming as much part of who I was as laughter or breathing or thought. I hated my father. Just that. I hated him most, of course, because he had deserted me. He had walked out, turned his back on his oldest daughter without a word. Of anything. Of explanation. Of farewell. And certainly not of love. But I also learned quickly to hate him for being a thief, a womaniser and a bully. And, almost worst of all, for being a Communist. That makes me smile now.

So there it is. All your lives you have had a Communist Grandfather living in Cuba. Which is, of course, why I am currently where I am.

You ought to know a bit about your Grandpa Bernard. I've given you the headlines so you won't be surprised that he was a roller coaster of a father. He was the son of a Yorkshire miner who was born with an amazing talent, which – miraculously, given his background – was not only spotted but also nurtured. He became, as I learned when I found an album of newspaper cuttings that my mother thought she had thrown out, a sort of boy wonder emblem of Seventies' Britain, a "rent-a-quote neo-Marxist" one bitchy columnist called him, fodder for both broadsheets and tabloids and of course the early days of television, gaining even more in newsworthiness when this working class Socialist prodigy – to gleeful charges of hypocrisy – married your grandmother the Honourable Lois de L'Isle, daughter of the Lord Lieutenant of Surrey.

My father – socialist and hypocrite. I have no doubt that he was the main reason I wanted to turn my back firmly on the country of my birth and come to College in New York. My father had always lambasted America. Now I decided I wanted an end to pessimism, rainy days, strikes and socialism. I wanted to be a good optimistic American. Without a father.

I don't want you to get the idea that our childhood was all bad. He was away a lot, for a start, on tour – or fornicating as Granny later told me. And when he did come home it was often exciting one way or another. Lots of presents. And hugs. He was good on hugs. And of course, screaming matches. Well, he screamed, my mother cried. What those two were doing getting married I have no idea. I think she had fallen hopelessly in love, poor woman. He was very good looking, a tornado of energy, talented, famous, lots of money (mostly hers). Women were apparently never in short supply. I used to think he had married her because he wanted to sleep with the enemy. But she always said he loved her once, and maybe he did. Didn't see much evidence of it at the time. Boy, the mouth he had! Firing off opinions like cannon balls. My poor mother decided it was best just not to respond. So after a while I started answering back for her and your then teenage mother and your Grandpa Bernard had some wonderful shouting matches while Auntie Poppy and Granny crept out of the room. He seemed to enjoy that.

But – particularly when he wasn't there, crashing around and barking orders – I remember it as a nice childhood. We had a lovely place in a county called Surrey. The house had a long drive and pillars along the front terrace, a bit like the White House only a lot smaller, of course, and horses and Range Rovers – all the things that any self-respecting Marxist would think essential. We even went to boarding school! Very Harry Potter – and certainly not politically correct for a card carrying Socialist. His one concession was that it should be 'progressive' which meant that it was coeducational (unusual in England then) and we called the teachers by their first names and held councils at which we discussed school policy and made recommendations, which were then ignored.

I was at school when the news came through. Of course I refused to believe it at first. There had been – at least as far as your Auntie Poppy and I were aware

– absolutely no warning. I had not the slightest idea that anything was even troubling him. He had groaned and crashed around since I could remember. I knew he had been to Cuba the year before on a concert tour and used to go on to anybody who would listen about how fantastic the health system, the education, the values and so on were, how Fidel Castro – second of course to Ludwig Van Beethoven – was his hero, but I didn't pay any attention. I don't think any of us did. Now, of course, I can see that his marriage, his whole life style must have been a desperate and even shameful compromise. But so what? He'd chosen to marry money and class, he lived like a squire. No one else was to blame. Certainly not his wife or two daughters.

Anyway, Andy, the Headmaster (Principal to you) called Poppy and me in one evening. Granny had rung him. Your grandfather (it is making me shiver even now as I remember it, Andy at his desk, us two on the sofa, the room smelling of strawberry jam) had told her in the morning, and flown from Heathrow the same afternoon with one suitcase mostly, I imagine, stuffed with a small fortune in notes – all belonging to her. He left a message for his agent cancelling all UK and American concert bookings. They were stacked up for the next three years. The press, of course, got hold of it and it was going to be in the papers the next day and Granny wanted us to be warned. Andy said she sounded bad and she didn't want us to see her in this state. It was good that we were warned. Somehow or other the whole school seemed to know by breakfast the following morning. Front page in many of the newspapers. All with photographs. One, I remember, called him a traitor. I totally agreed.

It's all a bit vague after that. Granny didn't cope well – particularly when she discovered he'd stolen from her. It seemed a cruelty beyond anything I could ever have imagined of him. Of anybody. Off the scale. Poppy got over it before too long, or seemed to. For me the pain and the anger, perhaps foolishly, took over my life for far too long.

It was in America I found hope and energy – a fizzy drink on a hot day – and it blasted away all my father's toxic bullshit.

And then, after a while, I met a shy architecture graduate called Marty and before long I married him. And the following year you were born, Tommy. And the year after, you Billy. All nice and neat and happy. Except we had no money. Who knows why your father wasn't getting hired? Not assertive enough? Too impractical? That snafu over the Hoboken pier? Just unlucky? Anyway – we were broke and somebody had to fix it. Granny paid for me to go to Law School. I graduated well and for the next 20 years went to work, often seven days a week, becoming senior partner two years ago. Seven days and usually upwards of 10 hours a day. So I wasn't really there for you, was I? Not the way Moms are supposed to be. And I was often tired and grumpy. Well, it can't be rewritten, however much I might wish it. At the time, I'll be honest, I was pleased with myself. Why not? I watched you growing up – from afar, maybe – and thought what a good job Marty and I were doing. Marty and Maggie, parents to Tommy and Billy. A good firm. I got pleasure from paying for the house – your faces when you saw the size of it! – the beach apartment, the vacations. I got pleasure from continuing to be a major contributor to the Republicans, despite the mess the Bush family made of it all, pleasure from the fact that John McCain showed up at my birthday party. Your father and I weren't Romeo and Juliet any more, but who is after a quarter of a century?

Was that me being 'cold'? I thought I was just doing what I had to do to keep you, your father, all of us on the road. I used to see other Moms high fiving their kids when they collected them after school or from parties and I knew I wasn't like them. I know some people thought I wasn't very 'feminine' whatever that means. If it means 'girly', I am fine with that. But I was happy – proud – to be a woman and I never thought of myself a bad Mom. I was doing a job – I was bringing home the bacon.

So as far as I was concerned, we were trundling along fine until the day your father broke it to me – very gently – that he was leaving me for someone called Barbara. And I was being deserted again. I was back in the headmaster's study with the smell of strawberry jam.

And when you two said you would like to live with him, I started asking myself – not surprisingly you may agree – why the men in my life walked out on me.

I admit I fell apart for a while. You saw some of it. I wasn't proud of myself. I knew of course that father-leaving-child, and husband-leaving-wife are not the same thing. But I couldn't help the two tumbling over each other in my overheated mind, round and round, like sneakers in a dryer. Always I came back to the same place. On both occasions I never saw it coming. Playing happily in the countryside and somehow, I'd stepped on a mine. What was next? What else was about to explode in my face that I ought to be able to foresee? Surely with Marty I should have seen some kind of sign? Boredom, restlessness? Absence even. How did he manage it? Where did they meet? Nothing, not a clue. Should have set bells ringing but it didn't.

What had I done to get it so very wrong?

That's the question that I foolishly allowed myself to be tortured by, because I was being weak and I was never supposed to be weak, not me – the question that came looping back endlessly, futile of course, easy to see now, but so painful then, as painful as it had been when my father left, that terrible cry of childhood – what did I do wrong? Daddy why did you leave me?

A week, maybe two, after you all moved out your father called one night to collect some stuff. I'd forgotten he was coming and had to wave away the cigarette smoke as I let him in. I had started again, only one, two a day. I wasn't proud of myself about that either.

I asked him, "What did I do wrong, Marty?"

"Nothing," he said. "You were wonderful. A rock. Perfect. So perfect there was no room for me."

"I got impatient. Yelled at you. I wish I hadn't."

"You had a lot on your plate. And I guess I was pretty maddening."

He was still being nice, of course, because that's what he is. But I sort of understood what he was getting at. Not that I was perfect, far from it, but that maybe I sucked all the oxygen. Is that what you felt? Was that what I did wrong?

As it happened, I was playing one of your Grandpa Bernard's records, a vinyl I discovered I had kept. Beethoven's 'Emperor'.

"Never heard you play that before," he said. "Nice."

And he left, carrying his racquet and sneakers.

I still didn't tell him about my father.

After he had gone, I put the record on again and listened to the music he had made thirty-five years ago. I remembered him telling me that the 'Emperor' scared him. I was learning piano at the time and I could not imagine that anything could scare him. Listening to it now, picturing his fingers skipping with astonishing speed across the keyboard I understood only too well. I looked at his young face on the record sleeve just as I used to know him and wondered how he would look now as an old man and whether he was still alive.

Why had he done it? Why had he left a family, a lovely home, fame, money, a successful career to go and live in an impoverished, brutal Marxist police state? Why had he left *me* for that?

It must have been several weeks afterwards that Howard copied me into his email reply to someone called Carlos Ruiz. A Cuban-American. I decided to sit in on the meeting.

Smartly dressed, Ruiz was quietly spoken, no trace of an accent, with a shy smile I didn't trust at all.

"For my father, Castro was a usurper who took away our business, our home, our way of life. But that was over half a century ago and my father is dead. I have no agenda, no vendetta. What is more –" that smile, "I live in New York, not Miami." So not one of 'them', he was telling us. I wondered just how popular he was with his compatriots. "This is a business opportunity, no more."

"What kind of business, Mr Ruiz?" asked Howard. He was sitting at the far end of the long table, the light from the window reflected in the gleaming mahogany space between them.

"I've only seen photographs, of course, I've never been to Cuba but our house, Casa Nueva – it has been the 'new house' for 200 years you understand – is large and very beautiful. Spanish Colonial, classical pillars, statues, formal garden, you know the sort of thing. It may well be falling apart, now. My one remaining cousin in Havana is getting old and hasn't been to see it for some years. But I have little doubt that it could brush up quite nicely as, I don't know, a hotel, golf club, maybe a fat farm. Depends on what market is going to emerge. Mister Obama clearly wants things to change between Cuba and the United States. That may be a good thing or it may not. But my guess is there is going to be a market and I want to get in early. It won't be easy. Private property has always been a hornet's nest there since Castro and nobody really understands it. But I want to try. My cousin told me he heard that there was a move to appropriate Casa Nueva as a Music Academy at one time."

I remember scribbling on my pad 'Music Academy'. I don't know why. I took very few notes.

"There may be other plans hatching. I want to try and make sure that what was in my family for over a century is still ours today."

"You have title deeds?"

"Copies," Ruiz replied. He took them out of his brief case and slid them confidently along the table to Howard. I watched, the observer, as Howard glanced through them.

"You'll bring me back my Casa Nueva?" Ruiz, as ever, was smiling. His voice was almost a whisper.

Howard saw him out. By the time he came back into the conference room I had made up my mind.

"Shall we put Luis onto it?" he suggested. "Or Phillip? His Spanish isn't as good, obviously but he's a fine old ferret. Do you think the Fed will give us clearance or should we route him through Mexico?"

"Howard, I think I'll handle this one."

"What do you mean?"

"I mean that I will do it. I'll go to Havana."

His expression. I almost laughed.

"Why for God's sake?"

"It interests me." I thought, for a moment, of telling him. We had worked together for over ten years. I trusted him as I trusted nobody else. But it had been a secret too long.

"Don't you think... A Spanish speaker...?"

"I'll manage. My dual citizenship, UK passport might help."

His expression changed. He knew me well enough.

"Well, OK. Maybe a break, change of scenery would be in order right now."

I wasn't having that. No one was going to think that just because my husband had walked out on me, I would need a trip to the Caribbean as solace.

"That's got nothing to do with it. I'm fine."

I was lying, of course.

He shuffled papers and got to his feet.

"You be careful, now. They lock you up I'm out of a job."

Ha.

HOWARD

Would you tell me something about your relationship with Mrs Barrington? How long have you known her?

Okay... Let me see... I think I joined the partnership ten, maybe eleven years ago. Yes, eleven years.

And your relationship with her was good?

Yes. Well, yes... Look I am not sure how much validity anything from me really has in this instance. As a colleague. And maybe even as a lawyer. But, hey, we have put it in your hands and I guess it is up to you to decide how much weight you want to afford it. And the Attorney General, of course. Or whoever is going to...negotiate. Do you know yet who ...?

Not yet.

OK. Anyway – as far as that is concerned, we always had a very good professional relationship.

Purely professional? Did you meet socially?

Oh well, yes, my wife and I used to have dinner with Maggie and Marty occasionally. Yes, we socialised to that extent.

So you could say you knew her well?

Oh, absolutely. Oh yes. That's why it was so incredible. I mean... well, that's it. Incredible. I guess as a lawyer you start to think nothing about human behaviour will surprise you. But this... I gather she is not denying charges... Hell, when I heard I just didn't believe it. Not credible. Period. It isn't possible. There must be something else. Something behind it, that we don't know. This could not be Maggie. Period.

Why not?

Oh... Gosh... Gosh, gosh, gosh. I suppose you would have called her in every way a decent, conventional woman. Tough. Immensely hard working. Dependable. Honourable.

A good lawyer?

Impeccable. Left nothing to chance. Always fair minded. A thoroughly collegiate senior partner whom all of us who worked with her respected. You could trust her to deliver and she would. That's why people came to us. She is – was – the secret of our success. I mean, sometimes I thought she was overdoing it. Sometimes felt she worked too hard, if you know what I mean. Felt she could lighten up. I don't mean she had no sense of humour. She had. A bit British, perhaps. A little ironical if you follow me. But I did sometimes feel she was driven, you know? Maybe it would have helped to lighten up. Might have helped her marriage. And, by Golly, that was hard enough to swallow, when those two

18

broke up. But this ... this ... shit.... That's not very lawyerly, I know, but that's how I feel. Still totally and utterly incredible.

[FROM HOWARD WISEMAN WITNESS STATEMENT]

Chapter 2

And neither of you were too impressed when I told you my plans, were you?

"They hate America, because we have elections and stuff," was your analysis, I remember, Billy. "Send somebody else. What's the point of being boss if you can't send somebody to do the crappy jobs?"

Well, now you know. I had decided to find my father.

I want you to imagine a warm Caribbean evening, the sun dipping red behind the Gulf of Mexico. I was standing on the promontory at the edge of the hotel garden watching the sea break on the thick wall along the side of the Malecon, the broad sea-front road below. At my feet was an old cannon facing across the water to Miami. Every so often the spray hung in the air, sailed gently across the road and misted my skin.

I hope one day, if things work out – no, *when* things work out – you will both be able to get to Cuba. My first impression of it was a big surprise. I think I had expected something halfway between an open prison and a shanty town – run down airport, potholed roads, ancient cars without bumpers, fearful, stressed-out looking people. Some of that is certainly there as I was to discover but I saw little of it the first day. The airport is modern, the architecture a little Stalinist perhaps, but generally glass fronted, gleaming and purposeful like airports all over the world, though the Immigration line is perhaps even slower than JFK. An efficient taxi sped me along wide grass lined avenues to my hotel the Nacional, which is about as grand as any hotel that I have ever stayed in, a monumental building, testament to the vast wealth of pre-Revolutionary Cuba. A maracas-and-guitar-wielding trio in gaucho costumes and big smiles greet the guests in the shade of the enormous drive-in portico. Inside are wide, softly lit corridors, a book shop, long wooden bars stacked with glasses prepared for *mojitos* with slices of lime already skewered on the rim, and deep, pillared terraces with rattan recliners, looking out onto elegant gardens with palm trees, and sandy pathways cutting between swathes of thick, springy grass. I knew, in theory, that tourism had saved the Cuban economy, but the images indelibly fixed in my mind were of dogs scavenging in the streets, poverty and repression. Certainly not the Hotel Nacional.

After checking in to my room (large, wood panelled, air conditioning, you could get CNN but not Fox) and taking a shower I headed for the gardens to breathe in the warm air and watch the sun set across the sea. At the far end just beyond the cannons a rock escarpment drops away down to the Malecon where kids in vests and shorts dodge in and out of the sea spray that cools them, rusts the cars and makes the beautiful old building crumble.

It is a glorious sight and I really hope one day you will get out here.

I was feeling good. I had made a choice, taken action. Here I was in the belly of the beast on a twofold mission – firstly to restore justice to an individual who had been dispossessed by a tyrannical regime, and secondly (OK, maybe firstly) to trace my father and put him on trial for crimes against his family. Justice. And vengeance.

I had taken out a cigarette and was putting it to my mouth when I saw him. I don't think I have ever thought of a man as 'beautiful' before. This one was. Quite shockingly so. And I don't mean 'sexy' whatever that implies. He was just beautiful. In his late twenties I guessed, astonishing coffee coloured skin, warm, smiling eyes, perfectly proportioned mouth, nose, jaw. Feminine in a way. Maybe that's why he seemed beautiful. And his hair. Dark, curly and coming down – I am trying to avoid the word 'tumbling' – over his right eye. A Caravaggio painting.

And tall. By which I mean taller than me. I don't know if you guys have been aware of it (I've usually tried to keep that kind of silly nonsense to myself) but I have always been a little self-conscious about my height. At 5'10 ½" and wearing any kind of heel – as I was then – I find myself all too often looming over the men I meet. Part of not being considered 'feminine' I dare say. I hated it when I was young, feeling gawky and awkward and although I've more or less got used to it now I have always preferred taller men. Like your father. And now this Caravaggio painting.

I don't know if I stared at him. Knowing me I probably didn't. But the moment seemed to hang in the air.

Not only was he beautiful, but somehow *familiar*. We couldn't possibly have met before. And yet. That seen-on-the-TV feeling. I know, I know. You'll just have to take my word.

Instinctively, I put the cigarette back in the pack. His smile broadened.

"Is good," he said. "Not smoking is good."

"You caught me. I am trying to give up."

"You American?"

I nodded, bracing myself for the attack.

"Good. Thank you for visiting us. We like it when Americans visit."

"Ah… OK."

"Your first time in Cuba?"

"Yes."

"I have seen you before, I think."

This took my legs away. Just what I was thinking about you, I wanted to say. I reached for the low wall surrounding the cannon and sat down.

"I don't think that's possible," I said.

"You an actress?"

I started to laugh. This was much easier.

"God no!"

"Angie Moore. You remind me of Angie Moore!"

I laughed even more. He started to laugh with me.

"No… No… You look like Angie Moore… Beautiful like her… Yes…"

Now, your mother is not used to being picked up. And certainly not used to being called beautiful. I have always known that my face can look rather severe, sometimes disapproving, even when I don't want it to. 'Handsome' is the kinder word when people are struggling for something to say. On the rare occasions when 'beautiful' has been used I have, of course, never believed it. Only 'feminine' women are allowed to be beautiful. But I knew what was happening here. And I quite enjoyed it. He was smiling, relaxed. But enough was enough. I got up to go.

"No please… You like tour guide round Havana?"

So that was it. Not that kind of pick up. I was a bit disappointed.

"I like very much to take you."

"That's very kind, but no thanks."

He nodded, smiling. He looked sad. Clever actor, I decided. Very professional. But I smiled back and returned to the hotel, hardly giving the beautiful young man another thought.

RAUL

You worked regularly at the Hotel Nacional?
No regular work. Not possible.
So where else?
Else?
Where else did you work?
Hotels.
Doing what?
Tour guide, why not?
Did you do other things?
Why not? Tattoos. I learn to give tattoos. Yes. I buy, I sell. Anything. Coconut oil, chocolate. Buckets. Fridges. Jobs. People.
People?
Of course.
For sex?
Sometimes. Why not? Also – drivers, musicians, clothes, people who make clothes. Translator. Anything. If it pays. Why you look like that? I was a trained teacher. I make $20.00 a month. You live on $20.00 a month? I do anything. Actor, sometimes. Yes. And musician. I play in club. But – tour guide, yes, mostly.
And mostly at the Nacional?
Richest people.
Just 'tour guide'?
I don't understand.
Sex. Did tourists pay you to have sex with them?
Why you talk about sex all the time? Of course sometimes sex. Why not? They want, they pay. Not big deal. Always with condom. I want to live.
The management at the Nacional – did they know about this?
Why must they ask?
Do they allow just anybody to be a 'tour guide'?
Of course not! Only few. Clean, speak English, Italian, German, maybe Dutch. Know Havana. Polite. Very few. And must have friends.
Friends?
Reception Manager. Clerk, maybe. Chef, I don't know.
Let's talk about Mrs Barrington.
OK.
That first time – you followed her? Why her?
I had just started work. She was the first I saw.
That's the reason? She was the first you saw?

23

Why not? She was by herself. She looked rich.

Were you attracted to her? Did you think she was beautiful?

Beautiful? …. No…. Yes. She didn't think she was. Serious face. Face of important person. Tight, you know? Closed. Like an oyster. And inside – the pearl. I liked that.

So you followed her into the garden. And?

No 'and'. We talked. A little. I told her she looked like Angie Moore.

Did she like that?

She laughed. The serious face laughed. We both laughed.

Did you really think she looked like Angie Moore?

Maybe a little. Maybe not …

Go on.

What 'go on'?

I thought you were going to say something.

(Pause)

She looked… like I had seen her before. Like film… or photo… in magazine… somewhere in my life…. Not a friend, of course not, but … like a friend… is hard to explain…

[FROM RAUL VENTURA WITNESS STATEMENT (1)]

Chapter 3

The practicalities of tracing somebody in a large city like Havana are harder than you might think. That little dot on the map miles away where you assume you will probably bump into your father on the streets turns out to be a vast anonymous sprawling mass. Police forces, I assume, have methods not open to the rest of us. Certainly not open to inquisitive foreigners from an 'enemy' country.

Under the assumption that your grandpa had not changed his name, my first, and most obvious, move was the telephone book which, surprisingly, had three numbers listed under people called Harris. I decide to wait until I – and, hopefully, whoever I was calling – had eaten. Pork had been the main offering on the Room Service menu and since neither of you liked pork so we never had it that's what I went for. Despite Cuba's reputation for indifferent food it wasn't bad.

Then the phone. First of all, I rang you and we had one of those OK conversations about nothing, which depressed me. Do you remember? Anyway. To my surprise there were three Harris' listed in the phone book. None of them, however, spoke English and as I speak – or spoke – very little Spanish we were struggling. What was evident was that none of them knew of a 'Bernard'. Or admitted to it.

I slept badly feeling absurdly sorry for myself.

The following morning, I was due to meet Abdel a lawyer we had found to guide me around Cuban property law but he sent a message saying he was stuck in Camaguey and his flight would be late into Havana and would therefore not get to the Nacional until 2.30.

So I was free to spend the morning looking for my curmudgeonly old father in the Havana haystack. Assuming he was still alive.

I did have one clue. To my surprise – and, to some extent, anger – he had always sent us birthday cards for several years after he decamped. The last that I could remember had been for my 21st birthday. It had an address inside with an invitation to write or even visit – which had made me even angrier. I had found it when I was rooting around in his old vinyls.

I joined the short line to speak to the Chief Receptionist. His chiselled good looks, grey hair and measured calm should surely have destined him to be an Airline Pilot. Later when I got to know him a little, I told him and he smiled and bowed – in a calm and measured manner. It was hard to think of him as a tool of a Police State but no doubt he was noting this American woman's comings and goings, just as some tired old tape, whirring away in the ceiling of her bedroom, was recording her telephone calls to her business colleagues and her sons and her night time breathing, snuffling and snoring.

I asked him if he could recommend a driver. I had barely finished my sentence when Miguel was at my side. I had no idea where he had come from. Miguel, black, serious, clean cut, freshly ironed, turned out to be, thank goodness, not a charmer like the Caravaggio beauty I had met the previous evening. Miguel peered at the fading ink on my birthday card. He showed it to the Chief Receptionist. They peered together, conferred, and finally seemed to agree on what it probably said.

Miguel led me to his car, a brown Nissan, not by any means new – the passenger door handle needed to be finessed to open and shut – but not quite the rust heap of Cuban legend.

I think I was still expecting the Havana suburbs to be a collection of shantytowns with pigs and chickens in the street. What I got was wide, graceful, tree lined avenues with grass verges, bougainvillea, mariposa, pretty Spanish houses, some areas of plaster a little in need of attention, maybe a new coat of paint would have been good, but for the most part lovingly looked after, residential streets of the kind found in old Californian towns. Miguel told me the district was called Miramar but I still couldn't decipher even that from my father's faded scribble. Occasional national flags fluttered from roof tops of houses where bored looking armed guards stood at the gates suggesting we were in Embassy territory. Clearly the old bastard had once lived in upmarket Havana. And still did?

What would I say to him if I found him? What did I want from him? Just to tell him that I hated him, that he had behaved shamefully? To find out why he had done it? To learn who he was, who my father was? Why do my men leave me? I realised as I sat in the back of Miguel's Nissan peering through the window that he was perhaps going to open a door for me into territory that I hadn't fully prepared myself for. I realised I was frightened. And I hadn't expected that. I told myself not to be stupid, there was no need for fear. It was over thirty years ago, we both had to take responsibility. When I had him in front of me, I would know how to handle it.

The house that Miguel stopped at looked far from upmarket. It stood out in the street like a rotten tooth. It was large and probably once imposing but was now cold and lifeless, the garden overgrown, the windows shuttered, soggy cardboard cartons on the front steps. Miguel peered again at the writing on my birthday card, rechecked the street sign and nodded.

As I pushed open the little wooden gate one hinge came out of the rotting wood making the gate slump drunkenly. Though reason told me the house was clearly empty my heart was hammering as I picked my way past dead gladioli and dahlias, and a few stubborn wilting roses, through the mushy cartons and knocked on the door. The sound echoed inside. No footsteps, no movement answered. I tried again. Still that echoing silence.

I levered myself cautiously up on a loose pile of stones that had once been part of an ornate little curved garden wall outside the front windows. I peered through what gaps I could find in the shuttering. All I could see were bare floorboards reflecting a stream of sunlight coming from somewhere. Empty walls, empty floors.

Movement from the window of the adjoining house – neatly painted, ablaze with mariposa – caught my eye. As I swivelled to look, whoever it was ducked out of sight.

I went back out onto the road. Miguel sat in the car, the driver's door open, his head tactfully down in a newspaper. I turned in at the neighbour's ornate tiled pathway and knocked on the door. Silence. I knocked again, making it clear I was not going away. Finally, I heard shuffling and a plump middle-aged woman with greying hair swept back in a bun, wearing slippers and a stained apron opened the door. She was sweating. She kept her eyes down, wiping her hands on her apron, clearly not wanting to look at me.

"*Por favor…*" I began. I was struggling. "Bernard Harris?" I pointed at the empty house. She shook her head quickly and went to close the door.

"*Mi padre,*" I said, holding it open firmly.

Now she looked at me. It was hard to tell if there was sadness in her eyes or anger. Was he dead? Or did she hate him? She certainly knew him.

"*Lo siento,*" she said quietly and pushed the door shut. I'm sorry.

I was sitting in the back of the car wondering what to do next with Miguel in the front, his head still down in the paper – as though he regularly took overwrought American women around Havana in search of missing fathers – when the neighbour's door opened again and this time a portly grey haired man came out, also wearing slippers. He was smoking a cigar and had a piece of paper in his hand. He hurried towards the car, glancing around discreetly to see if he was being watched.

As he arrived at the car he leaned in the window, thrust the scrap of paper at me and hurried away leaving the inside of the car smelling of cigar smoke. The paper had three largely illegible words scribbled on it in pencil. They meant nothing to me. I passed it over to Miguel. His eyebrows lifted.

"Musicians' Union," he said.

We retraced our steps to Central Havana. Having manoeuvred into a tight parking space, Miguel pointed across the road at an anonymous looking building with a glass door. '*Syndicato de Musicos*' was stencilled on it in gold lettering. The street was busy not only with cars and buses but bicycles – mostly old and upright – as well as bicycle-rickshaws and ponies and traps for tourists, motorised tricycles in egg-shaped cocoons; and people, lots of people, black, white and coffee coloured like the beautiful young man (only none so beautiful). Ample women in figure hugging lycra licked ice creams and laughed at obviously sexually loaded remarks thrown at them from lazily smiling, confident young men sitting on low walls. I felt not only ungainly but very much a foreigner. My dress was sticking to me in the heat.

I could hear an accordion playing from inside the building. I pushed the door open, glad to be coming in off the street, out of the stifling air and the high, hot sun. The door led straight into a large gloomy room, full of people and cigarette smoke. Some sat on plastic chairs reading newspapers or tattered magazines. One was restringing a violin. A thin, heavily lined grey-haired man was quietly teaching a younger man some guitar chords. The accordionist was nowhere to be seen. I noticed only two women, both black. Mostly the room was occupied by a long line of people waiting patiently for a man who ignored them, sitting behind a large trestle table stamping forms, occasionally checking something on the desk top computer in front of him. Behind him, on the wall, in fading blue paint was written '*Viva La Revolucion Siempre!*'. Either side of the slogan were the now familiar paintings of Che and Fidel, also fading.

The air of resignation that seemed to hang over everybody changed as they became aware of me. I felt even more overdressed. To my embarrassment the line of people waiting at the trestle table seemed to melt back making way for me as though instinctively they wanted this intruder to be dealt with and ejected as soon as possible. I hung back, shaking my head. The faces stared at me, not unfriendly, just a little puzzled as to why I was being so hesitant.

Then the man behind the table, aware of the change in atmosphere, lifted his head. He nodded, indicating I should step forward. One of the women in the line smiled and nodded too.

This wasn't a conversation I wanted to have in front of so many people but it seemed I had no choice. The man behind the desk stared blankly at me as I approached.

"Do you speak English?"

He nodded.

"I am looking for Bernard Harris."

Silence.

"Why?"

"He is my father."

The room seemed to draw in its breath. The man's eyes did not leave mine nor did they change expression. I felt myself beginning to bristle.

"Do you know who I am talking about?"

"You are an American?" An accusation. Now it was my turn to nod.

"Can you tell me about him?"

"I am not authorised."

This guy was really getting me going.

"Can you at least tell me if my father is still alive?"

"I am not authorised."

I walked out.

I was so angry – and also blinded by the sun when I came out – that at first I could not see Miguel and the car. I stood there a moment trying to get my bearings.

"Senora!" I turned and recognised the man who had been restringing his violin. He hurried to me across the pavement, now empty handed. He took my elbow gently. His eyes were hot with anger.

"I'm sorry," he said. "Your father was great friend to Cuba. Great man. Not dead. I don't know where but not dead. And that man in there is bad, stupid... *marecon.* I'm sorry."

And he went back inside before I could thank him – or ask him what the word meant.

Miguel was looking a question at me as I walked across the road. I shook my head. He opened the passenger door solicitously. Behind him a long crocodile of schoolchildren dressed smartly in yellow skirts for the girls, yellow pants for the boys made their orderly way along the pavement chatting happily, not looking at all oppressed.

It was not yet midday. I had one more idea.

The British Council, you guys need to know, is an exporter of cultural and educational propaganda. I had always thought of it as formal in a 'jolly' kind of way and very British. Bob, on the other hand, was shaven headed, deeply tanned, and was wearing shorts held up by braces over a bright green T-shirt. And, worst of all, socks with sandals. He spoke with a strong Scottish accent.

"I know well who you mean. But before my time, you understand. No, I'm sure we would have heard if he was dead. He used to be a regular on our guest list, I'm told – he was a big fish in those days, so he was, and wherever he had chosen to live he was still a Brit. But I'm afraid your father didn't like us too much. I daresay you know. From what I gather my predecessors got a wee bit bored of having him turn up to our parties and then slag us off as useless and decadent while necking a bottle or two of rum. He liked a dram, your father. But I dare say you know that, too."

It wasn't said unkindly.

"His poor wife used to get embarrassed, apparently, then angry and take him home. It was said to be quite dramatic."

"His wife?"

"You didn't know? I'm not sure they were married. There was a woman, anyway."

Of course there would have been a woman. Women. I just hadn't thought about it.

"Do you know how I can trace him?"

"I can put in a call to my man at the Ministry of Culture. They are usually very helpful. If I find anything out, I'll contact you at the Nacional."

And that, for the time being, was all I could think of to trace your grandfather. At least, it seemed, he was still alive. Which meant that the moment when he and I would meet again was probably approaching. And I was dreading it more and more.

I showed Miguel the address on the copy of the Casa Nueva deeds and asked him if he could find it. I thought it would be good to have at least seen it before talking to the lawyer in the afternoon. Miguel consulted a map in his car, then folded it away, nodding to me.

By the time we had gone slowly up and back down the same wooded road on the outskirts of the city it was clear he was lost. He got out of the car and hailed a passing motorcycle and sidecar. To my surprise it stopped obediently. Later I learned that, transport being problematic, people habitually stop for each other out here, for rides, to barter some gasoline, to help with repairs. Luckily the passenger seemed to know where Casa Nueva was. He pointed further up the road where the trees were even thicker.

Miguel looked doubtful, but when we got there it was possible to make out a gap, which might once have been a drive, forming a winding passageway between the trees. We followed it slowly down a slope, carefully negotiating tree roots and potholes, until it opened out onto an enormous meadow surrounded by trees, incongruous so close to the city, like a secret. And in the middle of it, even more mysterious, the ghost of a large classical mansion, a sugar baron's castle from another age, now a bleak ruin, windows shuttered, vines curling around the pillars along the front terrace and disappearing into cracks in the walls. Senatorial statues, some still standing, mostly lying face down in the ankle high grass formed an avenue marking what had once presumably been a triumphant approach to the house. Around the back stood roofless sheds and outhouses, one nothing but a pile of masonry. In the woods beyond were what seemed to be the remains of an army assault course. I felt at the time like I was walking through a dream but in truth it was more nightmare. You might have recognised it as a scene from Disney, but to me it was from the British Hammer House horror films of my childhood. Although it was much larger, of course, it also reminded me of the house we grew up in, Windings, which was down in a hollow and had pillars on the front terrace, but here, now – magically transplanted into Cuba – had for some terrifying, quite unexplained reason become ravaged and diseased and menacing. I took photographs from every angle so that my client would know exactly what he might be letting himself in for and then left feeling cold, despite the oven like interior of the car, which had been standing in a sun hotter even than on the holiday in Florida you hated so much Tommy.

When we got back to the hotel Miguel shyly suggested $10.00 for the morning's work. I gave him twenty and asked if he would be free when I had finished with Abdel. Until 6.30, he said. Then he was on night shift.

What kind of night shift? I asked him.

"Hospital," he said. "I am doctor. Trainee oncologist."

He smiled patiently at my reaction.

The lawyer, Abdel, turned out to be well dressed, charming, spoke good English and had both the briefcase and the manner of the experienced professional. He was also utterly useless.

I had ordered coffee for us both and we took it on one of the verandas sitting on the rattan chairs under a big fan. He started by directing me to the 'American Interests' office, where copies of title deeds to properties once owned by now expatriate Cubans were all logged. I might have sounded a bit impatient with him. We were beyond that, I said, what we wanted to know was how to go about establishing title in Cuba. He backed off, spreading his hands.

"If your client did not assert claim to the title within five years of leaving Cuba, the Government deems the property to have been abandoned. I have made enquiries for you and I understand Casa Nueva is now so badly neglected that it has been taken over by the Cuban Housing Association."

"Bullshit. They can't take over what belongs to my client."

Another smile, another spreading of the hands.

"I do not speak for Government, of course, but I think if it were possible to consider your client as claimant to title Cuban Housing Association would seek compensation for maintenance."

"What maintenance? They have let it fall to pieces."

"Nevertheless. And with US embargo how would he make payment?"

"Well let's assume the embargo is lifted, let's assume my client is prepared to make some payment. Where do we go to establish title?"

"Is difficult."

"I know it is difficult. That's why I am talking to you."

"I think maybe Property Register. Yes. If no good – International Courts."

Maybe he just didn't want to get involved in something that could be politically toxic. Maybe he was just in it for the dollar fee we had already agreed. I paid it in cash with bad grace. You've seen me do the same in stores.

It was still mid-afternoon. I found Miguel in his car under a tree, this time reading a copy of the British medical journal, The Lancet. He did not know where the Property Register was but within minutes he had found out – there seems to be a brotherhood amongst the tour guides – and shortly afterwards we were parking in the shade of a ground floor car park underneath a high-rise government building standing on pillars. It was quiet here, the traffic light. The only sound was the shrill, competitive cries of a group of boys playing sandlot baseball on a piece of dusty waste ground nearby.

"You like me to come with you? Maybe they don't speak too good English."

Without him I would probably not even have got past Main Reception. The immense friendliness I was to find in Cuban people seems to have been surgically removed in their bureaucrats. None more so than the guy in the Property Register. Maybe it was being in the intolerable heat of the very top floor with a little table fan instead of air conditioning, but Senor Jimenez when he finally came to the counter was sweaty, suspicious and dour.

He began by pointing out (through Miguel as translator) that the title deed copies I showed him were in the name of Hector Ruiz, not Carlos, my client. I assured him that Hector had left Casa Nueva to his son Carlos in his will. He said he would have to see it. I told him I would arrange to have it faxed or sent as an email attachment. Oh no, he said it would have to be the original.

In the flabbergasted silence that briefly followed he launched into an attack on the Ruiz family for abandoning what he seemed to think of as a national treasure like Casa Nueva and allowing it to fall into such disrepair that the Cuban Housing Association had been obliged to take it over. The logic of this was so twisted that I decided not to even try to answer. I asked if there was a file on Casa Nueva. Of course, he said. Could I see it? Only for Cuban nationals he said and almost smiled at having outplayed me. I told him I represented a Cuban. If he has an American passport, he is not Cuban was the predictable answer. Trumped again said the gleam in his eye. Then Miguel said something to Senor Jimenez and it was his turn to be speechless. What? I asked. Miguel said he had pointed out that he was a Cuban National. I started to laugh. Even Jimenez was forced into a little smile. I put a $10.00 bill on the counter. The file arrived.

I am not sure what I thought I would learn from an official Spanish document. Howard had said we should send a Spanish speaker and of course he had been right. I saw various Ruiz names and title changes going back to the 19th century. The last entry was Hector who had inherited in 1952.

Below his name I saw an entry referring to 'Escuela de Musica' which I noticed in particular because I remembered what Carlos had said when we met him. There followed a paragraph that included dates and sums of money and at the end a reference to 'El Director – Senor Bernard Harris'.

And I had to hold onto the counter.

My client had led me to my father.

"Are you OK?" Miguel asked.

It took me a moment.

"Fine. Can you ask Senor Jimenez if he knows how to contact this Senor Harris? I'd like to talk to him."

Jimenez shrugged. It all took place before he joined the Property Register, he said, closing the file.

"You want to meet Senor Harris?" asked Miguel as we drove back.

"Can you arrange it?" I was calmer now.

"Me, no. But perhaps someone else. I ask for you."

I didn't ring you that night because I didn't want to have another depressing conversation. (They weren't easy for you either, I understood that.) I rang Howard to tell him I thought we were on a wild goose chase and that we would be better going through the international Courts – something we had already warned Carlos was possible. Then I decided to eat in the restaurant.

As I came into the lobby the handsome Chief Receptionist signalled to me.

"Someone wants to speak to you, Senora." He was already looking over my shoulder. I turned to find the beautiful young man approaching. He was smiling – but more circumspect, with not quite the same swagger, on his best behaviour here in the lobby.

"You would like to meet Senor Harris, Senora?" Laid back. As though we had known each other a long time.

"Can you arrange it?"

"Of course."

My stomach turned to ice.

"When?"

"You go to dinner now?" I nodded. "I wait. Then I take you. Is good?"

I couldn't eat, of course. And I didn't want to drink. I wanted a clear head. I was back out in what felt like a few minutes. He was sitting in the lobby, waiting.

"I'd better know your name," I said as he stood to meet me.

"Raul Ventura."

He reached out his hand. We shook. Lightning shot up my arm. I find it hard to believe it myself now. But that's what happened. And I am, after all, trying to tell you the truth.

"I'm –"

"Senora Barrington."

He was staring at me, intimate, cocky again.

"Maggie."

"I know."

So he'd been doing his homework? I hadn't told Miguel my first name. It hadn't occurred to me. Smooth bastard. Beautiful smooth bastard. Who seemed, once more, incredibly, to be making a play for me. And was about to bring me face to face with my father whom I hadn't seen for over thirty years.

Change in this island, seemed to be carried on the wind. And it was carrying me with it.

He led me to a car parked outside on the dimly lit road. As we approached, I recognised it as Miguel's.

He laughed at my expression.

"He is my friend. Tonight he is working."

"Where are we going, Raul?"

"To the apartment of Senor Harris. Ten minutes, maybe less."

"Does he know we are coming?"

"He has no telephone."

"He may not be in?" A reprieve?

"I think he will be in."

'Theeenk…' Long and thin and nasal. Hanging in the night air. I tried to concentrate on that, the almost musical sound of it, not on the terrifying prospect of meeting my father again. 'Theeenk…'

Raul had walked to the car and was standing waiting. I remained on the pavement. I wanted to turn around, go back into the hotel. I had hated the man, wanted to kill him for 34 years. Was I really going to meet him now? He wasn't expecting us, nobody would know, the whole idea was a terrible mistake. What could I say to him? Or he to me?

Raul prised open the passenger door, holding it open for me. And that was the decision made. I walked towards him, got into the back seat and we drove off, Raul and I, still in our innocence, about to meet my father, your grandfather and set all those life-changing wheels in motion.

Chapter 4

The street was narrow and dimly lit. Raul edged the car past small boys playing football, men pushing furniture in hand carts, others peering under bonnets. Older men sat around a table playing dominoes by lamplight. Teenage girls, gossiping and surreptitiously smoking squatted on dark doorsteps leaning against heavy, ornately carved doors, while mothers chatted in open doorways through which grandparents and toddlers could be seen watching television in brightly decorated rooms. Candles flickered on the walls next to vibrantly lush prints of forests and sunsets. Richly painted folding screens acted as room dividers behind which double beds with equally colourful covers could be glimpsed.

I want you to get the picture because I don't think you've ever seen anything like it, not even that night we drove around the back streets of Miami when your father got so nervous and you said you wanted to get back to the hotel. I'm not sure you would like this, either. But I did. To my surprise, I admit. It was warm, we drove with the windows down and the kids stopped playing football and trotted along beside us calling things – asking for money, I guess. I was beginning to realise they could spot a foreigner a mile off. The boys had lovely big grins and cheeky eyes. And the air was thick with music, pop, rock, salsa, rap, classical sometimes, all fighting to get a look in. It came from balconies and windows and from radios in the street, in cars, even in a bicycle basket as its owner pedalled past us.

What I didn't expect was this to be the street my father lived in. "Here?"

Raul nodded, switching off the engine. He looked uncomfortable about it.

I got out. The smell of drains was like a body blow. The kids gathered around us, chattering, pushing through each other, standing on tip toe to make eye contact, waving their arms in the air excitedly. I followed Raul as he made his way through them, ignoring the babble. Instead of ringing the bell or knocking, he took out some keys and unlocked first a wrought iron gate, then a heavy wooden door. Did Raul live here? Was he my father's neighbour? His face looked set, not in the mood for questions.

I followed him up four flights of clean, well-scrubbed stone stairs. The yellow and blue walls gleamed, smelling of fresh paint. With every step my legs got heavier, my heart beat faster. Different sounds percolated through at each floor, voices from television sets, music on the radio, a child doing violin exercises. On the top floor came the strains of an orchestra playing classical music. What had brought my father (if that really was him behind that door), now an old man, from a once imposing house in Miramar to live four flights up without a lift in a downmarket tenement building? I wanted to turn back, even now not to know. But my legs kept moving. On the last flight of steps, galvanised into a decision, I reached out to touch Raul, to tell him to stop. But he was already knocking on the door.

Once. Then twice in quick succession. His head was bowed as we waited. No turning back now. The door was in the side wall immediately at the top of the stairs. The landing was narrow so I had to stand two steps below Raul. I couldn't see through the doorway, for which I was grateful.

The music was turned down. Then the door opened. My father was, apparently, standing a few feet away from me. Raul spoke in Spanish. I heard no reply. Raul spoke again. The only thing I made out was 'Casa Nueva'. Another silence. Then some sort of grunt. Assent? Raul stepped back, indicating I should go in.

I gathered myself. A meeting, that was all. A little journey. Life would go on as before. Part of me watched from outside my body as I climbed up the two steps and stood in the doorway.

Nobody. An upright piano that seemed to crowd the little room, some huge modern paintings dwarfing the walls and a glass topped table with two alloy garden chairs with pink plastic strips wound onto the frames for seating. Only the piles of books and empty food cartons on the floor suggested any kind of life.

"I wait for you downstairs in car," said Raul and eased past me.

"Come in," said a voice that I didn't recognise.

I stepped in and closed the door. Some of the paintings, I now saw, were erotic. So explicit that I hadn't at first realised. I heard sounds coming from behind an arched entrance to my right. Then a man appeared through it.

A little walking scarecrow was coming towards me. Robinson Crusoe, dishevelled and sun baked on his island, skeletal, with a frail looking leather brown face almost invisible behind half-moon glasses and a tangled explosion of wiry grey hair, cascading down his shoulders and flowing from his chin to settle on his chest. Only his eyes, gleaming demonically, suggested it might be my father. But this man was shorter than me. It couldn't be him. Or had I grown? Had he shrunk? Both?

"You're an American who wants to talk to me about Casa Nueva or some such crap, is that right? I don't know about that but it is a good excuse for a drink, not that we need one. Sit down, sit down."

Now the voice, the Yorkshire accent, sounded more familiar. It *was* him. This little man was my fearsome father. He clearly didn't have an idea who I was. Why should he? I hadn't planned it – I hadn't planned anything – but something, I don't know what, made me decide not to tell him, to see how long it could last.

"Will you?"

"No thanks."

"Oh well, sit down, at least. I've never minded drinking alone."

My mother had left me in no doubt about that. On closer examination, the impression of a derelict or a castaway was inaccurate. Though he was barefoot, his clothes – a kind of safari suit from, I would guess, the nineties over a white vest – looked pressed and clean. Under his left arm he had a bottle of rum, in his left hand two glasses. His right arm hung limply by his side. Using his teeth to remove the bottle top and only his left arm to pour he helped himself to a generous measure and sat down opposite me. With his left hand he lifted his right arm onto his lap and turned to look at me as though inviting comment.

I looked away. Not because he had stared me out. Because he had had a stroke. A brief, instinctive surge of pity tugged at me. Then – serve the bastard right. My selfish bully of a father had had a stroke. And right now, he didn't know who I was. The whip was in my hands.

Not very nice, I know. Do I sound like the mother you thought you knew? It was anger that had kept me on track in the years after he left. It was anger that served me now.

"What's this nonsense about Casa Nueva?" He threw back his head and downed his rum.

I reached into my bag and passed him my card. He picked it up and squinted at it. My father. Two feet away from me.

"M. Barrington, Senior Partner. Gender neutral they call that don't they? Does that make you Miss, Mrs or Ms?"

"Mrs."

He poured himself another glass of rum before speaking.

"Presumably as a New York lawyer" – every word varnished with contempt – "you are not here for the bracing Cuban air. Presumably you are interested in Casa Nueva on behalf of some Cuban mobster – ex-Cuban – from Miami or some such hellhole who now wants to claim it as his own. Though why you think I could help you – or want to help you – I don't know."

I could feel the adrenalin gathering at the back of my throat ready for a fight, just as it did over thirty years ago. Only this time I wasn't a child. This time I would stay in control.

"Your name was on the Casa Nueva file at the Property Register. I hoped you might tell me something about the house and why your application foundered."

"I am right, aren't I?" Leaning forward, staring at me.

"I represent a client who would like to reclaim the family home the Cuban Government confiscated from his father."

He uncoiled.

"Bullshit. Those who stayed lost nothing. Your client chose to bugger off and get rich in America. Fuck him. *Gusanos* we call people like him. Worms."

I remember – or think I remember – every word. Afterwards I replayed it, moment by moment, looping it through my mind all through that night, and many more.

"Casa Nueva could be a very beautiful house, Mister Harris." It felt good calling him that. It helped me stay cool.

"Ay, it is." He was looking at me suspiciously. Surely not?

"It needs money spent on it. My client would like to restore it."

"What's he thinking? Hotel? International bloody conference centre? It's not going to happen Mrs Barrington. Cuba is for the Cubans. Not for the fucking Americans. Never again."

At which point the lights went out with a slight 'thunk' that seemed to judder through the building. From the floor below came the sound of ironic cheers.

"Sod it… I'll just…"

He was scrabbling about laboriously.

"Can I help?"

"Fuck, no."

I heard him shamble off in the direction of the arch. Then drawers being opened and slammed shut. Then a crash.

"Buggeration!"

I tried not to laugh.

"Are you all right?"

No reply. I heard a match strike. Light flickered through the arch. He reappeared holding a lit candle fixed in a bottle, breathing heavily. He put it on the table between us and sat down again.

"It shouldn't last long. Now… Where were we?"

"Casa Nueva."

"Yes. Sure you won't have a drink? Cuban rum. The best."

"No thank you."

"Smoke?"

"I'm trying to give up. Again."

"Don't. Keeps you healthy. Look at me."

He laughed, wheezing, took a cigar out of his jacket pocket and lit it off the candle. As he exhaled, the lights came on again to further muffled cheers from the floor below.

"And all's right with the world. Now – Casa Nueva."

"I thought you might be able to help."

"Best help I can give Americans is to tell them to keep their noses out of other people's affairs."

"I'm sorry you don't care for us Americans, Mr Harris."

"You and your kind been systematically trying to bring my country to its knees for over half a century."

He was staring at me, his eyes cold and hostile. I returned his stare. He was making it so easy for me to hate him again.

"You think of yourself as a Cuban, do you?"

"Ay. Pretty much." Then suddenly he smiled, as though at some private thought. "And you think of yourself as an American do you?"

I stared back, going cold inside. Now I wanted a cigarette. Badly.

"Tell me… Did Casa Nueva remind you of anywhere?"

He knew.

"And it is not why you came here is it?"

Jesus.

"You're Maggie, aren't you?"

37

BERNARD

I'd always thought that if it came from anywhere it would come from her. Not little Poppy. And not their poor mother, certainly. But our Maggie, yes. Bloody minded. Sanctimonious. Pain in the fucking arse.

I didn't recognise her when she arrived. Father didn't recognise his own daughter, shock, horror. But why should I? It's been…. What? Thirty-four years. Fuck. A third of a century. More.

I've just played this back. Got it wrong. Not "IF it came from anywhere etc" It HAD to come. They, rather. My Furies. My Eumenides. Yes. The tragical history of Bernard Harris. Hubris without catharsis. My very own Eumenides. Chasing me across the fucking ocean. And the years. Quite right, too.

No – bollocks. Self fucking pity. Stop it. Every man has the right. Only one life.

And mine almost gone. On the way out, anyway. Useless fucking existence.

Calm. Got to keep calm. At least until after tomorrow night.

So…. My daughter. Fuck her. Won't see her again. She's done what she wanted, looked her ogre father in the eyes, seen he's still a pile of shit and she'll fuck off back to wherever it is with the pile carpets and the Jacuzzis. Not an ethical bone in her sanctimonious body.

Fuck this. Got to keep calm.

I always thought they would make her Head Girl at that bloody school. Wonder if they did? Always knew what she thought was fucking well right.

The way she said "my client". That ineffable smug moral fucking certainty. And then the way she looked at me, squaring for a fight. And then … the mouth, I think. The jaw? That square, almost masculine jaw. Something. She had been tall even then. Now Maggie writ even larger. My Eumenides.

Well, she got as good as she gave. Better.

[EXTRACT FROM BERNARD HARRIS TAPED DIARY (1)]

Chapter 5

"You said you were trying to give up."

Grinning, impish in victory.

I hadn't even realised I had lit up. I was tempted to stub it out, but didn't want to give him the satisfaction. I exhaled at length.

"I thought you might turn up one day."

"And I never thought I would see you again."

Dead skin. Oh, the comfort of that.

"Aye, fair enough." That accent. My father. This scraggly little stranger filling the space where a father should have been.

"When did you recognise me?"

He poured himself another tot.

"And if I hadn't? What? You'd have walked out?"

I had no idea. What had I been I trying to do? I didn't want this man back in my life. Suddenly the whole thing seemed pointless. We had nothing to say to each other.

"Are you really here grubbing for Casa Nueva?"

"Not how I'd phrase it."

Now I stubbed the cigarette out. I wanted to leave, I wanted never to have seen him. Did he sense it? When he spoke, his voice became suddenly querulous.

"I don't know a single thing about you. I don't have a single bloody scrap of information about you. Nothing, fuck all – since you were twelve."

"Fifteen." Jesus, he can't even get *that* right. I could feel myself becoming fifteen again. Don't let him, don't let him.

"Nobody answered my cards, my letters, not you, not Poppy, not –"

"What the hell did you expect?" Anger. Much better.

He flinched, blinking. Good, I thought. I can handle him.

"No, no, fair enough. It's just – this blank, this great zero, then you... turn up. A property dealer from Manhattan. Fuck me."

"Lawyer. I'm not a dealer."

"What is it? Revenge?"

Guilt? This man feels guilt?

"I thought it was time."

"Well. Here you are. Here we are. Father and daughter. Very nice."

Suddenly perky again. A clown, not a giant. He puffed on his cigar, put it down and then with the same hand picked up his glass of rum, this time holding it under his nose savouring the smell, his right arm folded limply on his lap.

"What happened?"

"What do you mean, what happened?" That impatient, angry tone, the question apparently fatuous, the questioner imbecilic. Once it frightened me.

"Your arm."

His face relaxed, no longer threatened.

"Oh. The pendulum. Useless bloody pendulous appendage. Stroke. About five months ago. Maybe six."

Momentarily it was almost possible to feel sorry for him.

"You weren't easy to find."

"No."

He looked away. Angry?

"I had the address in Miramar. Nice house. Why did you move?"

He drew on his cigar, then turned back to me, now grinning defiantly.

"Bit down market here? A touch insalubrious?"

I said nothing, staring him out. His face clouded again, irritated that I wasn't playing.

"It doesn't matter."

"Doesn't it?"

His eyes flicked up at me. Nervous, hostile again. Was I mocking him? I continued to stare. Making moves like we always did. He seemed reassured.

"I don't suppose I shall ever know." His voice quiet now, level. "Bureaucrats. We breed them in Cuba, you know."

"So?"

"While I was in hospital. With this bloody stroke. Good hospital. We do good hospitals out here."

"What *happened*?" To hell with the propaganda. He looked chastened.

"Usual crap. Whisper, fucking whisper."

"What about?"

"About bollocks and lies. Doesn't matter."

"What lies?"

He wouldn't look at me. It was like talking to one of you when you were hiding something from me. It was a while before he spoke. When he did it was with a funny sort of giggle.

"I had been judged 'anti-Communist'." He glanced across at me as if to see if I was getting the joke. "'Counter Revolutionary'. When I came out of hospital I had been rehoused. Here. In 'Mon Repos'." Again that little anxious glance to see if I found it as funny as he did. "My Cuban pension – for what that's worth – stopped. End of story."

I couldn't speak. Rage. He'd made his bed. The bastard had made his bed. This was what he had left us for.

"Managed to hang on to the piano. God knows where the grand is now. Wouldn't fit here anyway."

Or had he learned his lesson after all? Had he finally turned his back on the comrades?

"Are you 'counter revolutionary'?"

"Am I fuck! Jealousy, that's all. Little bastards in the Musician's Union – always resented me, especially when Fidel made me Director of the Music School. I was always a bloody foreigner to them. Waited until I was in hospital. Then put the knife in. Or is it the boot? My English is a bit rusty. Don't even try to understand. Nobody does. This is Cuba."

I could not sit still. I got up, started to walk around.

"You've had a stroke and the comrades put you four floors up in this... shithole without a lift. Is that right?"

He looked at me, warming to my anger. His face set. Battle.

"Oh, dear me, yes, oh yes, this is what you wanted to hear, isn't it?" His voice was thin, spittle started to fleck his lips. "Yes, yes, serves the old bugger right. You want me to apologise, don't you? You want me to say how I've fucked up my life and yours."

Tiredness swept through me as fast as the anger had fired.

"I don't know what I wanted. Or what I want. I didn't even know if you were alive –"

He was sitting forward in his chair jabbing his cigar hand at me.

"Look at him, the father who walked out on you twenty years ago –"

"Thirty, damn you – more –"

"Look at him now! Fucked, completely fucked. Is that right? Yes? Is that what you think?"

I went back and sat down. I remember putting my head in my hands. I was close to tears suddenly.

"You always were a sanctimonious number. I remember your School report. 'Head Girl material,' they said, and I thought, *Yes, fuck it, they're right, she is, my daughter is Head Girl material.* Did you make it, then? Did you make Head Girl? Your mother, your sister, pushovers. But you always managed to get up my nose. Don't waste your time, woman, I'm not... I don't want to... Just fuck off now, why don't you – Please? Thank you. Just... just leave me alone."

His voice puttered out. We both sat in silence. It was all spinning away from me. I had to get it back. Get just a little something back.

"Look... Look, maybe all this does serve you right," I spoke deliberately, trying to be gentle. "But I also wanted... I wanted to see you... because I was hoping, God knows why, we might get to know each other. I thought it might...resolve a few things."

It was true I had wanted revenge. Even at some level to kill him. But this wasn't a lie either.

"You came here to punish me. Nothing more."

Oh God. Try. Try and be reasonable. Even if he is right.

"You were well known, respected, rich even. What was it about? Politics? *Politics*? Or did you want to get away from Mum? From us? I've wanted to kill you, I've blanked you for over thirty years, but I still don't want to see you like this."

The cigar was shaking in his hand. Spittle foamed on his lips.

"Then trot off back to Manhattan. If you've blanked me all this time, a few more years won't be difficult."

Refusing to look at me. A wizened, malevolent little boy.

"I need to know. Was this worth more to you than us?"

"Oh – fuck off. Fuck right off now…Values are what matter. *Values*. That may be hard for an American to understand. I am not going to apologise."

"Jesus, who's asking you to apologise?" I was fighting panic now, a child going under. "You make me feel 14 years old again… I came here to try to understand, to… I don't know – to heal. Not to brawl."

Still holding in there. Just.

"Sanctimonious shit. You came here for revenge. Do you think I haven't been waiting for it?"

No longer. The bolts snapped, spinning into a void.

"Fine… Fine… If that's all you've got to say to me, if that's all you've got to say to your daughter, then yes, yes, revenge, that'll do." I think I was screaming by now. "Don't you think you earned it, you selfish, selfish thieving monster… you…monstrous man… You… I wanted to kill you. Do you hear me? I – WANTED – TO – KILL –YOU. I still do. God damn you, you deserve it… I want to… Oh fuck…"

It all drained away. I felt helpless. But I had told my father I wanted to kill him. That was something. He stared back at me quite calmly, almost pleased, as though he had got what he wanted. He seemed in that moment truly demented. Even to me in my demented rage. A wave of sadness washed through me.

"You have no idea what you did to us have you? None at all."

"I left you. Fathers leave families."

Pointless. I gathered myself to leave. Again he seemed to sense it.

"What happened to Poppy?" Spoken quickly, a by-the-way enquiry.

For a moment I struggled to think who he was talking about. Then I remembered. Your Auntie Poppy. My sister.

"Primary school teacher. In Yorkshire. Headmistress now. Three kids."

"That's good. That's very good. Are you sure you won't have a shot of rum? It's very fine."

Now fresh and full of energy.

I got to my feet.

"Is that it? Finished have we?" Still smiling, still triumphant, but also suddenly uncertain.

"We're getting nowhere."

"No. No, probably not."

"Goodbye, Dad."

It just slipped out. I wished – immediately – that I hadn't said it.

A victorious grin spread across his face.

"Oh now. No, you won't get past me like that, No. Mission NOT accomplished, madam. Off you go and goodbye. My sanctimonious daughter. Goodbye forever if you please. Yes, that's it."

He flapped at me with his left hand, shooing me out. The right remained impotently, pathetically in his lap. I stared for a moment, transfixed by the sad grotesqueness of the image. Then turned to go.

As I got to the door, he lobbed his grenade.

"By the way – that young man, the one who drove you here – he's your brother."

Chapter 6

I hadn't wanted to speak as we drove back to the hotel and he seemed to sense it, keeping quiet the whole way. I wondered if he knew and was frightened, too. No, not that. I wasn't frightened. Not then. I was reeling – both from the awful, brutal meeting with my father: and now trying to accept the wholly impossible truth that I had a half-brother. Your half uncle. This man sitting beside me, his hands lightly on the steering wheel, his knees close to mine. His beauty, once breath-taking, now for some reason distasteful. He, the professional charmer from Cuba. I, the respectable lawyer, the matron from New York. Total strangers. And somehow – apparently – siblings.

Should we just talk about it matter-of-factly, get it out of the way and then carry on being strangers? We had nothing in common but our genes. Our father's bullying mean-spirited genes.

When we parked at the hotel, he had switched off the engine but stayed in his seat as though he knew we had things to say to each other. How could he? Because he already knew about me? Or simply because I had made no move to get out myself? We sat side by side in a silence that got heavier with every moment. The plaintive sound of the trio singing in the hotel foyer mingled with the cries of the seagulls over the Malecon. I was grateful for his silence. Suddenly I wanted to take his hand, to hug him, to hold him in my arms, my brother, my flesh, to sign the pact now between us. Close the perilous gap.

"Do you know? Have you guessed?" I asked at last. I sensed him tense but he shook his head – almost imperceptibly – still staring ahead of him through the windscreen. The light from the hotel fell across the lower part of his face leaving his eyes in darkness.

"You know, don't you? He's my father, too."

He made a little sound. A puncture, a sigh. His head dropped. Still he said nothing. Then he opened the car door, got out and went to stand under the shadow of a tree.

After a moment I followed him.

"Are you all right?"

He still didn't look at me.

"Maggie…" he said. "Maggie and Poppy… my sisters from England."

"You knew about us?"

He nodded.

"And when I saw you… I… You looked…"

"Like the film star – Angie Moore. Rubbish."

He smiled.

"And when I knew you were Maggie… But you were American Maggie Barrington not English Maggie Harris sitting on pony in photograph…"

He shrugged. Tears glistened in his eyes.

"Then you want to meet my father and I think maybe… and then I think no, she is lawyer and Casa Nueva and… But when you come back to car and your face is so sad…" Now he turned and looked at me for the first time. There were still tears in his eyes but he was smiling. "My sister. My lovely sister."

I let his words warm through me like coals. No charmer, now. A boy.

"I knew nothing about you. You've come as a shock."

Now he laughed and, stepping forward, put his arms around me. I eased myself away. He stepped back, seeming to understand.

"Why didn't you tell me when you knew I wanted to meet this Bernard Harris that he was your father?"

He shrugged, looked down.

"My father… doesn't like to be my father… Doesn't like it to be known that he has me for son." A little nervous grin. "Particularly, I think, to American lawyer."

I digested that a moment. My heart opened to him.

"You know something Raul?" I said. "We have something special in common. We share a terrible father."

Now we both laughed. And this time I moved to him and hugged him. Lightly. And it was nice. Very nice. The smell of him. The feel of him. The decision was made. We could never be strangers again.

He put his arm through mine and automatically we turned away from the hotel and walked across the road to sit on the sea wall. It was a calm night. The sea trickled around the rocks, swishing gently below us. A couple of children were swimming, dark heads bobbing in the still, moonlit swell, calling to each other, laughing. Further along the wall a pair of lovers embraced, she leaning back against his chest while he nuzzled her neck, his arms around her, his hands lightly cupping her breasts. Cars buzzed by on night time business.

And we talked. So easy now, so much to say. The air was warm but I was shivering with excitement, though trying to hide it from him. It was so strange to hear of my father as part of another family. Raul told me about his mother, Rebeca, and growing up in the house in Miramar. It was clear that Rebeca wasn't at all like poor Granny. From what Raul said she fought the old bugger, toe to toe, never mind that she was just a young singer in the chorus and he was Director of the Music School and a friend of Fidel's. (If either of you guys don't know who I mean when I talk about Fidel you can darn well find out.) Anyway, apparently the fights got to be too much and Raul and his mother left to go and live in the country with Rebeca's parents. But Raul hated the country, grew to hate both pigs and mangoes he told me, so they came back to the city and she retrained as a nurse and he went to school and then university and was planning to become a teacher. They didn't live with the old bastard any more but they saw enough of him and he was as cantankerous and evil minded as ever. At first Raul

45

said he was frightened of him but then learned to ignore him. He said he thought his mother and your grandfather always loved each other and always would.

"And you think he never loved you?" I asked.

"Perhaps… When I was little. Now, no. Ashamed."

"Why?"

"I do not love his revolution. The old man's revolution. Once good –"

"Was it? You think so?"

"Oh yes. Maybe. But now…" He made a face. "Where you live in America? California? Ohio? Florida? I know all the States."

"New Jersey."

"New Jersey." Tasting it, rolling it in his mouth. "You have big house?"

"I guess so."

"One house? Two? Cars?"

"Oh Gosh…"

"I want to live in America."

"OK. Maybe you will. Why not?"

He laughed excitedly and took my hand and kissed it and we were both laughing and it was so easy to laugh and talk with this beautiful, now suddenly vulnerable young man with whom I shared so much and of whom I knew so little.

It was good to be able to talk about the horrors of my meeting with the old man. As I described it to Raul I became a teenager again burning with adolescent anger at the awful, irrational unfairness of the man and I started to cry and it didn't seem to matter in front of this stranger my brother and he held my hand and nobody had held my hand like that for God knows how long – it wasn't something your father ever did – and it was so nice, such a deep comfort.

And when finally, very late, we said goodnight he hugged me again, very close, almost fierce, and it was wonderful to feel I was in the arms of a man, my brother, who seemed to care for me, and this time I hugged him back and felt tenderness, optimism, a sense of past, present and future all in one embrace, that overwhelmed me, and that did not feel the slightest bit wrong.

At Reception as I collected my key, they told me the British Council had called to say that they had the address I wanted. I went to bed smiling and slept well.

In the morning Raul was waiting for me in the lobby. He had said he wanted to show me the Old City. If we greeted each other awkwardly it was not because we doubted our new found intimacy but because of the stern eye of the Chief Receptionist. My half-brother still looked very handsome in the morning sun. And very pleased to see me.

RAUL

What was your reaction when you realised she was your half-sister?

(Long pause.)

Is impossible question ... It was ... everything. Upside down but right side up also. So strange ... impossible ... a dream... but also real.... So strong ... like magnets, you know? Two magnets...click.

You mean sexually?

Again – sex. No. Love. Yes. Love. All my life I dream of my sisters in England. With their Queen Elizabeth. Maggie and Poppy. And now Maggie .... My sister Maggie here. Talking. Smiling. Beautiful.

You did find her beautiful?

What do you want me to say, Mr Attorney?

I just want to understand. You've always liked women, haven't you?

Like women? Yes, yes, yes. I like women. What do you want?

I mean sexually.

I know. I know you mean sex. Again. OK Mr Attorney – I fuck. A lot. When I see a woman – let's say any woman – I think of her naked, on her knees, her arse to me waiting for me to fuck her. What do you want me to say?

The truth.

Maybe it is the truth. OK?

And Mrs Barrington? Is that how you thought of her?

NO! ... No .... Love. I told you. Love for somebody who was part of me but I didn't know, somebody who jumped into my heart because she was already there, somebody I was allowed to love without ... all that shit...

So are you telling me you did not want to make love with her?

(Long pause.)

What is she saying?

Mrs Barrington is not denying any of the charges against her.

And me? Charges?

If that is what you are worried about, nobody is pressing charges against you.

Hug... That was all. To be free to hug this beautiful woman, this woman who was me*, to hold her ... Pure love... It was wonderful.*

And her? How do you think she felt about you?

Magnets.... Two magnets... Click.... So easy.... A lifetime in a moment... Oh, outside, in the front she is very... closed. You know? Very... strong. The big lawyer. The boss. But underneath her smart, expensive clothes from, I don't

47

know, 5th Avenue she is a simple woman who lost a father and found a brother. A friend.

So you did imagine her without her clothes?

(He laughs)

Oh, Mr Attorney, yes, I could imagine her without clothes. I am a man who can imagine any woman without clothes. But her, it was gentle, shy, loving. Not sex. Just hug. This beautiful woman. Naked in her soul. Let's say Eve. Not fucking. I didn't think about fuck.

No?

I don't know why you want me to…. Well, maybe I do. But no. NO.

[FROM RAUL VENTURA WITNESS STATEMENT (2)]

Chapter 7

I had seen photos of the Old City, *La Habana Vieja.* I remember thinking how romantic it looked, a relic from a more graceful age before Castro and Communism. The reality is even more beautiful. Cool, ornate squares, and narrow streets, in my mind now, from where I am writing this, all ochre and green and blue. Blue for the shadows I suppose, the sun beating down through the green of the palm trees in the *Plazas* onto the creams, ochres and browns of the crumbling old buildings with their exquisitely ornate shuttered windows and balconies. Statues on proud plinths surveying fountains, little strips of carefully tended grass, second hand book stalls in the cool of colonnades, others selling children's toys, colourful dolls – everything seemed colourful – paper hats, wooden, carved diabolos, old-fashioned biplanes painted garish red with CUBA stencilled on the wings. Tables and chairs were set out in the shade in front of terrace cafes and bars, an old woman sat on a low wall smoking an enormous cigar. She was wearing traditional dress, billowing skirt and blouse in red and white, fanning herself with a delicate lace fan, at her feet a rusty tin in case any passing tourist chose to drop in a coin.

A young man with a sketch pad followed us as we walked, his pencil flying across the paper and by the time we had ambled across the *Plaza de Armas* he was tearing the sheet off the pad and presented it to us with a flourish and a big smile. It was astonishingly good – by which I probably mean flattering. A professional. I gave him some money, dollars of course, and he seemed pleased. Raul asked to keep the sketch, which made me blush like a teenager.

While I saw all this, I was not really taking it in. I was walking next to a brother I never knew I had, his arm casually in mine, guiding, possessive. At first it had felt strange. Like holding hands, it wasn't (isn't?) your father's style. But as we talked and listened and laughed and shared lives it felt natural, more than natural, paired, one of the happiest, most untroubled, most innocent hours (two hours?) of my life. We talked about your grandfather, of course, and the horrors of growing up with a bully. The relief of being able to share these memories! With Auntie Poppy it had been impossible. It wasn't that she didn't suffer from it, but I always felt she suffered less than me, probably because her solution was to shut down and try to ignore it. So I couldn't talk to my sister and I couldn't talk to my mother, of course, and by the time I married your father I had buried it, or thought I had. So the relief of finally being able to talk to someone – above all being able to laugh – was heady. We talked about you, of course, and about your father (I told Raul that he is a good man), and our life together, and he wanted to know every detail I could dredge up about America, about the stores, the television (he had seen some and loved it), the clothes, the cars. The cars! He took me to a classic car museum they have in the Old City. It was nice to come in out of the sun and see these beautiful old vehicles, some going back a century, all lovingly kept. Raul's eyes shone as he touched them. I wanted to take him back to America with me and buy him the latest Chrysler, or, better perhaps, a Jaguar, something disgracefully polluting and extravagant. Then he took me to see the old Cathedral, vast, dirty grey, with its towers and intricate pillars. In the square in front of it was a craft market. Clothes and carvings and paintings, hundreds of paintings spread out beneath awnings and sun umbrellas, customers and sellers flirting, teasing, laughing and, like the school children, not looking at all oppressed. On the steps of the Cathedral there was a white headless chicken, a little blood smeared on the flagstone. Raul explained it was a religious sacrificial ritual. He told me how Santeria was practised by many in Cuba and that it is a mixture of Catholicism and the worship of the ancestral deities of the Yoruba people of West Africa who were brought over as slaves and could only practise their ancient religion by pretending it was a kind of Catholicism to fool the slave owners. He made it sound so normal, so 'respectable' even to a WASP like me. I began to feel I was losing my bearings – and didn't want to stop.

This island of change.

We were having lunch – or, more accurately, still talking over largely untouched plates of food – on a covered veranda that curved around an old cobbled courtyard when Miguel brought us the news of your grandfather's arrest.

I remember the moment very well. Raul was telling me about being made to help roast a pig when he was living in the country as a child after he and his mother left your grandfather, how the custom is to stick a long branch in the pig's mouth and force it right out the other end and then turn it on a spit over an open fire, and how much it revolted him and how he had never wanted to eat pork again, and how it was another reason he wanted to leave Cuba and go to America where – apart from anything else – pork wasn't the main dish, when suddenly he stopped and looked down into the courtyard apparently alarmed. Miguel was running through the tables set out below us, glancing up nervously. He bounded up the stairs to the veranda and hurried across to our table. He nodded apologetically to me and then started to speak rapidly to Raul in Spanish. The only words I could make out were '*tu padre*'.

"*Mierda!*" Raul threw his napkin down on the table as though his father could always be guaranteed to spoil things.

"His neighbours saw him being taken away by Police this morning," he explained. "He rang my mother at work, she rang Miguel. He has cell."

As the clearly lucky bastard with the cell Miguel joined in. "I knew you going to *la Habana Vieja*, I ask everybody – you see Raul? Where is Raul? I find you here like detective." He looked proud.

"Does anybody know why? Has this happened before?" I was the only one who seemed shocked. My elderly father. Arrested. In a Police State. This didn't seem a time to be calm.

Raul shrugged, shook his head.

"This is Cuba." He got to his feet.

"Where are we going?" I asked.

"Police Station."

"Come," said Miguel easing back my chair like an old-fashioned Southern gentleman. "Maybe mistake. Police make mistakes sometimes. My car is here."

I threw enough dollars down on the table and hurried after them.

As we hurried up the ramp towards the old grey stone walls of the Castillo del Morro overlooking Havana Bay and the Straits of Florida where the main Police Station is situated, we could hear a woman's voice, hectoring, insistent. Inside it was dark, the shutters closed to keep it cool, the only light coming from a single ceiling lamp. Although it took my eyes a little time to adjust, I could make out a grilled reception desk at the far end of the room. A middle aged, bespectacled man in police uniform was nervously fingering his moustache as he listened to the short, buxom black woman in a nurse's uniform haranguing him. She paid no attention to us. We sat on a bench out of her eye line. Raul didn't need to tell me this was his mother.

When she seemed satisfied that she had made her point she turned back into the room. She saw us, fixing instantly on me. The blaze in her eyes cross-faded to a warm glow. She smiled and came across, her hand held out.

"Maggie... Not so little Maggie. My husband say me you are in Havana. Rebeca." We shook hands. I found I was already smiling back. "Is OK. Police make mistake. I explain. They bring him now. Is good. So... How you like Cuba?"

I started to laugh. She was like a waterfall. She laughed with me. The handshake became a hug. I was instantly bewitched.

"I am your new mother-in-law, no?"

"My God, so you are."

"You must be very nice to me."

Everybody was laughing now. I even caught sight of the policeman behind the grill smiling.

So I want you to think of me at that moment in the central Police Station in an old sea front castle in Havana with a new brother, a new stepmother my own age, black, and a father just being brought up from the cells. The thing you have to understand is that at the time – far from thinking I had gone through the looking glass – it all felt perfectly normal.

"Are there any other members of the family I haven't met yet?"

We were laughing even more, waves of laughter bouncing off the Police Station walls, a truly merry gathering, when the security door to the side of the Reception desk clanked open and two policemen came in. Followed by my father. The laughter cut off as though a switch had been thrown.

As he saw me, he stopped in his tracks, his face set. The silence stretched out.

"Say hello to your daughter, you rude man!" said Rebeca.

He turned away from us, nodded to the man behind the desk who pushed across some keys, money and a wallet. My father laboriously signed a paper with his left hand, his right arm still hanging inertly by his side, then marched out into the sunshine without a word or a backward glance.

Walking out on me again.

REBECA

Had you always known that your husband – am I right, you were formally married?

The day we received divorce papers from England. Like that. (Clicks fingers) *We no live together after few years but we never divorce. Now I am Ventura not Harris. My son also.*

Had you always known that he had daughters in England?

Of course.

And when did you know Maggie was in Havana?

At Police Station.

At the Police Station?

When Bernard is arrested his neighbour, Cristobal, call me. Always I say to Cristobal – look after Bernard, knock on door, how are you, do you want food, all this. Now Cristobal hear Police knock on door. He hear Bernard very angry, he hear him taken away, he call me. I call Raul's friend Miguel, I leave message on phone – tell Raul come to Police Station –

Why? What could your son do?

Hah! Nothing for Bernard. For me! *I leave work, go to the Police Station. I tell them I know who is doing this, I know what is happening. They say I cannot see him. I am angry. I make police call our friend, Jesus, Bernard's friend in Ministry. Jesus talk to Police. Police say I can see him, maybe they make mistake. I say – sure you make mistake motherfucker! I go to see Bernard. He is angry, he is frightened. Now he tell me about Maggie in Havana and she has met Raul and he seems frightened, and something hits me here, you know* (she puts her hand on her chest) *and I am frightened, too. I don't know why. Maybe with my son – always danger. But I make Bernard calm. I go back to Policeman and call him more than motherfucker. That is when Raul come with Miguel and woman who must be Maggie. So I meet my daughter-in-law and I think she is nice and we smile, we laugh. Then this stupid man, her father he won't speak to her and she is angry, too. Why not? Her stupid father. But I have to go with him because he is still my husband.*

[FROM REBECA VENTURA WITNESS STATEMENT (1)]

BERNARD

Rebeca has just gone…

(Long pause)

Fuck *but she's tiring…. Didn't say anything as we left the bloody cop shop. Found a taxi. Knew the driver. Of course. Free ride. Knows half the bloody taxi drivers in Havana. Fucked them, I dare say.*

She let loose behind closed doors, of course. Told me I behaved like a shit. Quite right. But the sight of that sanctimonious bitch sitting there with the boy, the two of them, suddenly a little team, both with a father they can hate, she thinking – look at him, look at that arsehole, arrested in his beloved Cuba, pathetic little man. What a fucked-up life, what a fucked-up father. Well, fuck her.

"She's come all the way to see you, you have no right not to say hello… nya, nya, nya." … It's all bollocks. That woman came here to gloat, to take revenge. Cunt. "I'm going to her hotel to tell her you are sorry", she says. "And I am going to invite her tonight." You fucking well are NOT, I said. But she will. Interfering busybody. Always thinks she can fucking MEND things.

They can all leave me alone. With my fucked-up life.

(Long pause.)

Better get some sleep. TRY. If they managed to pull a stunt like today, who knows what they will do tonight.

[Long pause]

I hope I get some sleep …. Oh fuck, please let me sleep…

[EXTRACT FROM BERNARD HARRIS TAPED DIARY (2)]

Chapter 8

For a while the fight went out of me. The sad, utterly selfish old man. I had done what I could. Why was I wasting my time in this grim unlit Police Station in this stinking Marxist hellhole? Let him dribble his life away. I felt drained. Time to go home. Back to Montclair. To work. To a life I knew.

The sunlight was blinding as we came out. Miguel offered to take me back to my hotel but I wanted to walk. Raul said he would come with me. I wanted to be alone but he told me I would get lost.

He seemed to know instinctively not to talk. This charmer, my brother. The skills of the professional gigolo? I didn't want to think about it.

After a while as we trudged along the back streets behind the Malecon, faces staring curiously at us out of ground floor windows, walls bearing slogans in fading paint – *Patria o Muerte!* or *Venceremos!* – now quite familiar, his silent presence became a comfort. I had lived most of my life knowing my father was a selfish heartless bully. Maybe I had hoped to find something different. It was painful to come face to face with the shabby mean-spirited reality but so what? There were no excuses for him, he was nothing but a tawdry egotist. Forget. Live. You. I thought of you both and how good it would be to get back to you. You were a help. Really.

When Raul took my arm to cross a road it was nice. It was nice when he left it there. I felt that a gap was being filled. Not replacing my pathetic father – and certainly I never thought of him as filling the gap left by your father, be very sure of that – but nevertheless a male reality that was part of me, of my childhood, that belonged to me and one that I could be grateful for and cherish. At one point our route took us past a park. An ice cream seller was just inside the gate, sitting on his tricycle with its icebox trailer waiting for custom. Raul broke away from me, went over to him and came back with an ice cream each. I wondered whether I should offer to pay but did nothing. The ice cream was wonderful.

"When shall I see you?" he asked when we got back to the hotel.

He was looking at me like Wowser used to when he was a puppy and we shut the door on him, leaving him alone in the house. Maybe he had guessed.

"I've got to get back, Raul."

"Back?"

"Home. The States."

As I said it, looking at him, I knew I didn't want to. Not yet.

"NO!"

Panic in his face now. Or maybe anger. I wanted to hug him. I took his hand.

"Look… You and I won't lose touch. It's been wonderful to meet you. To find you. Truly wonderful. But I can't deal with… that anymore."

"Forget him. Me. *Us*."

"I know, I know. It's been extraordinary. I've never got to know somebody, got so close to somebody so quickly in my life. It's a little frightening."

"Not frightening. Wonderful!"

"All right. Frightening *and* wonderful."

I squeezed his hand.

"But I've got to get away."

"Stupid… This is *stupid*."

"Please Raul – I won't go without saying goodbye, of course not. And we'll keep in touch. Maybe I'll come back, maybe you'll come to visit me in the States."

"Maybe, maybe, all maybes."

And that's when I made my mistake. I think probably something to do with feeling guilty about not paying for the ice cream.

"Look you've been very kind showing me around and I know that is your job, and I know things aren't easy here and I don't want you to be out of pocket, so how about –"

I was scrabbling around in my purse, my head down, when I sensed rather than saw him spin around and walk off fast.

REBECA

You were angry with your husband?

Of course! Stupid man.

Did you try to make things up with his daughter?

First my son come to see me. Like little boy. Very unhappy. Maggie say she wants to go back to America. All this ... bad stuff. Please Mami make her change her mind, I don't want to lose her so soon, I want to show her La Habana, please Mami talk to her. All this. My new sister. Don't let her go. Why you care so much? I say. You want her to take you to America? My Gucci boy.

Is that your name for him?

Is one name. He love money and clothes and cars. The revolution, what we are doing in Cuba was nothing to my son. He never understand what Fidel gave to us. Is sad for me. You want her to take you to America? I say to him. Is that what it is? No Mami I love her. You love your sister? You love her like a sister? How do I know? he say. I have never had a sister. Love is love. Hah, I say.

What do you mean?

(Pause)

Maybe I teach him wrong. Maybe Cuba teach him wrong. For us, sex is easy. My son is very beautiful. Everybody want to make sex with him. He doesn't understand love, maybe. Except he know I love him. He know that.

Did you think he wanted sex with his half-sister?

(Pause)

I think he love her.

So you agreed to talk to her?

I cannot say no to him. Not when he cry like little boy.

What would you have thought then if she had taken him with her to America?

(Pause)

Happy for him. Sad for me.

Angry?

(She does not reply)

[FROM REBECA VENTURA WITNESS STATEMENT (2)]

Chapter 9

I had just put the phone down on Howard. He had given me my regular business update. I had told him I was planning on getting a flight back the next day. My hotel room was very silent. No traffic, no sounds of television coming through the wall. Suddenly the thought of going back to that big empty house in Montclair, to the same deals, the same round of meetings and paperwork made me feel desolate. It was time to make big changes in my life. My life in America seemed set in concrete, my identity – lawyer, Republican stalwart, wife and mother – immutable. Only I was no longer a wife and mother. Or, rather, I was a failed wife and mother. So it was not immutable. Change had already begun. And now in this puzzling, seductive, alien island of change, a new family, a new identity.

It was Raul, of course. Largely. I don't know whether you can possibly understand what an extraordinary discovery it was. I can't justify it, can't explain it. It was just *there*. It was he who had turned the page. It was he who had lifted my heart in some inexplicable way, who had made me walk lighter. Every moment with him was a discovery of myself. And now I had offended him and I was planning to leave the next day and had no idea how to contact him. The thought of never seeing him again was frightening.

Then the telephone went and it was Reception telling me that a Rebeca Ventura was downstairs to see me and I whooshed with relief. Maybe Raul was not lost to me after all.

It was cooler now and she and I took *mojitos* out in the garden to sit by the cannon, where Raul and I had first met. She had changed out of her nurse's uniform. She looked gleaming, hair glossed, lips glossed, high heels, low cut dress. Vibrant. Carrying a bit of weight maybe, but very sexy, my stepmother. And beneath the energy a formidable stillness, a watchfulness that spoke of wisdom.

"So… You like new family?" Her eyes glittered across the tumbler at me as she sipped. I smiled back.

"Still in shock."

"I shock you?"

"A little."

"Because black?"

"NO! Because stepmothers are supposed to be old and we are almost the same age. And I suppose I never thought about him marrying again… Well, no, I just never thought about him. Or tried not to."

"Your father is good man."

I looked at her. She seemed to mean it.

"So why aren't you living with him then? What was so good about walking out on his wife and daughters in England? You left him, he barely acknowledges Raul. Please tell me – what is good about him?"

"Good people do bad things."

"Well, it is nice that you defend him. I'm afraid I can't."

She put her *mojito* down on the wall beside her and stared out across the Malecon to the sea.

"My father had a whorehouse by the docks – there." She pointed to her right along the sea front. "When Fidel came to power, it was closed down. For most black people Fidel meant freedom. My mother say when he came down from the mountains and the church bells were ringing, she kissed him, she kissed Che. I don't know if was true, my mother sometimes she believed her dreams, you know? But she was happy. Everything was going to change for us. My father not so happy. I remember his whorehouse. Big, painted blue. I thought it was a shop and I didn't understand why I wasn't allowed to go there. But I watched and I saw men go in and come out with nothing and I wondered how poor Papa could make money if nobody bought." She smiled at me. I smiled back, touched by the image but also mesmerised by her stillness, the calm authority that sat so easily on her. "When Fidel closed it down, closed all the whorehouses, Papa left us to go to America. So you see both our fathers left us. Your father loved Cuba, mine America. But he also loved us. He sent money every year until he died. Maybe he was gangster, maybe priest. Was he a good man? Was he a bad man? In my life here we have seen so many bad things, so many good things. Bad people do good things, good people do bad things. No?"

"At least your father sent money. Mine just took."

She seemed about to say something. Then appeared to change tack.

"Did you need it?"

The point was made.

"I can't agree with you, though. There are good deeds in the world and bad deeds and we should distinguish between them. We have to have values, absolutes."

"Your father loves you."

"For God's sake – you weren't there – he threw me out, he was vile –"

"He is baby. The old man is baby. Treat him like baby."

"Is this why you came to see me?"

"I don't want him to die before he has said you he loves you."

For a moment this stopped me. Then it made me angry.

"Blackmail, Rebeca. And he is not a child. He's a selfish cantankerous old bully. If he wants to be treated with respect, let alone affection he should show some."

She sighed.

"Is true… I want to say only… I know him better than you. Don't go back to America. Not yet. If not for Bernard then for Raul."

"Raul?"

"Also baby. My men are babies. Is my fault?" Again those glittering, teasing eyes. "He call me just now —"

"I offended him, I know. I feel bad."

"He did not say so. He said Mama you must stop her leaving. My new sister. I want to know her, show her Havana. Please stop her. He say he like you. Very much. You like him?"

She seemed to be watching me with particular care as though trying to measure my response. It wasn't easy. How do you explain a gravitational pull? And whatever I felt about Raul was mine, not yet to be shared.

"I do… Very much. I don't know him yet, of course, and meeting a half-brother like this is very…"

I trailed away. I didn't have a word. And Rebeca didn't seem to need one.

"Be careful."

Two words. A simple enough admonition. But not the way she said them. They hung in the air between us. She was right. But I didn't know why.

"Careful of what?" I wasn't sure I wanted to hear the answer.

"He wants to go to America."

This I could deal with.

"And I might be his passport? I had wondered."

"He love you also, I think. And that may be not so easy."

What was she saying? What was wrong with love between a brother and sister? What could be difficult about that?

She took a sip of her drink, which she had barely touched.

"Maybe you will be big wise sister to him. Maybe teach him good things. Maybe help both my men."

We laughed, gently, relieved to have moved on.

"I am flattered," I said. "But I will have to go back before too long."

"Why? You have small children to look after? Husband?" Did she know? I shook my head. "You need to work to make more money?"

"Not really."

"You are free! Try being Cuban!"

I laughed. She made it sound possible. My new identity? She put the drink down and leant towards me.

"Tonight is concert for your father. In his honour. A little bit secret because… well, what has happened. I want you to come. His old pupils want show support for him. Solidarity. He has many friends in music. But enemies also."

"Enemies? Why?"

"Politics. When he was Director of Music School. Always you make enemies. While Fidel was *el jefe*, was boss, Bernard was safe, well, a little bit safe, but now Fidel is gone and Bernard's old enemies became more brave. That is why he lose his house when in hospital, and why today police arrest him. They say for hiding money from abroad. What do you call? Royalties. His enemies – from Musician's Syndicate – tell Police yesterday to arrest him because they do not want concert to happen tonight. Now because our Government friend, Jesus, say to let him go I think the enemies will be there and maybe they will do things. Will you come? Sit with me and Raul. With your new family?"

My new family. A curmudgeonly, selfish, politically contentious Marxist father, a mesmerising black stepmother and a Caravaggio charmer of a brother. I thought of the two of you and Dad and our life in Montclair. Two families. Both mine.

Or, more accurately, neither mine.

Chapter 10

The church – grimy, ornate Victorian neo-gothic – squatted incongruously between two Soviet-style high rise mansion blocks, functional slabs of sky-blue painted concrete whose vast blankness was relieved only by miniscule windows in grimly neat lines, like regimented pock marks.

On the steps of the church a shirt-sleeved crowd had gathered, many smoking in the evening sun. They watched – unerringly identifying the foreigner? – as I got out of the taxi and counted out the $4.00 that Rebeca had told me to pay the driver. They continued to watch – not unfriendly – as I mounted the steps towards them, the stranger not knowing anybody at the party. They made space for me politely. I stood for a moment, uncertain, exchanging tentative smiles. Once again I felt over-dressed.

"Maggie!" I saw his grin first, white teeth swimming out from the darkness in the church, eyes shining, arms wide open. He hugged me as though we hadn't seen each other for days, and I had never offended him by offering him money.

"My sister," he said in English, turning to a group nearby. "My lovely sister from England. And America."

There were scattered smiles, a few welcomes. I recognised my friend from the Musician's Union who had been restringing his guitar and had followed me out into the street to tell me about my father. He nodded to me. On the far side of the steps another group was gathered. They stood in silence, their faces neutral, as though not wanting to be associated with anybody else. I recognised the dour Union Official from behind the trestle table. He looked now even more dour. My father's enemies? Neither camp, if that was what it was, seemed at ease.

"Where's Rebeca?"

"Inside. Is lighting OK? Is sound OK? Is piano ready? She like to be boss." He grinned, took my hand. "Is very good you come, very good you stay. Is true, you not going back tomorrow?"

"I'll stay a bit longer, Raul."

He was still holding my hand, proud, possessive. I gave his a brief squeeze, a signal of some secret society we had wordlessly signed up to, then eased mine away.

"Shall we go and say hello?"

Inside the church many of the seats were already occupied. Extra chairs had been lined up behind the pews and to the side of the building. There was a table by the entrance where tickets were being sold, and on it a pile of photocopied programmes. Near the choir stalls a small podium had been set up with a microphone on a stand. Behind it a large easel with a huge framed photograph of your grandfather, taken some years ago. He looked very handsome. There was a grand piano, music stands, microphones, a mixing desk, lights rigged on cross beams. There was an air of defiant, clandestine improvisation.

Rebeca was at the foot of a ladder shouting instructions to a technician who was refocusing a lamp. She saw us and waved but did not come over. She was wearing the same dress (the cleavage looking, if anything, even more generous) but had now put a white mariposa in her hair behind one ear.

"Should we get tickets? Find somewhere good to sit?"

"We have. Front row. Mama want us to sit with him."

I was about to ask if 'he' knew and if this plan was really the best one given that he wasn't speaking to me, when we heard a dry ripple of applause from outside. Raul grabbed my hand.

"Papa has arrived."

He hurried us down the aisle back onto the steps where the sun was now tipping the rooftops. At the foot of the steps a uniformed driver saluted a middle-aged man in a suit and got back into the front seat of an official looking car as your grandfather started to climb towards us using a stick, the man in the suit hovering beside him step by step. Once again I eased my hand out of Raul's. He didn't resist. Our secret society – if we had one – did not include our father. It wasn't clear that he had seen us. The sun was catching his grey beard and tangled bed head hair (maybe that's where you get yours from Tommy?) tingeing it red as though his face and head were sprouting smouldering ashes. He hadn't seemed so fragile before. A performance? Had he always been a ham? The gallant old man, the applauding public, the trappings of power now lost. Cuba's very own Lucifer. I now saw that the man in the suit had a hand under his elbow, as they climbed.

"Jesus Lopez," Raul whispered to me. "Papi's friend from Ministry. Brave man."

Then 'Papi' saw us and, for a moment, hesitated. I wondered if I should back away, save him the confrontation. It was his night. But he continued, heading straight for me. The applause built the nearer he got to the top of the steps as though climbing them was in itself an achievement. I noticed the silent group on the other side remained silent.

He was breathing heavily when he reached us. He held my look, ignoring Raul.

"My daughter Maggie," he said. The man beside him nodded briefly. "Jesus Lopez. My one remaining friend in Government."

Lopez smiled patiently.

"Your father have many friends in Government. *Encantado.*" He put out his hand. We shook.

"So where are they, Jesus?"

Lopez smiled a politician's smile. My father turned back to me.

"So she got you here, although I told her not to. I'm not surprised."

I did not reply. We stared each other out. "Did the boy tell you there might be fireworks? I could be in for a mauling." Still not acknowledging Raul he indicated the silent group behind him now watching, it seemed to me, with open malevolence. "You might have fun." A flicker of a smile as he moved on?

Raul and I shuffled along behind him and Lopez as we proceeded up the aisle. A ripple of applause followed his progress but it seemed half hearted, nervous. Rebeca approached, kissed Lopez and led us to our seats in the front row. Raul gave me another furtive squeeze of the hand as we sat. It was comforting. We were in this together. Behind us a desultory, hesitant hum as the church filled up. It was joyless, the voices low, tentative.

I looked along the row past my new family to my old father, staring rigidly ahead, his limp arm in his lap, his beard and hair perfunctorily brushed and combed for the occasion. On Rebeca's orders? I had travelled to this mythical, fearsome island, still harbouring fantasies of killing my father, only to find myself sitting in a disused church in Havana ready to witness – what? – his coronation? Defenestration?

Rebeca half rose and nodded at someone behind. Lights came up on the podium and the photograph of the former Director of the Cuban Institute of Music. Your handsome looking grandfather. Silence settled. Lopez walked up to the podium, his footsteps echoing on the stone floor and took his place at the microphone.

The whole church seemed to hold its breath. Was this the moment? Would they try and shout the minister down? Could it turn violent? Armed police positioned themselves in the aisles, scanning the audience, unsmiling.

He began to speak. The microphone boomed, then whined, then settled. Raul leant into my ear, his breath on my cheek, and whispered a translation… Senor Harris a distinguished friend of Cuba for many years… Given so much to our country… Always controversial figure… Now a chance for us all, his supporters, his opponents to show our gratitude… As Raul whispered to me, I sensed him glancing over his shoulder to watch for any signs of unrest. But Lopez' speech passed off peacefully to polite applause. A string trio set up their instruments, offered their personal tribute to their former director – he acknowledged with a graceful nod of the head – and the concert began without any interruption. It was a Mendelssohn piece, I can't remember what. They played beautifully and although music had meant less and less to me over the years, for a while it cast its spell and I began to feel safe. Maybe we all did. The applause was prolonged and generous, my father pounding his knee vigorously with his working hand.

As the trio gathered their instruments and sheet music, Lopez got to his feet to go to the microphone to introduce the next item. At the same moment we heard footsteps slapping up the side aisle and the official from the Musician's Union ran past us and jumped up onto the podium, cutting Lopez off. Immediate uproar. This was what everyone had been waiting for. He tried to speak into the microphone but could not make himself heard. He waited, glaring patiently. Lopez went to the podium and gestured to him to hand over the microphone. He refused. The uproar grew. Impasse. My father watched the proceedings, apparently calm, utterly inscrutable.

I felt Raul's hand lightly on my arm. Protective. Was it all going to end in a noisy stalemate? Or worse?

Then Rebeca walked up to the podium, stepped up to the man – considerably taller than her – and spoke to him, he leaning down to hear. He seemed to demur. She spoke again. Then to everyone's surprise he abruptly stepped back and left the microphone to her. She gestured for quiet.

Everyone knows, she said – Raul translating once more – that Manuel has many differences with her husband… In Cuba we should be allowed to have differences… She asked that Manuel be heard with respect… and then her husband be allowed a right of reply… She asked him if he agreed. My father nodded, a little smile playing on his lips. Was he enjoying it?

In the uneasy silence that followed, she stepped back and returned to sit with us.

And Manuel, as I now knew him to be, began – looking and sounding at first a little hesitant, wrong footed. But as he got into his stride any pleasure my father may have had about the coming battle must surely have evaporated. Maybe to him the litany was ancient. To me it was not. A picture emerged of him in Raul's translation that confirmed my life long view of him as a bully and a tyrant. As Manuel ploughed relentlessly on, heard in grim silence, I felt simultaneously deeply ashamed – and vindicated.

During his twenty years as Director he had, Manuel said, held back indigenous Cuban music in favour of dead European composers who no longer had anything to say to us, placed an outright ban on modernism, pop, early rap, virtually anything American, had destroyed careers, persecuted anybody perceived as a dissident and sent suspected homosexuals to prisons, euphemistically known as 'correction camps'. It was intolerable that such a man should now be honoured, he said, and – looking at Lopez – that a Government Minister should endorse it, however unofficially.

He walked off to the thin baying approval of his clique and a continuing uneasy silence from the main body of the audience. The Minister stared ahead as though nothing had been said. Rebeca was looking down, her jaws working. Raul's mouth was pursed, his head nodding slowly, metronomically, managing to appear both sad and, like me, vindicated. It wasn't just us. It wasn't just with his children that the old man had been a bully. I couldn't look at him. I felt sick. And bitterly angry. My father sending gays to prison?

Nothing seemed to happen for a moment. Then he shuffled to his feet and made his way slowly to the podium, stepped laboriously onto it and settled behind the microphone. He lifted his head pugnaciously and stared at us. I could feel my heart thumping, almost audibly.

He started to speak. The microphone was barely picking him up. He tapped it. A technician leaped onto the podium and adjusted its angle.

He started again, now very clear. Raul leant across to me translating… He came to Cuba, he began, his voice firm and level, because for him and for many

Europeans of the Left it represented a place of hope and enlightenment. It was a society that he believed cared about values more than value. He wanted to be part of it and to contribute what he could. (Here he got his first – muted – round of applause.) He had heard Manuel's charges before and had answered them in private. Now he was pleased to have the chance to do so in public. Many of his audience, he assumed, would know that Manuel had been a student at the Institute and that as Director – on the advice of teachers and staff – he had felt obliged to expel him for being both disruptive and lazy. (Boos from Manuel's clique. I had some sympathy. It felt a cheap shot.) He knew, he said, that since those days Manuel had gone on to become a useful member of Cuban society and had done good work in the Musician's Union but he believed his views should be seen at least to some extent in the light of their early history. Turning to the charges themselves he denied absolutely that he had suppressed indigenous Cuban music. He insisted he had always loved it, that several of his students had gone on to successful careers in *son* and *trova* and he looked forward to hearing from two of them tonight – Manuel permitting. (A nervous laugh. But on his side. Maybe he was winning?) He agreed that he had concentrated more on classical music. That was because, he said, he venerated it and believed it held eternal values. (Warmer applause.) He accepted, however, the charge of disliking punk and most forms of modernism, especially those that came from America. (Laughter.) But he denied that punk was suppressed. It was ignored. And to his regret, he said, it flourishes today. (Big laugh) Turning to the most serious charges of persecuting dissidents and homosexuals… (He paused. I watched him, my spine rigid. The room was breathlessly silent. He seemed to be chewing, moving his tongue in his mouth to find saliva.) He could only say, he went on finally, that he was guilty and very sorry. (The silence was now rock-like. It was as though nobody could breathe, not a muscle could move.) The Revolution, he said, had been under attack from abroad – as none of them needed reminding – and from inside. Its values, health, housing, education for all, were as precious to him as they were to Fidel, to any decent Cuban. It was the view of the Government at that time – and it was a view he shared – that dissidents and homosexuals threatened those values and had to be contained. He said that he took action of that kind against – to the best of his memory – six people in his twenty years. And that, he now wanted to say, was six too many. Now as an old man he felt able to say publicly that the Government had been wrong, his beloved Fidel had been wrong and he had been wrong. And he wanted to apologise. He had acted in what he believed at the time were the best interests of a country he had adopted, for whom he had given up an international career and deserted a family – one daughter was here tonight – a country in whose values he had always deeply believed – and continued to believe. He thanked them for listening to him in patience.

He turned abruptly and left the podium – walking, I noticed, more smartly now – as cheers erupted. Had he got away with it? Despite my cynicism, even I was touched. And, despite myself, a little in awe of the scale of his influence. His achievement. Marxist bully and thief that he undoubtedly was.

As he took his seat beside Rebeca she suddenly leaped to her feet and, cheers still bouncing off the roof, marched up to the podium and gestured for silence.

What her husband didn't say, she wanted to point out, was that this morning at Manuel's request, Police arrested Senor Harris and took him – nearly eighty years old – into custody on suspicion of not declaring income from old recordings sold all over the world. She knew, she said, that this was a trick to stop tonight's concert from taking place and thanks to Minister Lopez it was quickly proved that all foreign earnings had been notified and her husband was released. She wanted everybody present to know that due to the baseless accusations of the Musician's Union her husband now received not one peso from the State despite having worked here and paid taxes and contributed so much for thirty years. He lived very simply – some may say in poverty – the only money available to him the few royalties he still got from abroad. That and occasional help from old friends. Our world-renowned concert pianist, she said. (She was steaming now, leaning forward, venomous with anger.) You should also know, she went on, something that has never been disclosed before in public but now, perhaps, particularly in the presence of his daughter needs to be said – he arrived in this country by our standards a rich man. All the money he brought with him he gave to the Music School. How do you think the Concert Hall was rebuilt and equipped? The rehearsal block? This man's money. All given to Cuba.

She was flushed now, short of breath. I swivelled to look at my father. He was already staring at me his eyes round with embarrassment. And guilt? He seemed to make a decision. He stood up and made to go to the podium as though to speak, to explain that it hadn't been his money, he had stolen it from his wife, my mother. Rebeca saw him and wagged a finger.

He had already said enough, she told him. He stood, frozen, as people laughed with her. He turned back to me as though he was about to apologise. He saw Raul leaning in to me whispering his translation. His face froze and he sat down again. So what? I was thinking. It wasn't his money. Philanthropy by theft. Rebeca at the same time was calling for the concert to continue. This was greeted with enthusiastic applause. As it died down, she invited Manuel and his friends to leave suggesting they might be more comfortable. More applause mixed with laughter. As Manuel and the others got to their feet, some smiling defiantly, boos broke out around the church, but Rebeca called instantly for silence, asking with obvious sarcasm for respect.

It didn't last long. The sound of their departing feet on the stone floor echoing through the church commanded instant derisive laughter. Manuel's rout was complete. As they disappeared into the dusk, I wondered what revenge he would plan.

Rebeca sat down, triumphant. Lopez, laughing, embraced her and went up to the podium to announce the next item. The concert continued, now something of an anti-climax. Until, that is, at the end, one of his former students played part of the 'Emperor' for which your grandfather had been famous in his day. It was magnificent and the entire audience stood and cheered, not only for the performance they had just enjoyed but for the memory of Bernard Harris all those years before.

He got up at the end and went across to the pianist and shook him by the hand and together they bowed to the ecstatic applause and cheers and tears of a packed church full of Cubans paying homage to my father. No one, I admit despite my best endeavours, more tearful than me.

Rebeca walked across to him and took him by the arm. Lopez stepped over to accompany them. The concert was over. They were taking him home. As they reached our pew he broke off and took a step towards me. His eyes were neutral, guarded, as though censoring any warmth. He said something. It was hard to hear above the noise, and his voice was now very weak, but I understood he was asking me to go and see him the next day. I nodded.

It was worth a shot, I thought. Even if only finally to kill him.

I watched the frail figure of my father walk away, his arm through Rebeca's as cheers from his supporters and former pupils filled the church.

Don't be a sucker I was telling myself. I knew the truth of the man. I felt Raul's hand connect with mine.

He knew too. I wasn't alone.

Chapter 11

For years pleasurable fantasies of all kinds of prolonged, painful acts of revenge against my father leading to his slow agonised death had been part of my life. Not talked about, not lingered over, less visited as time went by, but always there somewhere. When I first saw King Lear and watched Gloucester's eyes being put out, I saw my father. Nancy pushing Bill Sykes to his death – my father. In my heart, in the long nights in my school bed, I had killed him many times over.

Now as I walked back to my hotel with Raul I knew, of course, that I did not really want to kill him. He was pathetic and tawdry – I wasn't going to let myself be deceived by the public show of contrition and heroism. But he was human. Hatred had become contempt. Even pity.

Worst of all, I realised I wanted his approval.

"Do you still feel you want to please him?"

Raul knew exactly what I was talking about. His reply was instant.

"Yes."

"Even now?"

"Always."

The street was almost empty. A solitary bicycle trundled past. We walked side by side, his arm still comfortingly through mine.

"So do I. Strange."

We were walking past a large full-length plate glass window, brightly lit, the only one in the street. Inside was a counter with stools and a bored looking woman in a chef's hat. Above the window it said, quite simply, 'PIZZA'.

"Are you hungry?" he said.

It didn't look inviting. But I hadn't eaten for a long time.

"A bit."

When it came, it was at least hot. A half-moon of 'pizza' each, served on paper to be eaten by hand. A lot of melted cheesy topping with occasional sightings of ham and a great deal of dough.

Raul laughed as he watched me take my first bite.

"Not as good as American Pizza?"

"Different."

"Throw away. We find somewhere else."

"No, no, it's fine. Thank you."

He had insisted on paying. And it filled the gap. I managed one section and threw the other into a rusty bin by the side of the road.

"In America big beef burgers, big hot dogs, big pizzas, yes?" He held his hands wide apart to suggest the dimensions of a foodie Nirvana.

"Too big."

"Not for me."

He laughed and once more slipped his arm through mine. We walked gently down a slope towards the Malecon below us. We stopped at the sea wall, listening to the surf, looking out across the Straits of Florida towards Miami, somewhere out there in the dark.

"Ninety miles. Maybe I could swim."

"And leave your mother behind?"

He hesitated.

"She has her life. I have mine. My only life."

He continued to stare ahead picturing, I imagined, a world of big cars and big burgers and big money. I doubted if sub-prime mortgages, fiscal stimulus, failing health insurance or even the virtues of democracy featured at all.

"How about a drink?" We were walking up the slope to the hotel entrance. "I think we deserve one."

I don't remember who it was that suggested we went to my room. I think he asked me what the rooms were like. I was a little cynical. I imagined he had seen the inside of hotel rooms at the Nacional many times, courtesy of lonely female tourists.

He ordered for us both downstairs, fruit juice for him but insisting on a *daiquiri* for me. We sat, waiting, at opposite ends of the large sofa at the foot of my bed. Raul knew the waiter who brought the tray up. He introduced me as his sister. The waiter nodded. Unconvinced? As he closed the door behind him, we caught each other's eye and exploded with laughter.

I asked him if he had known of the charges against our father, and what had happened to the homosexuals he had apparently consigned to these prison camps.

"I was young. But it was normal then. Now not a problem. Some people don't like, but homosexual not secret. I met Jose last year, guitarist, I play with him in club in San Antonio de Los Banos. My father send him to camp. Jose say me – so what? Your father doing his job."

"Generous."

"Me not so generous. But… he is my father. We have to live. What they have done to him now is bad. When Fidel was *el Comandante* would not have happened."

"What was it like under Fidel?"

His eyes opened wide, amused but also shocked. He pointed to the ceiling and put his finger to his lips.

"It was good," he said loudly. "Very good." He was trying not to laugh. It had been foolish of me to ask. But I felt a rush of tenderness for him – flesh of my flesh – for the life he had to live, with a father like ours, in a country where simple conversations could be monitored by Police. More than tender, I felt angry for him. I reached out my hand to him along the sofa to give his a sisterly squeeze. He took it and raised it to his lips.

"Maggie… My lovely Maggie…" he said.

The flamboyance unsettled me. The feel of his lips on my fingers was too intimate. I withdrew my hand but not sharply, not so he would have noticed.

We talked, still sitting at opposite ends of the big sofa, about our childhoods in England and Cuba. The *daiquiri* took hold and I was getting tired and said I thought I had to sleep.

He immediately got to his feet.

"I leave you," he said, clicking his heels, giving a little smiling bow.

"How will you get home, Raul? It is after midnight."

"Walk. No problem."

I looked at him, my courteous Caravaggio charmer, still smiling. I felt bad about reacting like a stuffy Anglo-Saxon to his Latin charm. I didn't want him to go. I loved him.

"Oh, for God's sake…"

I picked up two of the four pillows on my bed and threw them onto the sofa. From the top shelf of my wardrobe I took a spare quilt and sent that after them. He continued to watch, a cautious smile on his lips.

"Why not?" I said. "Brother and sister. I just hope you don't snore. Do you mind if I use the bathroom first?" I was light headed now, reckless. Not me at all.

When I emerged wearing the full-length night dress your father called my 'passion killer' – or used to when it still meant something – Raul was watching a film on the television.

"All yours. Feel free to borrow my tooth brush." I slipped into bed zinging with toothpaste. It was fun. Like a sleepover with a girl friend. Only better.

I was drowsy, on my way to a *daiquiri* fuelled sleep when he came back out. I was lying on my side, my back turned. I heard him pad quietly over to the bed.

"Good night," he said quietly. I turned and opened my eyes. He was naked except for a pair of boxer shorts. His body was as shockingly beautiful as I had imagined it.

Which was when I realised I had imagined it.

He leant down and kissed me lightly on the cheek. Without thinking I cupped his shoulder with my hand. The touch of his warm flesh jolted through me.

"Good night, Raul."

Maybe I lifted my face to him and he misunderstood. Very lightly he brushed his lips against mine. Just a brush. No more.

"Good night," he said.

The last light clicked off. I listened to him settle, my heart still hammering. Soon his breath became steady. I pictured him, stretched out, warm, near my feet, imagined his chest rising and falling as he breathed.

RAUL

And in the morning?

I am sleeping.... I like very much to sleep, you know? ... Her hand on my shoulder... Raul... Raul... A cup of coffee on the floor in front of me. Good Cuban coffee ... Yes. She was dressed. But no make up. She looked ... still beautiful, still... special. That mouth always ready to smile. But older. The eyes, you know? The lips... Sometimes older women in the morning ... is not so good. But with her it was nice. "I must finish in bathroom," she says. She is looking into my head? She sees me thinking about her face without makeup? "You get dressed now. It is late." She goes to bathroom door. I think maybe I have not woken, still dreaming. This is my sister. She turn to me. That smile. "You sleep well?" She close bathroom door. My whole world is new. I drink my coffee. I hurry to be dressed before she come back in.

Were you shy?

No...! OK, a little, perhaps. But it was ... normal... She made it normal. When she come out – hair, make up all perfect. "Your turn," she say. Normal. I feel brave, good. I kiss her on cheek. "Good morning," I say. "You need shave," she say. She push me to bathroom door. Still smiling. "Hotel has electric razor. Use. And shower." Is so good. Water hot, powerful. I feel clean. Strong. My new life. When I come out she is working on computer. "What do you do today Raul?" she ask. I didn't know how to tell her. My friend want me to deliver cell phones. But secret, you know? Special Cuban market. But I cannot say to her in Nacional hotel room. So I say I work with cell phones, is all. She look at me. Her American-teeth-smile. Point at ceiling. She understands? "You need me?" I say her. "No – you work," she say. "I am going to see –" She stops. I remember it well, so well. "– our father." Still so strange. Our father. "Can you give me his address?" "You want me to go with you? I ask Miguel for car –" "No!" she say. Angry? "I want to go alone." OK. I think why? Why she want to see the old man? He make her unhappy. Like he make me unhappy. My mother unhappy. What is more to say? I give her address. She stand, closes computer. "Breakfast?" she say? And I stare at her like fish. What to say? Of course I have slept at Nacional before. Always in the morning the lady go to breakfast by herself. I go down the stairs to the kitchen, see my friends, they give me breakfast, I give them a little of the money the lady give me.

Is that how it works?

Of course is how it works, why not? Always the same. Poor Mister Attorney your wife not make sex with you?

Please go on. Did you have breakfast with Mrs Barrington?

"You want we go together?" I ask her. She look at me – why you ask this question? Then I see in her eyes she understand. Always she understand. "Of course we go together. Brother and sister. Why not? And tonight we have dinner together. Are you free?" She is smiling again, I am smiling. I go to her and give her a big hug. I keep holding her. Hard. I feel her thighs against mine. Then I feel her arms come up onto my back and she give me little hug. Then suddenly I know I am beginning to get erection – there Mister Attorney this interests you? Maybe my sister, my half-sister but beautiful woman, strange woman in my arms, what can I do? – and I am embarrassed and pull away at the same time that she does, though I don't think she has known. "Come on," she say. "I am hungry." And I am very happy. And also a little bit … I don't know…

And that's all that happened?

Why you ask? What does she say?

Oh… Pretty much the same. Though nothing about the… you know, erection.

So. The truth. Is all that happened. Mister Attorney. Friendship and love. And a little bit of an erection. Is a sin?

[FROM RAUL VENTURA WITNESS STATEMENT (3)]

BERNARD

Fuck knows why I said it. Bloody meaningless. It's all gone that life, long gone, another universe. The wench may not be dead but I nearly am. Nothing to be changed, nothing to be made of it. Onwards. So why?

Not sure she heard anyway. And why would she want to? She can tick the fucking box now. She's been to see me, she's done what she had to do. Thought she had to. Though why is beyond me. Revenge, of course, well, yes. But what fucking revenge? I am here, she is there, no connection left. What's past is past. An accident of spermatozoa, no more.

All of us. Accidents of spermatozoa....

Wonder what she made of the hullabaloo last night.... That prick Manuel... Self-righteous little shit... Routed him, though. Saw the buggers off. King of contrition, that's me. And the money.... Oh fuck it.

I don't know why I keep this bloody diary going. Except it's what's left.

Well at least it's been a life. What is there to say? More than some, less than some. Not Ludwig, but there you go, I did what I could, can't apologise for ever. He didn't. Never. Got to keep moving. Until you fucking drop. Yes... that's about it, really...

(Long silence on tape.)

Why should I fucking apologise at all? It's not just a life, it's a life I fucking chose. *How many people can say that? I had a gift. Not like yours, Ludwig, long accepted that but a gift. Nothing to be proud of, just a gift, something that was given to me out of a clear blue sky. But special. Music lived in me, dribbled from me, sweated. I ejaculated music. And I chose to bring it here, to share it with people who seemed to me – no, who* were *– trying to make a better world.*

Fuck it, they did *take on the world. And I helped. That's something. Nothing wrong with that.*

Don't know where the fuck this place is going now, blah blah, who does? Certainly don't know where I am going. Except to my grave, of course.

It is all a mess.

But I did make a choice. I stood up.

She can see that can't she?

(Long silence on tape.)

She probably won't come anyway. I probably won't see her again.

Sanctimonious cunt.

[EXTRACT FROM BERNARD HARRIS TAPED DIARY (3)]

Chapter 12

I knocked for a second time. Still no movement. I strained to hear anything, a shuffle, a creak. Nothing.

His body, lifeless on the bed? The floor? Staring at the ceiling.

Out. Why not? Shopping. Seeing a friend. Maybe he had never invited me. Maybe I misheard. And in any case, he never set a time.

Of course he's not dead.

Arrested?

I knocked again, loudly, startling myself.

To continuing silence.

The neighbour. Raul had said the neighbour one floor down kept an eye on him.

The smell of freshly-painted walls got stronger as I went down, my footsteps echoing. Here there was a bell. My heart was still hammering as I rang it. Footsteps. They paused at the door. I positioned myself so I could be seen through the peephole.

The door opened cautiously, held by a chain. A pair of eyes gleamed in the darkness, gender indeterminate.

"*Si?*"

Male. I struggled to assemble some Spanish.

"*Lo siento … Senor Harris? Yo su hijo… er hija.*" He could probably see I was a daughter and not a son.

Now the eyes lit up, teeth emerged below them, the chain rattled back and a beaming grey-haired little man emerged and pumped my hand, speaking enthusiastically.

I waited for a gap.

"*Muchas gracias, Senor…Mi padre no esta … Er, Policia?*"

Now the eyes opened wide, the grin became even bigger, he shook his head vigorously, drowning me in a waterfall of Spanish as he made it plain that no Police were involved. He took me by the arm, pointing down the stairs, obviously indicating directions. Seeing my blank expression, he tapped me on the arm to tell me I should stay where I was and disappeared back into his flat, a rabbit down its burrow, re-emerging a few seconds later with a notepad and a pencil, scribbling something as he walked and talked.

He tore the sheet out of the notebook and presented it to me. It was a beautifully drawn map telling me quite clearly to go down the stairs, turn right out of the house, then right again down what looked like a narrow alley where he had sketched out a single storey building with a pitched roof with 'C.D.R.' written beside it. He slapped me on the back encouragingly and leant over the balcony waving and smiling as I went down the stairs.

You remember Pinocchio's Dad in the film? That was him.

The moment I stepped outside the heat hit me, followed by the now familiar smell of drains. Faces watched with blank curiosity. An intruder. For the first time I was without any kind of guide, Raul, Miguel or even a taxi driver. Maybe Pinocchio's Dad had not understood what I was saying and had sent me on some other mission entirely or his map was an enjoyable invention to confuse a stranger and pass the time, and he had launched me on a magical Cuban mystery tour that had no destination. But there was the alley as shown on his map and I picked my way down it past old car tyres and plastic crates, eyes watching me from cracked windows; and exactly where he had indicated was a wooden hut with a pitched roof. *'Comite de la Defensa de la Revolucion'* was painted above the double door, the C, D and R in bold letters a foot high.

One of the doors was open. The sound of a piano came from inside, stumbling, repeating the same phrase over and over, honing it, before moving on, still hesitant.

I walked quietly through the door into the cooler but still stifling darkness of the long, narrow hut. As my eyes adjusted I could see a young boy, 12, maybe 13, sitting at an upright piano at the far end, at the foot of a small stage, lit by the dust-beamed sunlight that had managed to force its way down the narrow gap between the adjoining building and the only side of the hut that had windows.

Next to him, sitting very still, his back bowed in concentration, was my father.

The boy faltered, tried again. Still stumbled. My father said something, very quietly. I could barely hear his voice. Then he reached out with his left arm and played the phrase slowly, deliberately. The boy nodded, tried again, this time succeeding.

There was a single chair, looking abandoned, in the middle of the floor. Stacked against the walls were more chairs, a blackboard on an easel, some mats, a vaulting horse and what looked like ropes and uprights to form a boxing ring. The Committee for the Defence of the Revolution building was also a gym? A classroom? Concert hall? The chair was facing the piano. I tip-toed over to it and sat down to watch.

When Poppy and I were children your grandfather had issued resounding proclamations about not giving us music lessons. Too busy, he said, much too busy, and anyway, parents made lousy teachers. But occasionally when I was practising on the piano at home, I became aware that he had stopped at the door and was listening. At first it made me nervous but as I watched him now with the little boy, leaning in to him intently, making quiet noises of encouragement, I remembered how his advice on these occasions had always been gentle and concise.

The memory disorientated me. For most of my life I had carried a version of childhood with my father that had largely consisted of an inferno of shouting matches and raging confrontations. This skewed it. And as I sat there another memory flashed at me with shocking clarity, coming from nowhere, unfamiliar – almost unwelcome – of how I had watched from the ground floor window of our school room as my father walked my mother up and down the garden, his arm around her. She had her head on his chest, a handkerchief held to her face, weeping copiously. She had bought a golden-haired retriever, which she had called Sandy. Sandy had got out and been run over by a tractor and killed. We were all upset, but she was devastated. My father was gentle and comforting. I followed them, my own eyes blurred with weeping, as they walked from the yew tree to the herbaceous border and back, back and forth, back and forth, and her distress – so much greater than mine – stilled my puny tears and I continued to watch in dry-eyed awe at the sight of my father loving my mother.

Why had I denied myself such a memory? Did I not want to think that at one time they might have been happy together? That he might have been a kind man?

But as I sat there, I remembered also his tyrannical, fearsome rages – this gentleman, now leaning solicitously towards his pupil at the piano. I remembered standing outside their bedroom door in the afternoon. I must have been eleven.

"You vacuous, insipid bloody woman! Can you not just accept and move on? Or is your blue blood too thin for that? Just sit there fucking well snivelling. Five hundred years of inbreeding, no wonder all you do is turn to jelly! That is my reality – you hear me? If you can't take it crawl back to Mummy and Daddy and breed sheep –"

Raging now, utterly reckless I had thrown open the door.

"Don't speak to my Mum like that! You horrible man! Don't speak to her like that!"

For a moment they both stared at me, frozen, he red-faced, she watery-eyed. She was the first to move. She got up from the bed where she had been hunched and hurried towards me.

"Ssh, darling… Ssh, ssh…" she was saying.

From behind her, he yelled, "Get her out of here! Get that abortion out of here!"

"I hate you!" I screamed from the corridor as the door was shut on me.

My father. Now a shrunken old stranger.

I became aware that the boy was on his feet, collecting his music. He thanked my father who waved him away, muttering. As the boy turned to go, he saw me and froze.

Sensing this, my father turned also. After a moment he nodded to the boy who hurried past me out of the hut.

"Been here long?"

"Few minutes."

I got off my chair and went to sit on the stool the boy had vacated next to him.

"You give music lessons?"

"Nothing else I'm good for."

"The money must come in handy if they have cut off your pension."

"I don't take any fucking money."

He turned away from me irritably and started doodling notes on the keyboard with his good hand.

"You said you wanted me to come over."

"Did I?"

On guard, like a child. I waited. Clearly, I had not misheard.

"There's this bloody worm," he went on, still fingering the keyboard but more sporadically now. "Can't remember its name but it flourishes in the Cuban climate and attacks the particular wood used in these pianos. Russian pianos these are, half our pianos came from Russia. Half practically everything came from Russia. Used to. So there it is. The most musical nation in the world and its pianos are fucked to buggery."

"Is that what you wanted to talk about?"

"Not really." His eyes were wandering around the room, refusing to meet mine. With his left hand he was now massaging the knuckles of the inert hand in his lap as though hoping to bring them back to life. "You've travelled a long way to see me. I thought perhaps I owed you –"

"Not just to see you. I had business here."

"As you wish, lass."

Staring at me. Suddenly confident. It was me that looked away. Fingers of bright sunlight, poking through the window frame, hit the floor just behind him, the particles of dust dancing above his head like gnats.

"Isn't it a bit late to talk about what we owe each other?"

He puffed out his cheeks and blew a long breath. Now his eyes settled vaguely on the keyboard.

"What did you make of all that, then?"

"All what?"

"Last night."

"Turned out a bit of a coronation for you."

"I meant the music."

"No, you didn't."

Definitely my point this time. He smiled.

"Lawyer."

"You really sent people to prison for being gay?"

He shifted in his chair.

"Correction camps."

"Sure."

"You heard me. I'm not proud of it."

"And you spent Mum's money on the music school?"

"My half, fuck you. I took my half. My legal entitlement."

"*Her* money. Not yours."

"Her fucking father's money, her grandfather's, great grandfather's, money made on the backs of West Indian sugar workers, from grubby properties in Balham with outside lavatories."

"Money you married!"

"*Exactly!*"

"What does that mean?"

"Haven't you worked that out by now? I'd had enough. I'd compromised my whole life. My fault, of course, not hers, never hers but I'd had enough – of being sneered at, of being the Bollinger fucking Bolshevik. My hero, my God-substitute – from when I was very young, first learning about music – was the immortal, eternally bloody-minded Ludwig. Your mother never tell you about that? Well, she probably thought the whole thing a ridiculous obsession. He didn't give a shit, our Ludwig, who he offended or what he did, he saw only one duty, one noble truth. To his art and his integrity. Ludwig was who I always wanted to be. And here I was, a miner's son for fuck's sake, a miner's son living in a sodding great Georgian pile in Surrey while the poor bloody miners were fighting for their lives. Everything – apart from my music, and then only occasionally – was a lie."

"Including your family?"

Silence. Eyes on the floor, shifting ever more in his seat. It was an effort.

"Yes." Quietly. Then – "YES. I'm sorry. Maybe people like me shouldn't have families."

"Which is why you immediately started another one over here."

"That... just happened."

"Another mistake?"

"Oh... probably. The boy is... The whole of his generation seem fucked up to me. But what I am trying to say to you – about you, Poppy, your Mum, is that I couldn't take it anymore. I had to get out. I had to. And if you're on about the money, Christ it wasn't as if she needed it, was it?"

I wanted a cigarette. I had been good. Raul's disapproval had helped. But I wanted one now.

It was not long after he had left us. My mother had been at her desk – the one with the secret drawers you both always liked when you were little, the one I still use in Montclair. I had come to tell her that Poppy and I were going to muck out the stables. But then she always wanted to know exactly where we were at any time of day. It was irritating but we went along with it.

"Mum, we... what's the matter?"

Her shoulders were shaking, her head bowed, her hand on the telephone.

"Mum..."

She shook her head vigorously like a dog coming out of water. I hurried to her, uncertain, frightened, tried to hug her.

"What is it, Mum? What's happened?"

She pulled away from my arms, head averted. This was not for me, she was saying, this was not a child's business.

Slowly, insistently I pieced it out of her.

She had got her bank statement in the post that morning. The main deposit account was half what she had expected. She called the bank. They told her that your grandfather had taken the rest of it in cash the day before he flew to Cuba.

I wonder now if this wasn't the moment when I first began to see myself as responsible for my family, head of the household, the role I found myself playing (assuming?) in our family, with you, with Marty and which in the end he found so difficult?

It was certainly the first time I found myself mother to my mother. I tried again to cradle her, but after the first shock and disbelief my own bewildered rage was volcanic, overwhelming. She saw what an effort it was and – still fighting her own tears – became the parent again, trying to comfort me.

"It's OK," she said. "We'll be OK. We'll sell Windings and find a smaller house. We'll be fine."

But I didn't want to sell my home. I wanted to kill my father. I wept uncontrollably as my mother in her turn held me and I wrapped myself in the comforting prospect of murder.

"I think it is best we don't talk about it," I said to him.

He nodded.

"You do know, don't you…" He cleared his throat. "Well it's perhaps not even worth saying, but I always hoped you might join me… School holidays and things…"

I agreed. It wasn't worth saying.

"No. She never said."

"I didn't want to lose touch. I just… had to do it."

Now he was looking at me and I knew he was telling me the truth. His truth. And hatred and dreams of murder shrivelled – as, in truth, they already had – as I saw him now through the other end of the telescope, frail and old and in some perverse way heroic.

"I sent you birthday cards. Every year until you were 21. You never acknowledged them so I gave up. Did you… get them?"

I nodded.

"That's how I had the address in Miramar."

He sighed.

"Well, here we are. It is good you came over."

"Yes, probably."

"You don't sound too certain?" Smiling. Uncertain, suddenly vulnerable.

"Should I?"

A tacit. We both swung gently in the air.

"Do you still play?" he asked, indicating the piano.

I smiled, vengeful again, as the memory uncurled. No peace. Not yet.

"Not since you walked out on me. I haven't touched a note."

He looked nervous. As though he had guessed. Or knew.

He had left for Cuba on the Wednesday. The School Concert was due to take place on the Friday. In front of the whole school. Parents were invited. The irony did not escape Poppy or me. I was scheduled to play – Poulenc as I recall. Believe it or not, your mother was quite a good pianist in those days. And as my father's daughter my appearance on the school stage always carried a bit of a bow wave. On this occasion a tsunami. They were very nice about it. Miss Alcroft, my

Music Teacher told me I could withdraw if I wanted to. She said everybody would understand. But I said no. There was a violinist before me. A boy called Stephen. I had a bit of a crush on him. He was six foot at least. I liked tall boys even then. He finished, took his bow and we crossed on the steps up to the stage. He smiled kindly at me as he stood to one side to let me pass. Such silence as I walked to the piano. I could hear my own footsteps. I sat, adjusted the stool, arranged my music and prepared. And suddenly there were his hands on the keyboard, my father's hands and the piano became his thing, his world, tainted, treacherous and I couldn't touch it because it was him, it was a betrayal of my mother, the sound of it loathsome, the keys poisonous. I tried to move my fingers but they didn't want to. I tried. I tried again. I could feel the whole school waiting for me. I don't remember what I did. Poppy told me I said "sorry", shut the lid and walked off backstage. She said I seemed quite calm. What I do remember is that Miss Alcroft – for some reason, perhaps because she wasn't a full member of the staff, we always called her that, not Susan or Betty or whatever – had found me in the girls' changing room and was holding me and rocking me. I was certainly crying then, howling from the darkest, loneliest part of me, in humiliation and deep, raging loss. And I swore in my heart never to touch a piano again.

My father was looking away through the widow as I told him. When I had finished, I thought I could see tears in his eyes but it might have been a trick of the light.

"I'm sorry," he said at last. His voice was husky. "There is nothing I can say except that I am very sorry."

"It's a start."

He turned back. Now I could see the tears. They were drying on his cheek, his eyes still glistening, but he ignored them. He looked brisk, determined. He shuffled his chair closer to the piano.

"Come," he said beckoning me closer. "We used to play duets. Do you remember? Saint-Saens. My left hand, your right. Come on."

It took me a moment to understand. Then I slid the stool back, horrified.

"NO! I am not going to."

"Yes, you are. Come on."

"No! And I don't remember them."

"You will. Come on!"

He stared at me, my father once more. Slowly, mesmerised, I moved the stool back next to him. He reached out awkwardly with his left hand, took my right and positioned it limply on the keyboard.

"I don't want to do this."

"I want you to."

Infinitely reluctantly, still in a kind of trance, I shuffled even closer and half prepared my fingers.

"Just listen."

Gently, slowly, he played two phrases. They echoed from somewhere inside me.

"Remember?"

"No."

"You play the response. *Da-da-da-DAA-dee.*"

"I can't."

"Yes, you can."

Laboriously he positioned his left hand where my right should have been on the keyboard and carefully picked out the notes.

And I remembered them.

"Go on."

"I don't want to."

"Go *on.*"

And, of course, I *did* want to. I wanted to feel the sound of music coming from my fingers again.

I managed two notes. Then my fingers froze again.

He said nothing but reached across and showed me again.

This time I managed the whole phrase. Flat and awkward. But it felt wonderful.

"Good."

He played the echo and turned to me. But my mind was a whirling blank. I shook my head hopelessly.

He reached across and showed me. And again, I remembered. Not just the phrase. I remembered the music. It was – miraculously – sitting inside me.

I started to play with him – slowly, he had set the tempo – and the notes, the fingering seemed to swim towards me as I reached them, some other self in control, a memory that my body, if not my mind, had stored and was releasing. I was unaware of anything except the sound we were making together, flying in this little capsule and yet totally focussed inside it: when I went wrong I knew what I had done – or he showed me – and I was able to go back and pick it up without breaking the trance. It was as sweet, as exciting as anything I could ever remember having done in my life. I don't know how long we played – maybe only a few bars – but it was like a whole life coming back to me and when we stopped I don't know if it was because my fingers had run out of notes or because I needed to breathe or because I couldn't see the keyboard for tears.

"There, there," he said, patting me shyly on the shoulder as I sat there shaking. "Don't blub. You'll have me at it."

I accepted a shot of rum in the coffee he laboriously prepared for me Cuban style (short, strong, sweet) after we had climbed the four flights back up to his apartment (your mother puffing a bit, your grandfather wheezing noisily).

Still breathing heavily, he produced a cigar and lit it with much ceremony, holding the matchbox awkwardly between his knees while he struck the match.

"I have a good friend who keeps me in these," he said, shaking the flame out and releasing a stream of pungent smoke. "You disapprove, no doubt, but I would rather go to my grave with a good cigar than live a few weeks longer without."

"I'm struggling to keep off cigarettes, I can't talk."

"Give in, woman, give in. My answer to most things. But, I suspect, not yours. Am I right?"

"Probably."

"I know virtually nothing about you. Tell me about your life."

"You know I'm a lawyer."

"Tell me something I want to hear."

"Not sure there is much. I live just outside New York in Montclair. Two children, both boys, both at College."

"Husband?"

"He left me a few months ago."

"For another woman?"

"Yes."

"Younger?"

"No. That might have been easier. Just… better for him, I guess."

"Fuck him. Found another man?"

I laughed.

"That's not how it works with me."

"Well… At least I am now learning something about my daughter. So he buggered off?"

"Just like you."

"… I suppose so."

He flicked ash into a saucer, looking uncomfortable.

"You were angry with him and came to take your anger out on me?"

Now I was silenced. I had underestimated him.

"Children… they are the cards you are dealt. Partners you choose. Or something."

He gestured with the rum bottle.

"Top up?"

I put my hand over my coffee cup, shaking my head.

"What are your politics, lass? What do you vote?"

"Republican."

"Fuck's sake…"

I grinned.

"I warned you."

"*Why?*"

"I believe in personal responsibility."

"And Democrats don't? *Marxists* don't? What about corporate responsibility? Caring for the poor? Universal education? Healing the sick?"

"Like Cuba?"

"Why not? In that at least we have a record second to none."

"Look at you, Dad. Just look at what's happened to you. You served the comrades for over thirty years and they reward you by cutting off your pension, sticking you in a poky top floor apartment without a lift and tossing you in gaol on a whim. *Responsibility?*"

"A blip. Rough with smooth. I've had a good run. And I have friends. This won't last."

"You had Fidel, Dad. And he's gone. You're a gifted man who has given a lot to this island. You shouldn't have to live like this."

He waved his hand in front of his face flapping away both the cigar smoke and my words.

"I'm fine, lass. Fine. I made a choice with my life and I stand by it. Anyway, it's too late to change now."

"You chose a closed Marxist tyranny over a life that anybody else in the world would have envied. You chose this over your family. Over me, for Christ's sake!"

He sighed.

"It was nothing to do with you. Perhaps it should have been, but it wasn't. I chose a life of purpose and ideals over a class ridden, bigoted, decadent, directionless, post Imperial *mess*. Anyway, I've told you – it's too late to change now."

"No, it's NOT! Leave here – come back to America with me!" It hadn't – consciously – crossed my mind. But it was said now. "Get to know your grandchildren. You can learn to terrify them. It's over for you here, you know that. Try it. If you like it you could at least live out the rest of your life in some comfort. Come and make my life a misery for a bit – what do you say?"

And there it suddenly was. A plan. Mad, problematic but almost certainly workable. He teased the ash off the end of his cigar thoughtfully.

"You don't understand. I ought, of course, to say that it is kind of you. But you don't understand. You are an American, or have become one, so how could you? Please don't take this personally – I've had close American friends in my life and I have admired them – but my hatred for your adopted country, its imperialism, its bloated, arrogant sense of entitlement, its cruelty in the name of righteousness, its hypocritical venality, its blundering uncontrolled greed goes so deep that nothing, no change of administration, no superficial change of policy could persuade me to set foot in it. I know I deserted you, your sister, your mother. I have no voice in your life and I don't look for one. You chose America and I am glad if it has been good to you. I chose this country. I chose it for its values and however compromised they can appear to be now, I am grateful for what they inspired in me, the anchor they gave my life at a crucial time. So this is still where my heart is and where I would like to die."

"A tyranny. Noble in its way, perhaps. Once. But a tyranny."

"Still noble to me."

We sat in silence, nowhere to go.

BERNARD

I don't think I am going to see her again. Doesn't want me to come to the airport.

Can't stand them anyway.

So. Said goodbyes.

What the fuck. She votes Republican.

Wouldn't have minded a bit longer. Interesting woman. Despite everything. Tough. Like me. Maybe not quite as tough as she thinks. Like me? Meaningless. Genes are just a fucking accident. Nurture rules. Different worlds. Just happen to be father and daughter. Accidents of spermatozoa.

Wonder if we will meet again? Said she would try and come back. But that's... what you say. What am I to her? An ogre, of course, goes without saying. And quite right. No excuses. But maybe something changed. She asked me to go and live with her. And seemed to mean it.

I didn't think twice. Not for a second. Did she understand? Do I? It is hard to fucking well remember sometimes. The certainty. The absolute.... conviction. An end to greed, racism, sexism. The liberation of the human spirit. Historical fucking inevitability. The tenth house. That was what did it for me. If a village built ten houses nobody could move into any of them until the tenth house was built. I liked that.

Music for the masses. That was important. The sounds of Cuba.

And the sex. Got to be. Those Cuban asses. Rebeca's ass. The most wonderful, glorious rump in all creation. Something I experienced that you didn't, Ludwig. Part of it. Definitely.

But not all. And the bones are still there. Housing, schools, hospitals for all. Every snot-ridden motherfucker. A testament of a kind. And to be proud of, why not? But the spirit has gone. Raul's generation. Mean spirited, envious. Gucci Raul. Another accident. Definitely. Chalk and cheese. I can see me in Maggie. Not in him. Except his love of women. His mother seems to think he's OK and she's usually a good judge. I'm out of touch. With everybody, not just with his generation. In my bubble. Old. And now useless.

Those fucking snoopers from the CDR have already been round. Knew they would. Who was she? A foreigner? An American? Nya, nya, nya. I didn't tell them she is my daughter. Fuck 'em, they make me sick.

Maybe I should have gone with her, got the fuck out of this place.

Except that I still love it. Sort of.

Capitalism shaking itself to bits, we should be cashing in. The new Marxist dawn. Bollocks. Nothing. Zero. But we're still here so maybe we got some things right. Even the bankers starting to talk our language, greed, responsibility, long term, blah, blah. While they pocket their bonuses.

Nothing going to change.

I think the truth is that I am not a real revolutionary. Sorry, Ludwig. I am somebody who made a gesture and is now trapped in it.

I wonder what she will tell her American family about me? Anything?

I wonder if I will ever see her again.

Fuck it. There's only me. We all die alone. That's how it is.

[EXTRACT FROM BERNARD HARRIS' TAPED DIARY (4)]

Chapter 13

The thing I remember most about that dinner we had the night before I came home was how Raul held my hand as I wept. Weeping is not something I am used to doing, as I guess you know. But Raul *listened.* He heard me. That was what made being with him so good. We had been talking and he had been listening. I wasn't used to that. The tears just came. From nowhere. Well, perhaps not from nowhere. We had been talking about your grandfather and they ambushed me. Sobs, great heaving, ugly sobs. I was ashamed. What was happening to me? I had cried in front of my father and now in front of Raul. But he seemed to think it was fine and just reached across the table and held my hand. Which made me cry a lot more but feel a lot better.

Looking back on it, it wasn't all that surprising. It had been a crowded few days, rediscovering a bloody minded old father I had killed off years ago, meeting a whole new family, Havana, the hot, disorientating haze of Cuba itself, and now sitting on a balcony with my beautiful half-brother who was being so kind and holding my hand as the sun sank fiery red into the Straits of Florida behind him. It was the perfect time and place for tears, and I obliged.

We were eating at what is known here as a *paladar*, a private house licensed to charge small groups for meals. This one belongs to the mother of a friend of Raul's and he particularly wanted us to go there. Raul explained with open envy that his friend, Pablo, had got away to America – legally or illegally was not clear – leaving his mother to live alone in this tall, thin, end-of-terrace house facing out to sea. Maruja is an elegant, aristocratic-looking woman in her sixties, tall and thin like her house, with cropped grey hair and a severe expression that at unexpected moments can be replaced by a glinting, probably mischievous smile, coming mainly from her eyes. Raul explained that she had inherited the house from her once wealthy family who, supporters of Fidel, had chosen to stay in Cuba after the Revolution and had lived, he hinted, to regret it. She is an artist, the walls of the entrance hall crowded with paintings. Some are hers – the abstracts, as she was at pains to point out – the others are traditional (by which she seemed to imply effete) 19thC European portraits and landscapes, very possibly valuable. The faded, shabby furniture, worn rugs and once beautifully tiled floors all speak of a lifestyle very different from her present role as chef and waitress in her own home. But if this had been a disappointment to her she showed no sign of it, leading us up the curved stone staircase with impeccable dignity, across a large living room that housed a spinette and a couple of violins on stands as well as yet more shabby sofas and elegant inlaid tables, out onto a narrow balcony on which our table for two had been set and laid with old silver cutlery and damask napkins in monogrammed bone napkin rings. The balcony continued, curving around the corner of the house where another slightly larger table had been set for four more guests, positioned so that both groups enjoyed some measure of privacy from each other.

Raul clearly revelled in the style and elegance both of his friend's mother and of the house, his eyes darting with a mixture of pride and anxiety that I should be pleased with what I saw. He told me he had been around earlier in the day to make sure that Maruja was properly primed that I was his new-found sister and that we would want lobster and a good wine. As you may possibly remember, I don't particularly care for lobster and one glass of wine is normally my limit, but of course I expressed great appreciation as a dusty bottle of Cote du Rhone was produced. Maruja opened it expertly and poured me a little to taste. Assuming expertise I nodded confidently and she filled my glass. As she reached across to Raul's he covered it with his hand. I knew he didn't smoke – thanks to his disapproval I was down to one furtive cigarette a day in my hotel bedroom – and now I remembered that he didn't drink either. No wonder his skin glowed. Faced with a bottle of wine I wouldn't be able to do justice to and lobster which I didn't like I knew the meal would have its limitations, but Raul was attentive and proud, the view magnificent and I was very much enjoying myself until I started to cry.

I had been telling Raul about trying to play a duet with the old bastard and what a hash I had made of it, at least to start with, and we were laughing. And then suddenly I was crying. I think the thought had flashed up at me that he might die at any moment and that I might never see him again. I might never again see this self-centred bully I had spent a lifetime wanting to kill. So, of course, I started to cry.

Still holding one hand Raul manoeuvred a napkin into the other for me to dab with. We continued to hold hands as I mopped and straightened myself out, hoping Maruja hadn't heard me from the kitchen.

"I guess that means I probably care for him a bit, doesn't it?" I said as, a little reluctantly, I withdrew my hand from his.

He shrugged, this time not returning my smile.

"You don't, do you?"

He shook his head.

"My mother, yes. Him, no. Hate, fear. Sometimes admire. Not love. For what?"

"Did he bully you? Beat you? He didn't with us, but being a boy I thought maybe he –"

"He try. My mother not let him. One day – I was ten, maybe eleven – he hit me. So my mother hit him – whap!"

He smiled at the memory.

"May be that's what my mother should have done," I said.

"When I was little, was nice. He took me swimming. Presents. Fidel was like my uncle. My father – our father – was important man. I liked that."

"So why did you guys move out?"

"My mother… She don't like his girlfriends, his bad temper. Everything. Don't want to live with him. We go to live with her mother. Work on farm. I hate it. Wooden house with kitchen smoke everywhere, cold when cold, too hot when hot. I share the bedroom with my mother, I sleep on a mattress on the floor. Is little village on hill with Catholic church at top and my grandmother she still Catholic and she try to make us go to church every Sunday and I hate it. Only good thing is the orange tree in garden and we get oranges down with stick with wire circle to pull down the orange. Beautiful."

"You didn't see him?"

"Not when we live in the country. But my mother know I am unhappy. I bicycle five miles to school every day. I hate farm, hate church, hate little wooden house. So we come back here and she learn to become a nurse and I go to school. We don't see him so much, is OK. Except we have no money, nobody has money and the girls in my school, some, they sleep with tourists, sometimes boys also, and everybody looking for ways to make money, money, money."

"And you? Did you sleep with tourists?"

His face darkened, both hands waving the thought away.

"I don't want to talk about it. The other boys they drink, they smoke, they do drugs if they can, I don't do that. I learn about sex, for sure. In Cuba is easy to learn about sex and sex is good. But always with condom. I have to be healthy. I have to be strong. For new life. One day. When capitalism come to me. Or I go to capitalism."

He grinned shyly, then looked away. I waited for him to continue.

"I went to University to become a teacher and I tried, I like to teach, but every day – where is the money? I have to live with my mother. What for? I am man, I want to live my life, not hers. Yes, I like clothes, cars, good food – is a crime? I see pictures, I see television, films. I see another life. Why not for me? My father think is crime. My mother, too, but she still love me. Not my father, he hate me. Maybe not hate, but he don't want to speak to me. How can I love him? He think the Revolution was good, so good, make lives better and maybe, yes, then Revolution was good, but is old man's Revolution, and we need change. Is prison here, people all frightened and looking for money to live. Pablo, my friend, Maruja's son he get to America and he is lucky. I want to go to America, stupid, stupid America –"

"Why are we stupid?" I thought he loved us.

"The blockade. Stupid, stupid. End blockade, end *socialismos* in Cuba. Finished. We sell to you – cigars, holidays, operations in hospital, mangoes, sugar, we sell, you buy. Friends. Instead we have prison. Fidel make our prison. America keep the key. I want to get out of prison. I hate it!"

His eyes suddenly flicked over my shoulder. I turned. Maruja was standing in the doorway. Behind her a group of people were admiring the violins. Her eyes flashed at Raul. He looked down at once, understanding.

So did I. Even though they would be seated around the corner this kind of conversation was surely dangerous.

Maruja settled her new guests in and then came back to our table, removing the lobster plates and bringing us Cuban ice cream and some kind of caramel.

We ate in silence.

I wanted to tell him I would take him back to America with me, would help him find his new life. But I had only known him four days. He belonged to his mother. His father, perhaps. To himself. Certainly not to me.

I took my diary from my handbag and tore out a page, writing my email address, postal address, home, office number and cell. I passed it across to him.

"You and I are *not* going to lose touch," I said.

No response. He was staring, looking sad, at the scrap of paper. Waiting for me to say more?

"Do you have a number I can contact you on? Email address?"

He shook his head, still not looking up.

"My mother at hospital."

I pushed my diary across the table, indicating he should write in it.

He did so, still looking forlorn, then pushed it back to me.

"You come back to see me?" he asked, looking up at me finally.

"Maybe… I'd like to. Very much. Let's just see what happens." Come and live with me in Montclair, I wanted to say. In my empty house.

"Shall we get the check?"

He nodded and signalled to Maruja who was passing through the room behind us on her way to the other guests.

He stared morosely at the table as we waited. He didn't want me to go. He really didn't want me to go. And I realised in that moment that I was loved. The shock, the dizzying newness of it was overwhelming. I reached across the table and took his hand.

He looked up at me, at first surprised. Then, when he saw my eyes, his face flooded.

It was true and it was good. This beautiful person was part of me and loved me.

I took my hand away and we went on as if we were the people we had been before.

It was dark when we got outside. Still warm. I could smell the sea.

My last night in Havana. That empty hotel room. And then the empty house in Montclair. Why did I have to go? Why not stay here a bit longer? With my new half-brother Raul who loves me.

"What shall we do? It is still early."

Miguel's car was parked at the kerb. Raul was leaning on it, his elbows on the roof, staring out to sea. He said nothing for a moment. Then suddenly seemed to come to a decision.

"I show you. Come."

We drove in silence, following the sea front road, down through a long underpass and then, after a few miles, as the city was thinning out, he turned right along a dusty track between tall heavy mesh fencing topped with razor wire. It felt military. I became uneasy. It got worse. Ahead of us was a heavy closed metal gate with a sentry box, flying the Cuban flag, beside it. We pulled up. He got out and waved to the armed sentry who had emerged purposefully from his box.

"Have you ten dollars?" Raul was grinning at me. I climbed out of the car. I must have been looking very nervous. "Is OK. He is friend of mine. But ten dollars is good."

I passed a bill across and watched as Raul went across to the sentry box. I didn't see money change hands but after a moment he beckoned to me, smiling.

The sentry opened the gate just wide enough to let us walk through, saluting me with a grin as I approached. It looked suspiciously like a leer. Was this where Raul took his women?

"Raul –"

"Is OK. I told him you are my sister." Reading my mind?

I looked back, still uncomfortable. The sentry was watching. He waved. Friendly.

"Please… come. You will like." Raul was waiting, his arm stretched out towards me. As I reached him, he slipped it through mine in his usual way. The path was getting sandy. You could just glimpse the moon playing hide-and-seek through the trees.

"*El Comandante* has a house over there," he said, nodding to his left.

I stopped in horror.

"And for a ten-dollar bribe, we can just –"

He laughed.

"No, no. Many more fences, soldiers. Maybe tanks. Who knows if he is there? He has many houses. Sometimes one, sometimes another. So CIA can't find him."

Grinning, he put his arm around my shoulder and we walked on.

"Here is safe. Nobody shoot us. Nobody see us. Is nice. I promise."

I could hear the swell of the sea before I saw it. As the path emerged from the woods there, ahead of us, was a small curved bay with scattered rocks and a gently heaving sea in the moonlight. And nobody but us. Perfection.

And a perfect place for him to fuck his women. I wasn't sure I wanted to go any further.

But he was taking off his sandals. He left them on the path. I did the same. We walked across the warm sand towards the sea. Stood side by side in the middle of the beach.

"Is this where you take your women, Raul?" I couldn't resist.

His head dropped. Sulky.

"It's *different*. I bring you here because is beautiful. I want you to see it."

He sat down on the sand, his knees hunched up, looking away from me.

"And because you go away tomorrow and maybe I never see you again. I want you to remember. This. Me."

A little boy. And I forgot about the all the other women and just wanted to cuddle him. I dropped down onto the sand beside him and put my hand on his arm.

"We're not going to lose touch. I told you that. Not now we have found each other."

"How? You come back to Cuba? I come to America? How?"

"We'll figure it out."

"You don't know –"

"Well – as I say –"

"No – you don't know about *me*. What you are for *me*. All my life I think… I go here, I go there. I am angry. With Fidel. With my father. Sometimes my mother. With… policemen… everybody…with Cuba. I want to do this, I want to do that, so I do nothing. Then I find you. And you are part of me. And you are wise and beautiful and you are like the good part of me that I didn't know. You give me peace and love that is good… not just money and fucking and orgasm and goodbye. But now you go – so it is goodbye. Yes. You forget me. Is true? You forget me?"

He was staring at me, wide-eyed. For a moment I could not speak.

"Do you think…" I had to start again. "Raul do you really think that meeting you has not been important to me? Has not changed me, too? I've never felt such… Closeness, such instant closeness, to someone I had only just met. It is very, very strange indeed. What you say – like meeting part of myself. It's a little frightening."

"*Not* frightening! *Wonderful*!"

He reached up and held my head in his hands with a big, beautiful, eager smile that seemed to burst across his face. I started to laugh.

"OK… All right… Wonderful."

Now laughing too, he leaned forward and kissed me – very briefly – on the lips. And it seemed the most tender, the most natural thing to do.

Just as suddenly he got up and walked down to the edge of the water.

"Come!" he called.

I followed him.

The water was lapping our ankles. Almost lukewarm.

"You like to swim?" he asked.

"Don't be silly. In what?"

He puffed out his cheeks dismissively and pulled his shirt over his head, throwing it back up the beach. Then in one movement his trousers and underpants came off and he was naked. He grinned at me – I was keeping my eyes firmly on his face – then turned and ran out into the water.

I watched as he waded in, the moonlight playing on his back and – I had allowed my eyes to wander by now – on what I decided instantly was the cutest butt I had ever seen. He dived in and started swimming. I watched until he was no more than a disturbance in the swell.

I felt a little deserted. And overdressed. Cluttered. So why not? If he could, so could I. I had not been skinny dipping for many years, a lifetime, but I could remember how much I had enjoyed it. And Raul was too far out now to see anything.

I stepped back onto the dry sand, pulled my dress off, then unhooked my bra and – very quickly, before I could change my mind – pulled down my panties, threw them up the beach and ran into the water.

That warm, welcoming, shocking embrace, took my breath away. The freedom to fly and float, utterly unencumbered. I lay on my back, paddling gently with my hands, looking at the moon. The water slipped between my breasts as they surfaced, intimately caressed my thighs. I forgot about Raul, I forgot about coming home, I forgot about everything except the utter pleasure of being where I was and doing what I was doing. A child again.

"*Hola!*"

Raul was ten, maybe twelve yards away. Even at that distance his teeth and hair gleamed in the moonlight, his chest shimmered milkily under the water.

Quickly I swung my feet down and trod water, hoping he had not seen my breasts.

"Is nice?"

"Beautiful."

"Good. You look beautiful. Have fun."

Glib little charmer, I thought. Don't come any nearer. Please don't come any nearer.

"Are you sure nobody else will come here?"

His grin got even bigger.

"Is guarantee."

And with a wave he turned and kicked back towards the beach, that butt breaking through the surface, creaming behind him.

At which point I realised I was soon going to have to come out of the water stark naked and get dressed in front of him. Putting it off I turned and swam slowly out to sea for a little, before deciding that there was no point and it was only nakedness. As I got closer, he was sitting watching me, still naked, his knees up, his arms around them. His modesty by accident or thoughtful design? Either way I was thankful.

I crouched in the shallows, still hiding.

"The air is warm. I am dry already," he called.

"I'm shy," I called back, laughing.

"Don't. Naked is just naked."

Well, yes. But my ungainly hulk? Stretch marks? With luck too dark. Here goes. I got up and strode towards him, wanting to cover my breasts and my crotch but determined to brave it out.

He seemed to ignore my nakedness, patting his shirt, which he had smoothed out on the sand a discreet yard or more away from him, for me to sit on. I joined him, no longer self-conscious.

"That was lovely," I said, aware even as I spoke of how inadequately the word matched the moment.

"I'm pleased you see it."

He lay back on the sand, naked, utterly confident and absurdly beautiful in the moonlight.

I continued to sit, my arms around my protectively hunched up knees, now see-sawing back to shyness again, sharply aware once more of aging flesh, imperfect breasts next to my Caravaggio brother staring calmly up at the moon.

He patted the sand behind me.

"Come. Share moon with me."

Very slowly, mesmerised, I lay back. Still that yard between us. Why did it matter? My brother. No threat. But it did.

"You know names of stars?" he asked.

"Some. I used to. I would like to learn."

"Me too."

We lay in silence. The air was warm, the sea soughed.

"You like your swim?"

He reached out and took my hand. This was easy territory for us now.

"Beautiful."

We lay in silence, holding hands, floating in a still, quietly shushing world.

"Tomorrow you go."

"Yes."

"I want to say I love you."

I felt no need to reply. Why shouldn't he? And why shouldn't I love him back?

He sat up, shifted onto his elbow, looking down at me. I glanced across. He was aroused. I looked away, but felt neither surprise not anxiety. We were naked. He was a man. It happened. I still felt no anxiety when he leant towards me. Then he kissed me gently on the mouth. I held my face to him. Now his mouth stayed on mine, and he kissed me slowly and deeply. And I kissed him back, my hands still by my side. It felt natural and good. The most beautiful, the most tender of kisses between two people who were part of each other.

Then he brought his whole body towards me, moved onto me and I felt all his nakedness on mine, his flesh hot and shocking on my flesh, his hardness on my thigh and I bucked and rolled away from under him, panting. He stayed where he was.

I stumbled to my feet, grabbing my panties and pulling them on, my back to him. By the time I had finished dressing so had he. He was waiting, looking at the ground.

I headed back across the sand towards the car. He followed. Neither of us spoke.

RAUL

Are you saying she led you on? Is that what made you angry?

*NO! ... No, she doesn't, what you call, lead me on. She is not that woman...
She is ... shy, she is ... No, because was STUPID.*

What was stupid?

To be shame. *To feel bad. Was not bad. Was ... oh ... love. Yes. OK, maybe
I don't know love. My mother she say that. She say I know only sex. Sex is easy.
Sex I do all my life, from fourteen years, maybe thirteen, first Cuban girls, then
tourists. Is easy. And I like. But with her ... so shy ... so beautiful, to me beautiful,
maybe not to everybody but to me, yes ... and she is naked and I want to lick the
salt off her back and she lies down beside me and she is so beautiful, her breasts
become small because she is on her back and now she is not shy, just beautiful,
her belly, little baby lines, little, little, her secret hair, still wet with sea. Of course
I want her. She is not then my sister, we have not been children together, she is
new woman I meet. Woman who is part of me. We can talk. Talk, talk. And she
cry. We hold hands. We kiss. Yes. And now she kiss me. She want me, I know. So
what must I do? Of course I want to show her I love her? How else I show?*

So she should have let you make love to her?

*NO! Why you say that? Think that? She not want to make sex we do not make
sex. She say 'no'. Finished. No problem. I stop. I still love but I stop. No problem.
Problem is to* make *problem. Is what is STUPID.*

**You think it was stupid of her to think it was wrong to have sex with
you?**

*Of course! She want sex me. I want sex her. Of course! Why not? Because
world say so? Church say so? Same blood. Bad, bad, bad, Who can see blood?
Taste it? We not make babies. We make love. From first time I see her... I* know
*her. She is part of me. She is sent to me, I am sent to her She change my life. Of
course I want to show her. Love her.*

So what did you do?

Took her back to hotel, what else?

And then?

(Mr Ventura starts to laugh.)

*Oh, Mister Attorney... You want me to say I went to find a Cuban girl friend
to fuck? I have sex with myself* (he gestures) *so all is finished and good? No,
Mister Attorney I went to see my Mummy... Such a bad boy I am ...*

[FROM RAUL VENTURA'S WITNESS STATEMENT (4)]

Chapter 14

The Departures Hall was bright and garish compared to the dour, characterless Arrivals of those five long days ago. I didn't notice her get up and come towards me as I trundled towards the Air Cubana check in desk for my flight to Mexico City.

"*Hola!*"

I was settling at the back of a mercifully short line fishing in my purse for my passport and ticket. I had no idea the voice was talking to me.

"Hello."

Now I looked up.

"Rebeca! What are you doing here?"

"Waiting for you. Say goodbye."

She appeared to gesture towards a gift shop selling Cuban flags, large dolls of black Cuban mamas with enormous breasts smoking enormous cigars, Che Guevara posters, Che Guevara T-shirts, sun hats in Cuban colours. I couldn't see what I was supposed to be looking at. A thick set black man with a straw hat on his knee, holding a newspaper, was sitting on a long shiny metal bench beside the shop. He was looking at us. Rebeca waved. The man lifted his hand in unsmiling slow-motion acknowledgement and unfolded his newspaper.

"My friend, Pepe," she said. "He drive me here. He drive me back." A little woman-to-woman smile. Dismissive.

"Well, thank you. That's very nice of you."

It was bad of me, I was thinking. She had been very welcoming. I should have made an effort to contact her before leaving.

But my mind had been elsewhere.

We had not spoken as Raul drove me back. I don't know what he was thinking, feeling. Guilty? Angry? But it wasn't what he had done that silenced me. It was how I had reacted. We parked at the hotel and he turned off the ignition. He started to speak. I cut him off. His face twisted, he thumped the steering wheel with his fists in... what? Frustration? Rejection? I wanted to tell him it wasn't him. But all I could do was rest my hand briefly on his arm, then I pushed open the car door and hurried up the slope to the hotel. It wasn't the goodbye either of us would have chosen.

I wanted to tell him I loved his kiss. And, yes, loved him. But we must not, could not fall into the pit. As I came out of the darkness into the cold, overhead light of the big drive in porch I shuddered at the thought of what had so nearly happened. A visible, uncontrollable shudder. The doorman looked at me. Was I all right? I hurried past him to collect my key.

It was nothing. Nothing had happened. I repeated the lie to myself endlessly. The sea. The kiss. The sea. The kiss. I did feel shame. Some. And revulsion. At first. But before long it became the idea of revulsion, not the thing itself, buried under the quivering high of excitement, which gnawed at me through a restless night.

I woke, tired, to a colder reckoning. I must leave. Get out fast. I felt tainted. The sooner the aeroplane lifted off the runway at Jose Marti airport the better.

"My boy ask me to come," Rebeca was saying. "Again. Why he cannot come this time I don't know. He say I must. He say you are family. Bernard won't come to airport, my son won't. So you have me. Stepmother."

I smiled back.

"Well... thank you."

Part of me warmed to her openness, wanted to trust her, take her into my confidence. But I did not know what my father had said. Or what Raul had said. She seemed to be hiding something. Implying something. Or was I projecting?

We talked inconsequentially as the queue wore down. The woman at the check in desk when I got there proved to be another unsmiling Cuban official of the kind I was beginning to expect. She spoke a little English but we were both grateful for Rebeca's presence as translator. She insisted that I got a window seat so I could see how beautiful the city was from the air and would want to come back, and I thought how foolish I was to imagine she had an agenda and how easy she was to be with.

"You have time for coffee?" she asked as I tucked my boarding card and ticket into my purse. "Half hour before your gate open."

"What about your friend?"

She glanced across. He was still buried in his newspaper.

"He will wait. You could call him my boyfriend." She grinned. "One of my boy friends."

"Oh... OK." So my step-mother had a sex life. And a varied one. Did I want to know? For a brief, irrational moment it felt as though she was bragging about cheating on my father and I was uncomfortable. Then I remembered she was thirty years or more younger than him. And he had always been a womaniser. And impossible in every way. So why not? But sleeping around? Or was she teasing me?

"Pepe is very good. He drive taxi. When I need him, he come. For driving. For fresh meat. For mend television. For sex." Grinning even more. Testing me? Telling me this is Cuba and Anglo-Saxon protestants like me just better chill? "With your father is different. We don't do sex so much, now." OK, I've got it, my old man can still be sexually active, and you don't do fidelity around here, whoopee-do, can we change the subject? "But if he need me, I go. For anything. I still hate him some times but I go." Probably what she really wanted me to know. I had, of course, seen it in action but it was reassuring to hear. "With Pepe is much easier. If I need him, he come. Is how I like to live. Woman is boss. Good, no?"

I agreed that being boss was fine. Unless it breaks up your marriage, I thought.

She took my arm, chuckling, homilies over. I decided that she was right and that Anglo-Saxon protestants should definitely chill. We walked past shops selling rum, books, more Che Guevara photos and, of course cigars, until we reached a freestanding circular bar in the corner of the hall. We perched on high stools. Rebeca urged me to try fresh, iced lemon juice with my strong, hot coffee. I sipped at both, still unaccountably, irrationally wary of this exuberant stepmother of mine to whom I was so drawn.

Nearby a woman in crisp white overalls, drinking a milk shake and looking bored, was sitting by a massage chair waiting for customers.

"We are becoming good capitalists." Rebeca had followed my look. "We try to sell everything."

I smiled back, still waiting for the agenda, whatever it was. Then it came.

"Did my boy say bad things? Do bad things?"

He's told her. Jesus. How could he?

"In what way?" I could feel the blood flaming in my cheeks. I took a long, deliberate sip of my cold drink. I could not believe he would tell his mother. "What did he say to you?"

She was looking at me, curiously.

"He say nothing. He just say he want me to say goodbye. But I know him. Did he do anything bad?"

"In what way?"

For a moment she said nothing.

"Did he ask you to take him to America?"

I took a long, grateful breath. I could feel my pulse settling.

"No… Well… he told me he would like to go there but… no."

"I think he love you."

That *theeenk* again. Staring at me, unblinking. Probing? If so, what was she looking for? I wanted to tell her to mind her own business.

"I've grown very fond of him too… To find a brother, half-brother like that is…"

Life changing? Bewildering? Erotic? What could I say to her?

She seemed about to speak. But then changed her mind and we fell silent.

"Your day off?" I asked. Safe.

"I work this afternoon." Another silence. "Do I make you nervous?"

That got under my skin.

"Of course not. Why should you make me nervous?"

She was right, of course.

"I am sorry."

"Meeting a whole new family is… Quite something. It's not something… But no reason to be nervous. Of course not."

"Your new family welcome you. Please know that. Raul, me, your father."

"Oh yes? Have you spoken to my father?"

"I know him. You come back to see us soon?"

"Maybe. I'm not sure at the moment."

"Raul be very unhappy if he hear you say that."

She paused. I said nothing.

"And your father."

She was getting at something and I couldn't hear what it was.

"You think bad idea to come back here?"

"I said – I shall think about it. My father and I have existed without each other a long time. Maybe –"

"I give you Pepe's number. He has cell. If you need to speak to me, your father... Raul... You call Pepe. He speak English enough."

She scribbled a number on a paper napkin and passed it to me.

"My family like you. I think they want you in their life. And why not? *Por que no?*"

She was smiling, very friendly. She reached out and put her hand on mine. Impossible to fathom, I thought. Like Cuba. Then all of a sudden, I realised what her smile was saying. *My family like you.* They are *my* family. Keep your distance.

REBECA

Why did you go to the airport to see Mrs Barrington leave?

My son. He ask. He came late. In bed with Pepe, not good time. Pepe don't like to be interrupt. (She laughs) *I took Raul to kitchen. Raul not like Pepe. Raul not like my boyfriends. None. Many people my son not like.*

Why do you think that is?

(She sighs) *My son not know who he is. He not like his father when he was little boy because his father fight with me. Frighten him. Not frighten me but frighten him. Then he not like the country, he say he not fit there. Then he say he not fit the city when we come back. We have no money, everyone has no money, because of blockade I say, but he say because of Fidel. Everyone looking for money. Sex, secret market, how you say, black market. My son he hate Fidel, he hate the Revolution because he cannot wear Gucci shoes. I think sometimes he is poet. I think inside maybe a poet but he write no poems. Instead he chase money. And he do sex. He want love but he do sex.... We never make him happy...*

Which makes you sad?

Of course sad! Now very sad...

Yes... What did he say to you that night?

I tell you, he came to ask me say goodbye her. To her. He tell me flight, time. I say – you go. He say he cannot. I look at his face. I think – something wrong. He done something wrong. Maybe he try to sex with her and she not like.

That crossed your mind then?

Why not? Brothers, sisters, not children together meet when grown. Well known We learn name in nurse college. Genetic... sexual ... something. So what? For Raul sex is like talking. Or maybe he ask her to take him to America. I think something has happened so I say OK. Goodnight, I say him and go back to Pepe. In morning I ask hospital to work afternoon and I go.

You went to the airport because your son asked you? No other reason?

What reason? I like her, I want to say goodbye. She family. Strong woman. But unhappy. Too serious, I think, She should be more Cuban.

(She laughs)

Did you tell her that?

I try to make her laugh. I talk about sex. She shy.

So no other reason?

(Silence)

Maybe little one.

Yes?

I think she is dangerous.

You thought that then?

Not because she want to be. Because she who she is. She been in city four days, five days? And so much change. Bernard change. Raul change. She come to us like ... hurricane. Hurricane Maggie. Always she was dangerous.

To whom?

Herself, of course. To my husband. My son.

And to you?

I did not say me.

Were you jealous of her?

Stupid question. Stupid. We finish now. You turn that off, please.

[FROM REBECA VENTURA'S WITNESS STATEMENT (3)]

Chapter 15

I flashed the remote at the windshield. The tall wrought iron gates slowly swung open. I eased the Audi up the short drive and parked under the jacaranda tree by the forecourt as the gates quietly clicked shut behind me.

The size of the house, its confident symmetry had always been a comfort to me. I did that. That's what I have done for my family. This time I stood beside the car, my suitcase on the gravel at my feet, and looked at the ivy making its way up the red brick walls, now almost up to the third and top floor, the elegant Georgian windows, the fluted stone half pillars either side of the front door, the ornate conservatory roof just visible above the yew hedge at the side of the building and thought I am going to put this place on the market. Time to move on.

I undid both locks, eased open the heavy oak front door which had so pleased me when the realtor showed me around ten years ago, disarmed the third tier of security that I had installed by hastily punching the code into the panel in the cupboard under the stairs, desperate to shut off its maddening bleep.

I thought of my father in his tiny apartment with only his erotic paintings and a bottle of rum for company. How did I come to be living alone apparently needing three rings of security? My fortress for one.

From the hallway I could see into the game room, the corner of the pool table just visible, the living room with its complementing sofas, its elegant lamp stands, the button-down armchair set in the bay for reading, looking out onto the garden with its English roses. So many possessions, so carefully, lovingly accumulated. Yes. Sell. This place is dead skin.

I had been away barely a week but it was not just in the house that I felt a stranger. Arriving into Newark had been noisy, bustling and alien. As I got in the Audi when I collected it from the long-term parking lot, I thought of Miguel's car: and mine instantly reeked of needless wealth and ostentation. The freeway, taking us past ugly power stations and construction sites, was jostling with aggression and reckless, misplaced confidence, all once familiar, now disturbing.

Maybe, I told myself, I still wasn't used to the new order of things. Your father always met me when I got back from a trip and when we got home the house would not be this silent mausoleum but full of you guys, friends over playing pool, music coming from an upstairs bedroom. Hi, Mom, good trip? A hug, then back to playing pool. Maybe I just hadn't adjusted.

But, of course, it was more than that. This time I carried a whole new world in my head, and as I stood now, once again in my familiar old world, at the foot of the old stairs, reflected in the old Sheraton mirror, the old Landseer print beside it, my other, new world was at that moment still sweating in the sun, black beans and rice being prepared, rusty cars being fixed, the sea still pounding on the Malecon walls. Was my father sitting at his table on that plastic seated chair drinking rum, glowering at the wall? Or gently helping some child at the piano with his one functioning hand? Was my new, mysterious stepmother adjusting a drip at a patient's bedside? I thought of her calling out lighting instructions to the man up the ladder at the church before the concert. I thought of Raul asleep on my sofa at the Nacional. I thought of him on the beach.

And even as I replayed all this in my mind, the pictures began to disintegrate. I wanted to keep them fresh and present, but the life was draining from them like a dream crumbling even as you try to hang on to it. I knew this was what happened, that it was almost impossible to carry one life into another but I hoped on this occasion it would be different. This had not been just another trip. This had been a journey to another part of myself: and it was disintegrating as I stood there.

Sell the house. Move on.

I took a shower and called you. It wasn't a good time, if you remember. You were both going with your father and (I presumed) Barbara to a concert. We agreed to meet for lunch on Sunday. You chose Carlo's Place for the burritos. I gritted my teeth. Neither of you ever remembered that I hate Tex-Mex!

It was good to see you. I think you know I tried never to make you feel guilty about deciding to live with your father. But I suspect you probably did all the same, and often tried to make up for it. Like this time. You were very nice to me. You both looked handsome and gave me lovely welcoming hugs. You made a good job of looking pleased with the tie-dyed T-shirts I had brought back for you. You said the burritos were great and that I looked good with a tan. I enjoyed it all, however dislocated I felt. Did either of you notice, I wonder? It was good talking about your Master's programme, Tommy. And about your new drum kit, Billy. Except that Barbara had given it to you. Silly of me, I know, it is good that she gives you things, but that hurt a bit. As I remember it now it hurts even more. Because at the moment I can't give you anything. Can't hug. Can't talk. Nothing.

Neither of you asked me about my trip.

"Don't you want to hear about Cuba?" I thought it might shame you. Just a tad.

"Sure," you said, Tommy, through a mouthful of burrito.

"You're back, Mom," you said, Billy, pouring the rest of your beer into your glass. "Nobody shot you, nobody kidnapped you. That's the main thing."

"It is not quite like that, Billy."

And you disappeared behind your beer glass. Which more or less closed the door.

I don't think I was ready to tell you, anyway.

We could have talked about the politics, of course, how it wasn't what I had expected, how the story was more complicated than it looked to us in the States, we could have speculated about whether the island was heading for capitalism or staying with socialism now that Fidel was out of it, we could have talked about whether we should end the embargo as Obama is hinting. But I doubt if it would have held your attention.

I didn't even tell you about deciding to sell the house, did I?

That 'truth'. So hard. The story of your grandfather and my new family might have held your attention, I guess. But I had lived the lie too long and wasn't ready to open up. And it was too raw a story for me to risk on your indifference. And I certainly could not have told you about Raul. Not 'the truth' anyway. Not then.

I am trying now.

The difficulty, of course, is that it is, in part, to do with sex, and I wasn't brought up to be open about my sexuality, the way so many women are now. I think that was wrong, I think we should be able to talk about all our experience, freely and without shame.

I am prevaricating. You can see that I do not find it easy.

I did have boyfriends before I married your father. Boys weren't the centre of my life as seemed to be the case for some of my friends at school. But I was 'normal' enough, whatever that means. And your father and I were good together in the early days. But as with most marriages – all, I dare say – the early passion faded and I did what I believe many women do, I put those feelings away somewhere, in the bottom of a drawer, and for most of the time forgot about them. Foolishly I imagined your father had done the same. It was fine. That was just how life was. There were other things, a career, paying the bills, making plans.

The reason I wouldn't have wanted to talk to you about Raul over the burritos at Carlo's – unlike now when I believe I must – is that he revived my long-buried sexuality. There. I have said it. (Maybe I have already made it obvious? All this is so difficult, believe me!) I knew what I felt was supposed to be wrong, even potentially illegal. But the fact is my Caravaggio half-brother stirred powerful feelings in me. The pulse and energy of the rest of my time in Havana receded all too quickly. But memories of him forced their way constantly into my thoughts. I tried to push them away. I was grateful I had not succumbed, told myself I could never succumb. It was clear to me that I would never see him again. But the memory, the image of that beautiful, vulnerable, restless man wanting me, telling me he loved me, would not go away. I shall always be grateful to Raul for releasing me. I want you to understand that I feel a better woman for it. I refuse to be ashamed. So I very, very much hope you won't be either.

He – and Cuba – changed me. In many ways.

America, for example, looks so different now. Our rate of consumption seems, if not obscene, then largely pointless. That's why the house went on the market and I sold the car. You weren't at all impressed when I traded the Audi for my Prius, were you? Made no sense to either of you. Green isn't your colour, I guess. I think you were actually angry, weren't you Billy? Why? For a status symbol? It was my lousy status symbol, not yours!

And it wasn't long before I emailed Rob Viner, the Chairman of our local Republican Fund Raising Committee and cancelled my quarterly subscription. I don't think I have told you this either, have I? Perhaps I didn't think you would be interested. You both told me you supported the Republicans but I didn't think it mattered a lot to you. Possibly in light of the size of my donations, Rob was on to me within seconds of my punching 'send'. He was spread-eagled with shock. I told him I wasn't turning into a Democrat, I still believed in small government, low taxation, personal responsibility. But I did say I thought maybe we should end the Cuban embargo. Quoting Raul, I told him that if we ended the embargo, we would bring about the end of socialism in Cuba. Enjoying myself I told him Cuba had taught me the story behind poverty. The world markets collapsed not just because they were inefficient or irrational but because folk got greedy. The Republican party simply hadn't heard the story. Poor Rob. I am, not sure he knew what I was saying. I did, though.

Everything was changing. Even work.

Opening a file on a new project almost invariably used to give me a little burn of excitement, even the dusty corporate deals we tend to specialise in. Where would it lead us? Would we get it right? Would we be quicker, sharper-witted than the other side? Would the client be pleased? Recommend us to others? Now I couldn't find the burn anymore. The files had no story for me.

Howard didn't seem to notice. He said he was pleased to have me back. He told me he had already confirmed to Carlos Ruiz that we had continued to hit brick walls in Havana and that we would be better off going through the International Courts. He said Ruiz seemed unsurprised.

I didn't feel ready to tell him, either, about my new family – and obviously not about Raul. We did talk about Cuba in general. I tried to explain how it had surprised me, what a contradictory, murky place it felt, dark, sometimes fearful and yet seductive, impossible to categorise as a mere tyranny. Or, of course, as a socialist Utopia. The conversation I might have had with you guys!

It was exhilarating shedding old certainties. And not replacing them with new ones.

Within days of coming home, I started playing piano again. Just as Raul had helped me rediscover my femininity, my father had given me back my music. I had the upright tuned, the one we kept in the little bedroom on the top floor and nobody had used after you gave up on it, Billy. Aged eleven? Twelve? I had it tuned in the first week I was back. I used to go up there after work for maybe an hour, just letting my fingers drift and experiment. Letting them remember.

Starting a new life.

I finally quit smoking, for one thing. And started jogging.

And I went on a date. I didn't tell you that either, did I? The first for over twenty years. It was a disaster!

Talking of your parents dating, did your father and his lady love tell you we met?

I was getting some groceries at Zeno's, the one on the corner by the Methodist church. I had parked my new and oh-so-worthy Prius on that sloping driveway. Your father's car must have been there at the same time but I didn't notice it. This was no longer his territory.

I was just reaching for some yoghurt when I saw them, further down the same aisle. Your father and – I presumed – this woman I had heard so much about, imagined so many times, but never met. My first thought – what the hell were they doing in my neighbourhood? Then – he is pushing the cart, she is selecting. Just like we did.

Your father saw me. She sensed something and turned. We all froze. Then started to walk towards each other because there was no way out.

"Hi," he said.

"Hi."

"This is Barbara."

"Hello Barbara." I think I managed a smile.

"Hello."

Tiny, barely reached his shoulder. Mousey hair, sloppy jeans, sneakers. But quite pretty.

"We were just passing," he said. "On our way to Barbara's mother. Always liked Zeno's. Know where everything is. Creature of habit." He tried a smile.

"Really?" I said. I couldn't help it. He got it and flinched. She looked nervous. Even more nervous.

"How are you?" he said. "The boys tell me you have started to play piano."

"That's right."

"How is it going?"

"The first concert is still some way off."

"Only a matter of time, I am sure."

Suddenly it was easy, just like we had always been and I thought I do hope they are going to be happy.

"Babs' mum is not well," he said. "We had better be getting along."

"I am sorry to hear that."

"Thank you." She seemed genuinely grateful for my concern. Very nice. Just the woman for him, I thought.

"Good to see you, Maggie."

"And you."

And they and their cart moved off.

And there it was. My marriage was well and truly over. As it had been for years, only I hadn't admitted it.

My new unencumbered life seemed, finally, to be good.

Then that night I got the phone call from Rebeca.

REBECA

Did your life return to normal?

What is normal? What you talk about? When?

After Mrs Barrington went back to the States?

Pffft… Normal? I am Senior Nurse in Children's ward. I like my work. I am proud. I see friends, I see Pepe. I go to cinema, I go to beach, I go to my Women's Committees.

Excuse me?

*Cuban democracy. (*Laughs*) You not heard of Cuba democracy Mister American Attorney??? Elections, many elections we have. Of course! The Assamblea Nacional del Poder Popular, the Consejo de Estado, the Consejo de Ministros, but also here in La Habana, in every city, everywhere we have little Municipalidad, many, many. And Confederaciones, Associaciones, all elections. I go, I listen I talk. Sometimes a lot, I talk. We talk, nobody listen! Aaaah …. You believe, me, no?*

(Wagging her finger laughing.)

I do.

Normal? I look after my children in Hospital and my two children in my family, my husband and my son. But… yes, it has changed …

In what way?

Raul not come to see me. Strange. So I go to him. He does not want to talk. I think – is it because of Maggie? Is something else. Something bad is happening. Is it Police? He has trouble with Police? He get angry. Why you say that? Why you not trust me? Then I go to see my husband. Are you well? Do you eat? I ask his neighbour Christobal, is he well? He say he is fine. Both – something wrong….Maggie has changed them. They are not mine now.

Hurricane Maggie?

Hurricane Maggie. Then …. it happened.

What happened?

A friend give me tickets for ballet They make Swan Lake. I take Bernard. Bad mistake, bad, bad.

Why?

We go. We sit. Some people know who my husband is. They point, they whisper. He doesn't look. Theatre full, full, full. Cubans like music, like dance. We have good seats, the best. My friend has friends, you know? But in front of us, here in front, six empty seats. Time to begin. Still empty. We wait. Five minutes. Ten. I know why. Government Ministers. "We wait for Ministers," I say to my husband. He knows. He is angry. His concerts nobody wait. One day – I was with him – he tell Fidel "I keep tickets for you but you late – we start. You don't come in."

What did Fidel say?

He laugh. He embrace my husband. He love him. Now we wait, we wait. Everyone go quiet. Then they come. Five men, one woman. I know them from newspapers. One is our friend Jesus Lopez. He is first. The people stand to let Ministers come. Jesus first. He is looking down, not tread on feet. Then he look up. He see Bernard, he see me. Bernard raise his hand a little, his good hand, to say hello. Jesus look away. He walk past us, here, in front of us, we can touch. He say nothing, he not look round, he sit down. And I know why. He come to my husband's concert and the Consejo de Ministros say he was wrong. Manuel has talked. He make his revenge. So now Jesus, our friend, in front of other Ministers must not say hello. Only his neck, we have, the back of his neck. It was red. I want to hit it, make it more red. My husband put his hand on my arm. At interval, everyone wait for Ministers to go first. Jesus not look at us. He is sad, I think. He like my husband. When they have gone and we stand, Bernard say he is tired and would like to go home. I take him. He is not angry, he says, he is tired. I am angry.

I am sure he was angry, too. It must have been painful.

Of course. That was when it happened. The next morning.

What?

I am behind my desk at hospital. I am telephoning for drugs. Everywhere. Sometimes is hard to find supply. This blockade make everything difficult. I put telephone down and Pepe is standing in front of desk. "You must come," he say. "Christobal call me. Your husband has had stroke. I take you. Come." Pepe take me to Hospital Simon Bolivar. Not best hospital in La Habana. But near to Bernard. My husband is in bed in big ward. His eyes are open but he not seeing. His pulse good, his breathing good so maybe seeing but not understanding. I sit with him, hold his hand, his good hand. It does not move. Empty. I talk to him, try to make calm. Make me calm. I ask him if he understand. He does – so – with his head.

Nods.

Nods. But very small. Very small. I say can you talk? He open his mouth a little. He spit, no, dribble, down side. "Si" he say. Very quiet. Not clear sound. Like too much rum, you know? Rest, I say, just rest – in Spanish we speak in Spanish – be comfortable, no hurry. Is anything you want? He say something. I cannot hear. I put my ear to his mouth. "Quiero ver a mi hija" he say. Behind me I hear footsteps coming. They stop by the bed. I look up. It is my son. Your father want to see Maggie, I tell him.

[FROM REBECA VENTURA'S WITNESS STATEMENT (4)]

Chapter 16

She was waiting for me at Jose Marti with Pepe, brisk and forthright as ever. But something was different. She plucked imaginary threads from the sleeve of my blouse as we greeted each other. Strangers, not friends. Because he had asked for me? Jealous?

"I can't think what I can do for him that you aren't already doing much better," I said leaning down to kiss her on the cheek.

She looked away, making dismissive, shrugging we're-all-a-team noises.

Pepe shook my hand with a shy smile and picked up my bag.

With her usual abruptness Rebeca changed gear. She thrust her arm through mine, warm and tactile as before – like mother, like son, I thought – and we fell into step behind Pepe.

"Is good, you come. Very good." She gave my arm a squeeze as though dispelling any notion of rivalry. "Everything good at your home?" she asked politely.

I thought – I have lied to my sons and their father again telling them I had to go back to Cuba "on business", and although I had told Howard the truth about my father he had been shocked that I had kept it from him for so many years and I feared it may have damaged our long relationship. Home was something of a mess.

"Everything is fine," I said. "How is he?"

"Each day a little better. Slowly. We go to hospital now? Then to hotel? He expect you."

"Fine."

As we walked, I took in the heat, the palm trees glimpsed through the plate glass windows of the airport, the signs in Spanish, the soldiers, guns casually slung across their chests, the stalls selling rum and trinkets. I was in Cuba again. The same bit of earth as my father.

And Raul.

It was a modest-sized building, formerly a hotel, Rebeca told me. You could drive past it and not be aware it was a hospital if you hadn't spotted the little blue cross over the front door. It wasn't, she said, one of the best in Havana but it had a good therapy department and that was the bulk of his treatment, so she was happy with it. She was speaking very much as my father's wife, the nearest relative.

Leaving Pepe in the car with my luggage we went in. Reception was dun-coloured, narrow, with a low ceiling. It was very quiet. A shirt sleeved man sat behind a desk in the full blast of a fan, which ruffled the papers in front of him. He nodded desultorily at Rebeca, a regular visitor, while eyeing me with curiosity. Foreigner – even American? – printed on me. A couple of old men sat, smoking, in a glass-covered patio to one side in ancient wheel chairs. My heart sank.

Even more so when I saw the ward. Also dun coloured – who decides on these colours? – also very quiet. About a dozen beds without privacy curtains, one large window at the far end letting in a paltry light. All men, mostly old, mostly sleeping, some reading '*Gramma*', some listening to earphones. A nurse behind the desk acknowledged Rebeca with a smile as we came in and then bent back to her task.

I couldn't see him. The light? All old men in pyjamas look alike? Then I spotted an empty bed. There was a chair beside it in which a young man sat reading, his back to us.

Raul.

He stood when he became aware of us, putting his book down on the bed. Neruda's Poems, I noticed. We embraced distantly, like strangers. He looked tense, seemed shorter than I remembered, ordinary, not the glowing Caravaggio I had been carrying in my head these last weeks. It was a relief. It had been easier than I had feared.

"Where is your father?" asked Rebeca, as usual speaking to her son in English in front of me. I realised, for the first time, that it was a courtesy I had blithely taken for granted.

"They make him walk," he replied.

He gestured to the now empty chair inviting me to sit.

"I'm fine thank you, Raul."

The formality of it all was good. I was conscious of the men in the ward who were not sleeping watching us discreetly. The foreigner. Tall and overdressed.

"OK," said Raul. "I leave you. I wait downstairs."

He nodded to his mother and left. I didn't watch him go.

"Why walking?" I asked.

"The stroke. His legs. His good arm also now not so good. Need therapy, is all."

I sat on the edge of the bed. I have always found hospitals grim. This looked clean enough, efficient enough. But grim. Almost the only colour came from the flowers that crowded his bedside table – and his alone. There was also a thick pile of cards including, I later discovered from Rebeca, one from his Government Minister 'friend' Jesus who she told me had publicly humiliated him the night before his stroke at the ballet. Good and evil in one. Rebecca's mantra. My father. Cuba.

A door at the far end opened and he came – or, rather, shuffled – in, a thin, frail figure under a top-heavy mass of tangled grey hair. He was wearing a dressing gown and was accompanied by two nurses, one man, one woman, in reassuringly crisp, clean, white uniforms, with nets tied over their hair.

He seemed to glance up briefly but it was impossible to tell if he had seen us as he made no acknowledgement, his eyes returning quickly to the floor. I watched them approaching shuffle by shuffle. The nurses leant in to him murmuring encouragingly.

He reached the bed still without acknowledging Rebeca or me but I was sure by now he had seen us. One nurse took off his dressing gown, the other helped him expertly into his bed, adjusting his pillows, the angle of incline of the back support, pulling the cover up to his waist. He continued to keep his eyes down, avoiding us like a sulky child demanding love.

Rebeca looked at me and nodded towards him. Your turn.

I took the chair, positioned it as close as I could and sat down. I leaned forward and took his hand. His skin was loose, unresponsive. My throat was dry.

"Hello, Dad. How are you feeling?"

There may have been a twitch. Impatient. Dumb question. I was floundering.

"I've just arrived. Wanted to see you at once. I am here for as long as you like."

Still no response. I turned to Rebeca. She smiled sympathetically. He asked for you, I reminded myself. There must be something you can do for him.

"Is there anything I can do for you while I am here?"

God, I was bad at this.

He seemed to mutter something. I couldn't be sure but I thought I knew what he was saying. I started to laugh.

"Are you telling us to fuck off? Is that what you said?"

His mouth creaked towards a smile, saliva gleaming on his lower lip.

"Oh well, that's fair enough," I said, on safe ground now. Behind me Rebeca was also laughing. I stood, leaned forward and kissed him on the forehead. "Get some sleep, you old bugger, and I'll come and see you tomorrow."

Still smiling? A nod of the head? Pleased with himself.

"Bye then."

Rebeca stepped into the space I vacated and said something sharply to him in Spanish. Totally at ease with him. I envied her. Then she turned and putting her arm through mine we walked out of the ward.

"What did you say to him?" We were getting into the lift.

"I say him – You won't get better if you don't try, silly old man."

We laughed. Sisters again.

Raul was waiting for us in Reception. He stood as we approached.

"I go up?" he asked his mother.

"Leave. Leave stupid man alone," she replied and marched on towards the exit.

He looked confused. Sick bed niceties were clearly as lost on him as they were on me. We caught each other's eye. I smiled. He smiled back. He took a step towards me.

"You staying at Nacional?"

"Yes."

"You go there now?"

111

"I think Pepe is waiting to take me."

"Maybe I see you later?"

"If you like. Maybe you and Rebeca and Pepe can all have dinner with me?"

"My mother, she work tonight. Late. Pepe also."

We looked at each other, both wary. Slowly he smiled.

"I like to see you."

I smiled back.

"OK. 8.00 o'clock?"

And I hurried after Rebeca. Friendly. No problem.

We had dinner served on the terrace. By candlelight. His suggestion. He looked very handsome. A shining white open neck shirt, tight stone washed jeans and what looked to me suspiciously like Gucci shoes.

And was attentive and polite. Listened. He asked about you, about your father, my work. We talked a little bit about Obama, American politics. We kept our distance. It was nice.

But something was troubling him. I didn't know if it was to do with seeing me again, or even with the old man's stroke. I offered him little avenues but he didn't go down any of them.

After the meal was over, without saying anything we took our tiny cups of thick, strong coffee and left the table to go out into the hotel garden. Still in silence we found our way to the place we had first met, the old Spanish canon overlooking the Malecon.

We sat on the low wall either side of its elegant black barrel against which we could both lean. I decided I should clear the air. If it was something to do with our past encounters, I wanted to set out the new rules very clearly.

"Is something bothering you, Raul?" I asked. Like a good sister.

"No. Why you ask?"

"Are you sure?"

"Why you ask?"

"Instinct. Sister's instinct."

His mouth set, as though irritated. He stared out to sea. The sound of the traffic reached us muted from below. From behind came plaintive snatches from the resident trio spilling their hearts out to the clear, starry sky.

"Maybe a little."

"Do you want to talk about it? Is it to do with Bernard?"

I hadn't got used to 'Dad'. 'Our father' sounded prayerful.

"No. Not that… Police. I have trouble with Police."

My stomach clenched. As a lawyer the police hold no terrors for me. As the chronically orthodox private individual I have – until recently – always been, they terrify me. And this was Cuba. Not only Cuba, Raul.

"Does Rebeca know?"

"No."

That serious.

"Do you want to tell me?"

He turned to face me, holding my look.

"You truly want to know?"

"Yes."

"Good. Is help to tell you."

Oh God, did he think as a lawyer I could defend him? As an *American* lawyer?

"Raul I –"

"You remember the cell phones? I work with friend? You remember?" I knew at once what was coming. "Is black economy. Police find out. Arrest me."

"Have they charged you?"

He nodded.

"I am 'doing things against the state' – phhh… Bad boy. I am 'dangerous'. Next month in court. And my friend – worse. He is boss. He import. I sell. I sell cells."

He grinned cockily.

"If you are found guilty?"

"I *am* guilty."

Still cocky.

"What's the sentence?"

"A year, maybe."

Now no longer grinning. I reached across the canon and took his hand.

"Everybody do black economy here. They know everybody do black economy. Fruit, vegetables, chicken, petrol, clothes, radios, everything. If we don't have dollars like ministers, baseball players, rich bastards, how else do we live? Mostly they ignore. Then, suddenly, no reason – BAM…!"

"Do you have a lawyer? I mean, are they expensive, because –"

"No, no. I have lawyer friend. He can do nothing but he try to help. Is OK. Thank you."

I let go of his hand.

"So what can I do?"

"Nothing. Is good to tell you. And you are still my friend?"

"Of course, Raul."

"Is good you are here. Is good I can talk to you."

"I am glad you can, too."

This beautiful, tender man trapped in a sleazy, repressive world. If the cannon hadn't been between us, I would have hugged him.

"I have missed you very much. Lovely Maggie."

I said nothing. I did not want to look at him.

"You? You miss me too? A little?"

"I… have thought about you, Raul. Of course I have."

"I love you. Still, all the time – I love you."

His eyes were fierce.

I sat up fast. It had to be said.

"Look, Raul… Listen to me… What happened… happened. And I don't deny… But not again. It cannot happen again. It is insane. Illegal. Dangerous."

"Who say illegal? Who say insane? Who make rules? THEY do. Not me, not you. Church make rules. Fuck church. Love is love. We are not children, we did not grow together as children. We met – man and woman. I love you like nobody I love before. You make me good, you are part of me, I want you, I want you so much –"

"No, Raul, no –"

"I want to kiss you again. All the time I think of kissing you. I see your breasts. Now I look at you, I see your breasts… I see your beautiful body… your beautiful body… Please… I must kiss you… just kiss… Please…"

Despite myself I felt naked, caressed, safe. He leant towards me. I wanted the kiss.

Footsteps behind us on the path, a middle-aged couple, the man smoking a cigar.

"Buenas tardes."

They walked past us to the far end of the rock face, until they were lost in the dark.

Raul continued to stare into me. I was shivering.

"Please," he said. "Your room. I must kiss you again. Let me love you with a kiss. No more, just to kiss. Is all. So little. So much. Maggie…"

So little. So much.

"You promise?"

Did I say that?

"I promise."

But as we approached the door to my room my throat dried up. I stopped, turned to him.

"No. No. We mustn't"

"Please…"

The lights in the corridor were harsh. It was empty. He leaned in to me and kissed me gently on the lips. I couldn't help it. I kissed him back. Then I opened the door and we went in to my room. We kissed again. After a while, he left, keeping his promise.

I don't think I have ever felt so confused, so ashamed of myself or so burningly alive.

And I am sorry if it is difficult for you to read this about me. But I said I was going to try to tell the truth. And you are adults now and you need to know it all so you can understand what happened to me, why I did what I did, and why I am where I am now.

Wring it down isn't easy. But it helps. Hope you really do understand.

RAUL

OK, Mr Attorney, I tell you. I try to tell you. I am thirteen years old, I am living in country with my mother. In my school is older girl, fifteen, I think. Called Yolla. I know she like me. She talk to me. She look at me. Other boys, they laugh, they say things but I don't believe them. Then one day she say me come to my house after school, I have fresh oranges. So I go and her mother, her grandmother they are not there and she take me to her bedroom and she show me to make sex. So. Is good. I like. She like. Very much. We make sex everywhere. School, sometimes, in fields, her house, in cinema. I don't say anybody I make sex with Yolla. I think is secret for us. But my mother is very clever. She know. So. She give me condoms. Many condoms. She tell me about SIDA. AIDS. All my life I am king of condoms because my mother is clever. So, Mr Attorney for me sex is always easy. I am lucky. Women like to make sex with me. I like to make sex with them. After Yolla other girls. Women, also. Older women. My cousin. She 30, me 15. Very lucky. But love is not so easy. At Teacher College I meet Liset. Younger than me, beautiful, write poems. Virgin. Blah, blah. I love her. After long time we make sex. Is so beautiful. Sex with love. I want to marry her, make babies. One summer – I am new teacher now, she is still student – she go to work on farm on Isla de la Juventad. Mean Island of Young. Very famous, Mr Robert Louis Stephenson, is his "Treasure Island". Yes. There Liset meet older man, very powerful man, Central Committee of Party, blah, blah. She marry him. I don't know what happen. I know only she marry him and leave me. So…. I think is the end of my life. Then I think – no. I am young I make new life. I stop being teacher. I think – where is money? Tourists have money. I go to work with tourists. I buy I sell, I fuck. Some women they say they love me but is not true. For me there is no love. No place for love. Until I meet Maggie. Maggie who is me. Who look at me and smile and make me feel good, who is tall and strong and frightened and shy and for me so beautiful. She is from another world, a bigger world, but she is also mine and part of me. I love the way she talk, I love the way she walk, the way her hips move, her breasts…. And we talk, talk, talk… A goddess in my life that I can touch, whose hand I can hold, lips…. She is up there, you know? Above me. And I love her… (Long pause) I loved her.

[FROM RAUL VENTURA'S WITNESS STATEMENT (5)]

Chapter 17

He was the only one with a tray still on his lap. The others had pushed theirs to the bottom of their beds or put them on their cabinets. An orderly was collecting them and loading them onto a trolley, the clatter disrupting the stillness of the ward.

I watched from the door as his left hand directed a spoon hesitatingly to the bowl on his tray, laboriously gathered a load and then began the shaky progress to his mouth.

I was the only visitor. I could feel eyes on me as I walked quietly towards him, not wanting to distract. I timed it to arrive just as he had completed a mouthful and the wandering spoon was empty. He looked up as I moved a chair into place. There was a large napkin across his chest, tied behind his neck. It was liberally splashed with red. Tomato soup.

"Hello, Dad." I sat, the chair scraping on the floor.

He didn't look pleased to see me. The dilemma. To carry on struggling clumsily to eat in front of his daughter, slopping soup across his chest, or to admit defeat?

He grunted a response, hesitated, then clearly decided that more was lost by admitting defeat.

His left hand – before this second stroke in his complete control – jerked up from where it was resting on the tray and then lowered itself unsteadily into the soup bowl like the bucket on a digger. Cranking itself up unsteadily it began the ascent up his chest, shedding part of its load on the way. His mouth opened tortuously, the lower lip jutting out to make a platform for the spoon. When it got there, it tipped jerkily inwards. More soup landed on the napkin on his chest, dribbled into his beard. He sucked it in, slurping noisily. I looked away.

As the spoon came down it hit the tray hard.

I hesitated for quite a long time.

"Can I help, Dad?"

"NO!"

He fumbled for the napkin and dabbed at his soup stained beard.

We sat in silence.

He mumbled something.

"What?"

"The-ra-py." Each syllable was a breathy, nasal struggle. "Got… to… do-it-myself… Get… move-ment back…"

"Right. Well, at least you re speaking to me now."

"Wha…?"

"Yesterday. You old ham."

Briefly his eyes glinted. It could have been a smile.

"Shock… to see you."

"Why? Rebeca said you were expecting me."

A silence as he considered his options, his jaw working.

"Forgotten."

"Rubbish."

That glint again.

"Thanks… coming."

"Did you think I wouldn't?"

The fingers on his left hand, still holding the spoon, twitched. The spoon clattered free. He looked away.

"More soup?"

"No."

I put the bowl, half empty, on the cabinet by his bed. A tortilla wrap remained on a paper plate in front of him.

"Try that. Easier to manage."

Parent to my parent. Whom I barely knew.

His left arm swung obediently, if hesitantly, into action, his fingers locking on to the wrap and getting it by degrees to his mouth.

He managed two mouthfuls. The more the silence between us stretched out the more it began to feel companionable.

He put the half-eaten wrap down on the tray with a thump.

"Had… enough."

"OK."

Now I put the tray on his cabinet along with the half bowl of soup.

"Not… food," he said.

"What?"

"Living."

I froze.

"Want… to go," he said.

"Dad, that's silly," I said. But I knew it wasn't. I could hear in his voice that he wanted exactly that.

"No… point… any more…"

Ice was forming in my stomach as I cast around. Nothing. I could think of nothing to say. I reached over and took his hand. Not lifeless this time. His fingers dug into my palm.

"I can't think about that," I said at last. "We've got you still and I want…" What did I want? What could I do? "I want to do what I can for you…The therapy may help… And then, I don't know, maybe find you somewhere you can be more comfortable. Anything… Is there anything you want now that I could organise for you? Anything at all?"

There was a long silence. He took his hand away. Angry? My response so inadequate? Patronising?

"Rum."

"What?" I didn't think I could have heard.

"Rum… Not… allowed…"

Was it dangerous? Would it kill him?

"Have you asked Rebeca?"

"Nurse… Won't…"

Of course it wouldn't kill him.

And so what if it does? He says he wants to go.

"OK. I'll see if I can get you some."

"Now?"

"What?"

"Rum… Now."

How? Where do you buy Rum in Cuba? Were there liquor stores?

"OK," I said.

His hand flopped towards me. I took it. A smile now, a definite smile.

Standing at the entrance to the hospital looking out I could see nothing but offices, apartment blocks, a small park. It was very hot. Two young boys across the road sat on a low wall, their arms around each other's shoulders staring at me with open interest. I wished I had asked for Miguel.

There was what looked like a church dome across the rooftops and for lack of any other landmark I headed towards it. I found myself in an old square, like a large court yard, flag stoned, with a fountain, a terrace café set out in front of a beautiful church, a wholly unexpected oasis in this drab, characterless corner of the city. Along one side of the square was a colonnade, wide stone columns in front of a parade of little shops, the largest a chemist with rows of empty shelves behind the wooden counter, a second hand bookshop, a hairdresser, a shoe shop, a cigar shop and through a little grilled window in the wall I saw a small dark room with a counter and rows of shelves, this time filled with bottles. Going in through a side door, also grilled, I found a large sweaty man in a vest reading a newspaper behind the counter.

"Rum… *por favor.*"

He got to his feet, folding the newspaper.

"*Ron?*"

"*Si. Ron.*"

He pointed to various bottles behind him. I was still adjusting to the dark. I hesitated. He took down a large bottle of red rum and placed it front of me. As he did so I realised that smuggling rum into a hospital needed more thought than I had given it.

"*Blanco, por favor…y…*" I gestured a half bottle with my hands.

Disappointed, he produced one.

"*Agua?*"

He reached into a fridge under the counter and brought out a large bottle of water. For my plan to work I needed a bottle the same size as the rum. I gestured to him accordingly. Slightly impatiently he reached down to get a smaller bottle.

I put a $10 bill on the counter and suddenly his shoulders straightened and he smiled, looking years younger. I waved away the change in *pesos,* miming a request for a bag. The prospect of wandering around carrying a half bottle of rum in my hands did not appeal. He looked worried, as though fearing this could be a deal breaker and spread his arms in a gesture of regret. So I pushed and squeezed the bottle of rum into my handbag, and marched out carrying the innocuous bottle of water in search of a quiet corner where I could turn water into rum.

But the business of emptying a water bottle and filling it with white rum felt not only furtive and sordid but was perhaps even illegal here? Where could I do it? The church? A park? An alley? A public lavatory? Nothing presented itself.

Providing my sick and aged father with the comfort of alcohol was becoming a much bigger undertaking than I had anticipated.

I came to a wide tree-lined avenue. On the other side of the road a hundred yards or more away I could see a large building with a sign saying Hotel Salvador Allende.

Outwardly brazen, inwardly anticipating arrest at any moment, I swept past Reception as though I was resident and found a door marked '*Senoras*'. Thankfully empty. I had just finished pouring the contents of the water bottle into the sink when I heard footsteps approaching. The management of the hotel coming to investigate what this strange woman was up to? The police? I slipped into a cubicle and locked the door. I waited holding my breath while a woman used the cubicle next to mine, then washed her hands and left. Silence. Sweating now, I held the water bottle over the pedestal with the lid up and carefully poured the rum into it, losing barely a drop. Then I put the empty rum bottle in the bin, flushed the lavatory because that was what people who were up to no good in lavatories always did in movies and left, my heart hammering. The Reception Clerk did not even look up as I marched, apparently confidently, past him out into the street.

It was with some sense of achievement that I placed the innocent looking bottle of water on my father's bedside cabinet. I had done something for him. I had been a daughter.

"Thank... you."

He was looking at it longingly.

I unscrewed the top and put the bottle in his left hand. It made the unsteady journey to his lips. A swallow. Then another. Now parent again I reached out and took it back. He didn't resist.

"Does that make life a bit better?"

He thought about it.

"Makes... waiting... for death... better."

I waited for him to smile, to signal that it was a joke. He didn't.

Chapter 18

"Phhht! He make opera. Always make opera. Baby. Want to you to be his Mummy. We must all die. So?"

I wasn't used to being the soft-hearted one. And Rebecca's indifference unsettled me. But she had her arm affectionately through mine as we walked, making dissent difficult. I chose silence.

It was early evening. We had agreed to meet after her shift. Over coffee we had made small talk. She had been friendly and warm but I detected stubborn wariness. I, too, felt constrained. There were big things we could not talk about. Raul being charged and facing a prison sentence. Me smuggling rum into the hospital for her husband.

I had trespassed into family politics and wasn't used to them. They never seemed to be part of our family, my other, my all-American family, did they? Did you guys grow up sensing rows, unseen tensions flying around you? I don't think so. There weren't. Until recently, of course.

After coffee she told me she wanted to show me the American Interests building on the Plaza de la Tribuna Abierta Antiimperialista on the sea front. The clue, you may have guessed, is in the name. The whole enormous space is effectively a celebration of anti-Americanism. It is particularly associated, she told me, with a nine-year-old boy called Elian who became a political football between Cuba and the States a few years back. The boy's uncle had got him across to Miami on a makeshift dinghy and then, vociferously backed by the expatriate Cuban community and the Republican party (I remembered it and remembered feeling uneasy at the time), had wanted to keep him there against his parents' wishes in Havana.

In Cuba – and in many parts of the world – the outrage was enormous with massive demonstrations on the Plaza outside the American Interests building, where a few lonely American diplomats work under the auspices of the Swiss. Finally a judge in Miami ordered the boy's return to his parents, and in celebration of the 'victory' the Plaza was turned into a massive, Stalinist monument to Elian, with triumphal arches leading to a large stage outside the American Interests building on which anti-American concerts and speeches have been regularly staged.

I guessed Rebeca was trying to tell me something but she remained politely neutral, her face set in a comfortable, lazy smile as we wandered arm in arm through the crowds, some just strolling like us, others flirting, or hurrying home with shopping, dodging the clowns on stilts, maybe pausing by noisy rock groups clustered defiantly round amplifiers, warily eyed by the police.

I decided to risk her wrath and try again.

"I can understand it, though, can't you?"

"What you can understand?"

"That he is ready to die."

"Death will decide when death want to come. Is not our right. We must live bravely. He make opera for you."

The Albert Hall, my father playing – was it Rachmaninoff? – fingers a dizzying blur, hunched, possessed, demonic energy flaming from him. I was maybe ten – eleven?

Now, my father struggling to raise a spoon to his lips, food staining his scraggly beard.

My little stepmother, her arm through mine, her head barely reaching my shoulder. Soft, warm. Spine of steel.

Was it principle? Or jealousy that the old man had confided in me and not in her?

"There must be something we can do for him, Rebeca. You said yourself that hospital is not –"

"Good doctors. Good nurses."

"But depressing. You have to admit."

"Same for all. No privileges."

Her jaw set. A clown on stilts lurched over and tried to engage us in conversation. She ignored him. He admitted defeat at once, waving to us in mock disappointment as we left him behind.

"Some of the other patients were listening to music on headphones. Does he have anything like that?"

Now her head snapped up, looking interested.

"I don't know. He listen to CD in apartment."

"Can you get iPads in Havana?"

She sniffed.

"In dollar shop. I don't go in dollar shop. For rich people. Dollar people. Before we had one Cuba. Now we have two Cubas. Peso Cuba, dollar Cuba. You try."

"Where?"

She nodded across the Plaza. On one corner a large building stood out. It was freshly painted in green and white with a massive glass front above which 'PANAMERICANA' was written in large letters. The windows were gleaming with white goods, spotlit and in some cases enticingly beribboned.

I looked at her. She shrugged and we started to walk toward it.

"I wait," she said sternly as we arrived.

Inside music was playing seductively, the staff – men and women – were in black pants and black T-shirts with name tabs on their chests. They looked the customers – mainly diplomats? – confidently in the eye and smiled. Behind vast large glass cases, kept firmly at bay until the magic dollars were handed over, were fridges, cookers, blenders on one side, pianos, guitars, brass instruments on another, computers, TV sets with enormous screens; even a little sailing dinghy was mounted on a rostrum, hungry to be sold. One large alcove was dedicated to 'luxury' food, ranges of different coffee, cakes, chocolates, exotic pickles. A consumer cathedral in Communist Cuba. Not quite Macy's but close.

As I explained what I wanted, the assistant's smile vanished.

"Apple. Not possible. Sorry. *Blockeo.* You want MP3?"

I remembered you telling me, Tommy, of the infinite superiority of the I-Pad over the MP3. I think it may have been suspiciously close to Christmas time? I passed.

"Maybe I could get one sent over from the States," I said to Rebeca when I re-joined her in the street.

"I ask," was all she said and turned to walk back to the Plaza. She was thinking of Raul, I knew. Don't ask him, I wanted to say. Don't even mention it. He's in enough trouble.

She was standing at the foot of the stage when I caught up with her, staring up at the forest of black flags with white stars.

"You know why all these flags?" she said.

"No idea."

"The windows behind, the big ones. American diplomat offices. American spies we say. They give money to our enemies. People against the Revolution. Why? Is our country not theirs? They send messages from windows. Electric messages, big, big letters. Propaganda. In our country – against us. Fuck America. Sorry, but fuck America. So we put up flags. Each one in memory of Cuban killed by American terrorism. Nobody can see messages. We are poor country, you are rich, but we win. Always we win."

Was this prompted by my visit to the dollar shop? Or was it why she had brought me here?

"We don't do terrorism, Rebeca."

"CIA. Kill many Cubans. Try many times to kill Fidel."

"Jesus... You *are* angry, aren't you?"

"Not you. You my friend. But America, yes, very angry."

I took a breath. My turn.

"Right... Look, maybe Cuba isn't what I expected, maybe I got a lot of things wrong, it is more complicated than I realised. But there is a bottom line for me as well. Democracy is better than one party government. Dictatorship. Period. I can't move from that, Rebeca. And I don't want my country to do so, either. Somebody has to fight for that. Right now, we can, so we must."

She looked at me. Her face softened.

"You Americans..." She was smiling now. "Always you believe you are right."

"In that at least, yes."

"Palestinians. Israelis, Muslims, Christians, capitalists, socialists, everyone believe – everyone *know* they are right. You say you have democracy. But big money buy your democracy. You cheat for your democracy. Where is your democracy in Guantanamo? You say you have democracy. We don't say. We say we have full bellies, houses, good schools, good hospitals. For everybody. Yes – good hospitals!"

She laughed and put her arms around me.

"You want to understand why your father left you? Yes?"

Jumping out of another rabbit hole. I had never said this to her. Once again to my surprise – though I guess I should have become used to it by now – I felt tears gather, anger evaporated.

"He believed in us," she continued. "Is a terrible old man but always I love him. You too, I think."

I broke from her, willing away the tears.

"I don't know whether I love him. Maybe I have hated him too long for that. I don't know what I feel about him. But he's my father and I don't want to think of him rejected by the people he gave his life for, dying in that grim little hospital…"

I could not go on. She put her hand on my arm, her face gentle.

"Tomorrow. I work in afternoon. In morning I take you to Tarara. I show you why your father left you."

REBECA

"Soy Historico." Means I am old! The young people – my son – they call us 'Historicos' if we can remember Cuba before the Revolution. If we remember, they say we are Revolutionaries. They think is stupid... I do not remember. I was 2 years old. But I am Revolutionary. Yes, still after so many years. I wanted Maggie to understand. My mother, my grandmother, they told me about life under Batista. Being black under Batista. Not just black, being woman, being poor. Everyone – everyone – say Fidel saved us. No – not everyone, not 'gusanos', not the 'worms' who ....

The people who fled to America?

(A pause.)

Si – gusanos…. Everyone else – everyone – say he did good things for Cuba. He made us proud, gave us schools, houses, hospitals. The dream was for ALL Cubans. Now they call us 'Historicos'. 'Dinosaurios'…. What do you say?

The same. Dinosaur.

I look at the West. Greed. Banks, greedy banks saved by Government. I see greedy men – always men – American, Russian, British, they have private aeroplanes, private boats, houses, many, many houses like palaces, and other men and women – usually black, like me – dying because they have no medical insurance. Is that crazy? Rich men sleep in palaces, poor men sleep in streets? Greed, greed, greed. Why should I want that? Did she want that? Maggie, did she want that? Does my son want that? My stupid, stupid son….Yes I am proud to be 'Historico'. I am proud to be Revolutionary.

[FROM REBECA VENTURA'S WITNESS STATEMENT (5)]

Chapter 19

She was sitting in the lobby sharp at 8.00 the next morning in her nurse's uniform. She smiled her approval when I appeared. We're going to travel like Cubans, she had said, you must dress like a Cuban. So she had taken me to a market stall in the Old City that was open late. For a few dollars we bought a long floral-patterned sleeveless shift, a sun hat and sandals. She laughed when I held the dress up against me, clapping her hands. I had put it on reluctantly when I got up. I thought I stuck out like even more of a sore thumb than usual. But it was cool and it felt like dressing up, being someone else. And now we were going on an adventure, which she refused to tell me about. No time for breakfast, she said, we take coffee with us and go.

There was nothing to indicate that the dusty turn-in at the beginning of a gleaming, modern highway leading out of the city was a bus stop. An anonymous, locked concrete hut that looked as if it had been dropped there and forgotten, a free standing metal rail fixed in the ground, against which a bicycle, whose front basket was perilously loaded with melons and potatoes was resting, and a crowd of about a dozen people waiting patiently, men in suits with shoulder bags, bare-chested men, men in vests and sweat pants, women in garish tops and loose slacks, a couple of school boys in red pants, clean white shirts and blue neckerchiefs, two obvious tourists in shorts, walking boots and back packs, all watched with open curiosity at this odd couple climbing out of a taxi apparently rejecting its comforts in favour of a bus.

Rebeca flashed me a secret grin, enjoying the little stir we caused.

Just across a dry ditch was a low tree with an old car seat invitingly placed under it in the shade. She walked firmly towards it across the litter strewn, dead grass. I followed.

We sat, ready to wait. But almost at once a bus (she called it a 'wa-wa') creaked and groaned off the road onto the turn-in. Silhouetted heads crammed every window. Dreading the prospect of trying to squeeze into this mass of bodies in the heat I started to get to my feet but Rebeca held me back. Sitting down again, I watched as miraculously all but three of the waiting passengers were somehow absorbed into the wa-wa's entrails, the bicycle hooked optimistically onto the back.

As it whined on its way Rebeca nodded to me and we re-crossed the ditch and joined the remaining three passengers, a woman in a multi-coloured headscarf, stripy top and loose grey pants with a pink flash down the side, an enormously fat bare-chested black man in a beret smoking a cigar and a beautiful young woman who might have been his daughter in a simple red dress with serious, soulful eyes. I smiled tentatively at my fellow travellers, without response.

We waited in silence. Rebeca offered no explanation, no reassurance. This was to be a little taste of daily Cuban life for me to experience unpackaged. To our fellow travellers this was just the start of another morning. To me, standing in line for a bus amongst Cubans with my Cuban stepmother everything felt sharp and new.

Within minutes, instead of a bus an old blue Buick, one of the city's famous classic cars from the Fifties rolled to a stop, a middle-aged couple on the front bench seat. The window was wound down, what seemed like a negotiation took place and the woman in the headscarf got in the back. The Buick heaved back up onto the highway.

I turned to Rebeca. Is this how it is done? She nodded, a little smile playing. It was very hot out of the shade. I was grateful for the hat and the occasional current of cooler air. I looked at my watch. Still not yet 9.00. What would it be like by midday?

Now a whining, smoky blue truck with high, latticed sides, piled to the top with a mixture of cabbages and green bananas creaked off the metalled road and lumbered to a halt in the dust in front of us.

Father and daughter (if that was what they were), followed by Rebeca went to the driver's window. Again, negotiations took place. The bare-chested man shrugged, took off his beret to scratch his head, sweat pouring down past his ears, and the two of them stepped back. Rebeca beckoned to me.

"He go near Tarara. He take us."

She climbed up into the cabin, hitching her tight nurse's uniform skirt up to make the step. I followed. As I settled into the cabin, slamming the door I smiled apologetically through the window at the dispossessed couple. They had, after all, been before us in the line. This time both smiled back without rancour, waving us on our way, the girl with the soulful eyes looking suddenly animated. There would be something going their way soon.

"*Muchas gracias,*" I said to the driver who neither returned my look nor replied, concentrating on easing the truck back onto the highway.

He was a dour looking, thin-faced man. He wore a dirty cream shirt without sleeves, held together across his bony chest by a single button. He stared grimly ahead of him at the road from under what looked like an army fatigues cap. The cabin was narrow, Rebeca's legs angled across towards mine to keep the gear stick free, the bench seat hard and shiny, bouncing and sliding us into each other. She watched me, grinning slyly, wondering how I was taking it. I grinned back, enjoying myself.

It was the first time I had been out of Havana and I devoured the landscape. Every so often on our left we caught glimpses of the sea, always attended, like sentries, by tall resort hotels, little dinghies and pedalos clinging to the shore line. I realised why the road was so good. This was tourist territory. To our right rolling green farmland with tiled barns, red ploughed earth and fields of cattle were interspersed with villages with wooden roadside shacks selling vegetables and small, modern towns with cinemas and gas stations.

I felt Rebeca shift beside me and became aware that the dank smell of cabbage, which had hung over the cabin, had now been infiltrated by something not unlike cabbage but far stronger. You've guessed. I knew it wasn't me. I looked at Rebeca who glanced back, her whole face oscillating desperately between disgust and laughter. Not her. Our host continued to stare out at the road, apparently oblivious. It was so awful I started to laugh too, though like Rebeca trying not to show it. This may surprise you. You have both at times been guilty of farting in public and while you have found it funny – as did your father to my annoyance – I never have. Compared to this man, however, you were beginners. It was so poisonous and the situation so socially fraught that the only possible response was choking hysteria.

"Open the window!" Rebeca hissed, her hand across her nose, pretending to scratch her cheek.

As casually as possible, my hand also innocently in front of my nose, I struggled with the handle cranking the window down, letting in a welcome blast of hot but mercifully clean air.

As the cabin cleared, we settled back into some kind of propriety. Then in the silence our driver host spoke for the first and only time.

"*Lo siento*," he muttered.

Apologising.

It was in its way courageous of him and Rebeca, I think, tried to say something reassuring, but I am afraid within seconds we had descended back into spluttering, suppressed giggles like the schoolgirls we had become.

The rest of the journey passed in shamed silence. Thankfully it was not long before he turned off the highway, descending down a gradual slope along an arrow-straight road leading to a small, neatly contained seaside town. Presumably Tarara. And presumably where I would learn something about my father.

Rebeca asked the driver to drop us on the seafront.

I thanked him, still embarrassed by our hysteria and climbed out. Rebeca followed me.

"Shouldn't I give him something?"

"No," she slammed the cabin door, waving to him. "Is what we do. His duty as Cuban."

The truck cranked on its way, in a trail of blue smoke, our poor driver humiliated by flatulence and us two hysterical women, now free to regain his dignity as a good Cuban citizen.

"But not his duty to fart," Rebeca added.

And we fell into each other's arms, once more giggling helplessly, now quite unconstrained, able to be as childish as we pleased, all wariness between us banished, my stepmother and I bonded by a stranger's fart.

Recovering, I looked around. In front of us the sea broke in gentle ripples on a golden beach. Fair-haired children ran through the shallows, screaming with laughter. A lifeguard sat on a step-ladder in the sand. At first sight an idyll. But something puzzled me. Then I realised what it was. Men and women in white coats were watching the children as they played.

What had this to do with my father?

"Are you going to tell me why we are here?"

She put her arm through mine and we walked back across the road and sat on a yellow metal bench in the shade of a colonnade in front of a municipal looking building facing out to the sea.

"All these children come from Ukraine. You know Chernobyl?" I nodded. "All have radiation sickness from the explosion. Now, still after so many years. They come here, we make them better. Sometimes they stay six weeks, sometimes ten years. Since 1989 Cuba has done this. Even in the bad times after Soviet money has gone. Ukraine pays air fares. We do everything else. Schools, hospitals, everything. One country holding hands with other country. This is the Cuba the Revolution want to build. The revolution your father came to fight for. Come."

She took me to an office where we met a friend of hers, a young smiling doctor called Jose who showed us around in his car. We saw the hospital, small, bristling with modern equipment, treatment centres, the school, playing fields, a cultural centre. Jose told us how over the years Cuba had treated over 20,000 children, all for free, suffering from congenital malformations, leukaemia, alopecia, vitiligo, muscular dystrophy. He introduced me to smiling children with artificial limbs, to a boy who had been given four months to live by a doctor in Ukraine and now five years later was playing football.

Rebeca had done what she set out to do. First, she had walked me through a little corner of ordinary Cuban life. Then she had presented me with a microcosmic Utopia that I could see and touch, and which demonstrated a social generosity that the most brutish Wall Street cynicism could not lay a hand on. It was real, humbling and immensely moving.

As she intended Tarara helped me to understand my father's Cuban dream, the apparently crazy dream that he had left me to go in search of – and finally impaled himself on. Understanding it freed me. And I need you to understand it too so you can understand what followed, and why I did what I did.

Chapter 20

Raul had his head down, methodically digging with his spoon past the shrimp into the flesh of the avocado in which they nested. We had made little eye contact. I knew why. I told myself – over and over – that I should never have opened that door to my room, we should never have kissed as we did. But the fact was I *had* opened it and no amount of wishing could shut it now.

"I went to see him this afternoon," I said. We had now taken to referring to our shared father as 'he' or 'him'. 'Dad', if it belonged anywhere, belonged to me, 'Papi' to him. Neither title felt comfortable between us. "He was listening to music on an I-Pad when I arrived. Was that anything to do with you?"

He shrugged, accepting responsibility while disclaiming any great effort or sacrifice.

"Thank you. I didn't want Rebeca to bother you."

"No problem."

"He seemed very pleased with it. Though it is hard to tell with him sometimes." Now Raul nodded in recognition, a trace of a smile on his lips. Still not looking at me. "He showed me the list of albums that was downloaded onto it. Was that you too?"

Again, the briefest of acknowledgments. I am not rejecting you, I wanted to say. I am being sensible.

"You're a good man. You must let me know how much it cost you."

This time our eyes met briefly. A little smile. Then he turned to look out across the headland to the darkening sea.

Another friend, another *paladar*.

We had arrived as the sun was setting at what looked like a bungalow under construction, parking Miguel's car between a pile of sand and a cement mixer. There was an unfinished wall with window frames unglazed but in place, a ladder leaning against it, a stacked pack of breezeblocks, a drainage ditch with a builder's plank making a rickety bridge. Our host Alberto and his wife Yamilys, were out ready to greet us before we had stepped out of the car, embracing Raul affectionately, and then coming around to me, Yamilys turning her handshake into a warm, sisterly cheek-to-cheek. They led us past the building hazards, explaining in enthusiastic if limited English what it was all going to look like, through their large, open – though as yet sparsely furnished – living room onto a small, canopied verandah looking out across the sea. The table was already laid, candles lit, fairy lights twinkling in the vine above us. Everything about them was stylish, energetic and ambitious, people who would succeed in whatever corner of the world they landed. Enterprise Cuba. Raul beamed with admiration as they sat us down.

Then he had disappeared, almost instantly, into a cloud again when we were alone.

He put his spoon down, the avocado now reduced to an empty, lop-sided skin, and dabbed at his mouth. This was getting silly. I reached out and squeezed his hand. He looked up, startled.

"How have you been?"

"No problem." Bright. Too bright. "You?"

I withdrew my hand. We circled each other.

"How did you think he was?" he asked.

Safer.

"Still telling me he wanted to die."

"Why not?" His voice turned suddenly hard. "This is not a good life for him."

I glanced at him, surprised, but now he was watching the lights of a fishing boat bobbing out at sea. Music was coming from the kitchen, Yamilys singing to it. At the table in the living room, now also candle-lit, a party of four German men who had recently arrived were waiting for their first course, talking quietly.

"Your mother thinks it is all nonsense. 'Opera' she called it."

He shrugged. She would.

"She took me to Tarara. Have you been? The Chernobyl project. It is impressive."

Another shrug.

"Oh, come on Raul, even you –"

"No, is good. I know of Tarara. But so what? Look how nice we are in Cuba."

Now we caught each other's eye, and something – I don't know what – made us both laugh. He made a self-deprecating grimace as he laughed, shaking his head.

"No, is good, is good. Not everything in Cuba is bad."

"Your mother is very proud of what Fidel has done."

"My mother is *historico*. She live in the last century."

Alberto arrived to clear the table for our main course. He and Raul chatted easily in Spanish, laughing comfortably at each other's jokes. Then Yamilys appeared with our steaks, roast potatoes and beans, hustling her husband out of the way and placing our food in front of us with a flourish and a practised smile.

"Buen apetito!"

And then – for no reason that I could see – the atmosphere went dark once again. We sat opposite each other in this little corner of paradise, the broken reflection of a low moon flickering like a vast swarm of fireflies on the sea, both wary, tongue-tied. Finally, I put my knife and fork down and once more reached out, laying my fingers gently on his wrist as it rested by his plate.

"What's the matter, Raul?" Better admit that the elephant was there.

He removed his hand from my fingers, lifting a forkful to his mouth, chewing carefully before he replied.

"You know."

I caught his hand again. I felt strong, clear headed.

"I love you too, my brother, and there's an end to it. Now let's be friends. Let's have a nice time."

Slowly he raised his eyes to mine. I kept hold of his wrist. Then he smiled, a deep, dark smile that made me giddy.

"You are right."

So we did. We had a nice time. He told me more about Alberto and Yamilys, how hard they worked, how determined they were to have a good life, how they knew powerful people so they had a license not only for the *paladar* but also for importing sewing machine parts from Poland, how they were able to get cement and building materials – even a truck – when other people couldn't, how rich they were becoming by Cuban standards, how their secret was that everybody liked them and their only sadness that they could not have children. Then he told me how his lawyer friend had said to him that maybe as this was the first time the police had actually brought a charge against him the judge may be lenient. We talked about you both. He wanted to know what interested you, what I thought you might want to do when you graduate.

Driving back to the City – and, as I thought, to the Nacional – I wondered if this was how it was going to be when we met from now on, friendly meetings, cautious, well-defined intimacy. Part of me was relieved at the prospect. Another part – if I am honest, as I am trying to be – less so.

Then, suddenly, he parked in a quiet street that I didn't recognise.

"Why are we stopping?"

He turned to me, his hands resting on the steering wheel. I could hear the distant high-pitched whine of a late-night electric saw painfully working its way through timber, the deep, rhythmic blood pulse beat of rock music, all melody muffled as it forced its way to us through air vents, past subterranean walls.

"My mother show you ordinary Cuban life. I show you, too. Here is where I live. My ordinary Cuban life. You like to see?"

The ticking of the engine as it cooled.

"Isn't it late? What about… the other people in the house?"

"No other people. I live alone."

I could have said no. I could have said I am sorry Raul, I am tired I want to go back to my hotel. But I wasn't tired. And I thought, yes it would be interesting to see how he lived, do it now before thinking about it. I was out of the car while he was still sitting at the wheel. See his place and then go. We both knew the rules.

He unlocked a wooden gate in a wall, opened it and stood aside to let me in. We were in a small courtyard with a cat's cradle of washing lines and cables criss-crossing above our heads, clearly visible against the night sky. Two rickety but once comfortable looking cane chairs were clustered around a dry miniature fountain. A pile of old carpets was stacked against the wall. Nearby was a children's tricycle lying on its side.

I was shivering, though it was still warm.

He pointed to the top of the building. An outside staircase ran up the wall to a squat, tiled building perched on the flat roof, with a wooden shed attached to it. There was a window in the side facing us and a door at the head of the stairs.

"My apartment."

I followed him up the stone steps, both of us treading lightly.

The door opened directly into a narrow, windowless lobby with a small electric cooker with two rings and a tiny oven sitting on a Formica-topped table, a sink dangerously close to it, and a small blue fridge whirring noisily. An acoustic guitar hung on the wall between shelves on which stood a few pots and plates.

He opened a door to his left and went through it switching on an overhead light. I followed. The room was painted dark blue and dominated by a double bed, which was covered in a beautiful tapestried throw in muted golds and browns. For the rest there was a standing wardrobe and a small TV set perched on a chair. Behind a half open plastic curtain in the far corner was a little alcove with a shower and lavatory pedestal. He bent down by the side of the bed and turned on a low lamp on the floor, then switched off the overhead light and closed the curtains – also blue – over the window. On the wall opposite was a large print showing Cuba as a naked woman with pine trees scattered across her body. At the head of the bed a pencil sketch of a woman was taped to the wall. It took me a moment to recognise myself, the long ago self of that first morning in the *Plaza de Armas,* the artist sketching as we walked and talked. Raul caught my look and smiled, the smile wrapping itself around me, proud and possessive. I was a schoolgirl again, flushed, absurdly touched. I had to look away. I could hear the hum of machinery coming from the wooden shed at the back, water trickling into a tank, through the wall behind the bed.

"I share the roof with pumps and water tanks." He put out his arms indicating the magnificent dimensions of his life. "How I live."

Almost his entire apartment, his life, a bedroom. It was a long time, it occurred to me, since I had been in a man's bedroom. For a brief moment I felt trapped, the walls closing in on me. Then it passed, as quickly as it had flared.

"Excuse me," he said. "I need the toilet."

He closed the plastic curtain behind him. It was translucent, offering little privacy, his shadow as he stood, distorted across it. I wanted to leave the room but it seemed over fastidious and prudish. Then he started and the sound of his pee drilling into the water – the alcove acting as an echo chamber – was startlingly loud and very masculine and sent me scurrying through the door to the little lobby / galley that was my only hiding place. Here the sound, though mercifully muted, still carried and made me realise that I needed to do the same. Hold on, I thought, you'll be back in the hotel soon. And then told myself off for being not only prudish, but ridiculous. That schoolgirl again.

As I heard the lavatory flush I marched back into the bedroom. He was closing the curtain.

"My turn," I said. "But you can wait out there."

He smiled, pulled the curtain back and stepped aside.

"And close the door," I said as he reached it.

I waited while, still smiling, he did so.

My knees were touching the side of the shower – which was also the only place I could wash my hands. We spent a week with the Bradshaws once, on their yacht. You probably remember. This was even smaller.

And here it was not a holiday. It was how he lived.

Coming back out I knew I should say goodnight and leave. I didn't. I sat down on his bed. There, on my left, was the sketch of me that he had kept – always by his bed? – for two months or more. If I reached out, I could touch it. It was as though it had been waiting for me, a patient dress rehearsal for the real thing. And now I was here, bringing it to life. It seemed right, pre-ordained. I felt trust. Total trust in somebody who loved me. We both knew the rules.

I was shivering again. The schoolgirl would not go away.

He came back into the bedroom as the last sounds of the flush trickled to nothing.

He sat beside me.

I knew that if he tried to kiss me, I could handle it. A kiss, no more. That would be fine.

I wanted him to kiss me.

I wanted him.

He kissed me.

I have never taken drugs but I imagine what followed was what it may be like to be drugged. Perhaps you know, so you may understand. I can only hope you will understand. But you need to know. Or rather I need to tell you. I lost all reason. I lost who I was, the carefully protected identity, the me I had lived with for so many years just was not there. But beyond any bodily sensation was tenderness, consuming tenderness, different from anything I had known, certainly – also beyond anything I might ever have imagined. And beauty. And trust. A beautiful being who was mine to cherish and who cherished me. Total surrender, total closeness.

With no trace of sin.

That is just how it was for that space in my life, however long it lasted, minutes, hours. Now, for me, belonging to another world, but still eternal. And something for which, despite everything, I will remain eternally grateful.

The first image I have in my mind, the first thing I can actually remember is his eyes, warm, calm, totally at peace as we lay side by side. And as I stared back into them the cold knowledge seeped through my body, starting somewhere in my toes, up through my belly, my heart, settling like dull poison in my head that what we had done was wrong.

Illegal.

I tried to push the fear away. Not us. Not this. This was good, this was love. But the poison continued to seep. My old me was coming back to life.

"I love you Maggie." His eyes staring into me.

I didn't tell him I loved him. I moved towards him and kissed him softly. Soft lips, soft kiss.

I could feel him stir towards me.

I eased back.

"Why?" He looked puzzled.

"Because."

"You want to sleep?"

"I should go."

"No."

"Yes."

"Tomorrow?"

"I'm not sure. I think not."

Now he half sat up, his eyes wide in alarm.

"Why?"

"You know why… Raul, dearest Raul, you *know*…"

"I don't know." Petulant.

"Jesus… What we've done is illegal."

"Is beautiful."

"Yes. But illegal. This has no future. We live in different countries, you are not thinking straight."

"Why different countries? I come with you to America. Of course. You take me to America,"

The earth began to spin away from beneath me.

"I take you to America?"

"Why not?" He was staring at me, seeming genuinely puzzled. "Family…" He gestured at the two of us in case I hadn't understood. "Family."

"Raul, you really aren't thinking straight."

I could feel my heart start to race, panic threatening.

"We love each other. We must be together. Of course I think straight."

He reached for me tenderly, full of confidence. I flinched. Was that what it was? I was a passport? He continued to stare at me, looking more puzzled than ever.

"Why Maggie? Why?"

Could he really not see it? Was he pretending?

"What was this? A passport fuck?"

Now his eyes slowly dulled in shock. He turned away from me and lay back on the bed.

I was ashamed. It was I who had not been able to see clearly.

"I'm sorry… Raul – I am sorry…"

I wanted to reach for him, touch his shoulder, but thought better of it.

Silence settled.

After a while I swung my legs onto the floor, my back to him, looking for my clothes.

"I must go, Raul," I said, pulling my blouse over my head, my back to him. He seemed not to have taken in what I was doing.

The silence continued. Then from behind me –

"I take you."

134

"NO!"

I swung around to him, doing up the buttons on my sleeve.

"Thank you." I reached out, touching him this time. "I would prefer a taxi. Can you call one for me?"

I passed him my cell. I finished dressing.

He made a call and passed the handset back to me.

"Ten minutes."

He was standing, buttoning his shirt, his eyes dark with sadness. I went around the bed and put my arms around him.

"I am sorry, Raul."

He didn't move, his hands frozen at his shirtfront.

"You don't seem to realise…"

What didn't he realise? That I hadn't made love for nearly two years? That the only person I had made love with for a quarter of a century had been my husband? My ex-husband. That I had gone mad?

"I do love you," I said.

"But that is not the point," he said sadly.

He *had* understood.

"I wait for taxi with you."

We stood in silence in the road. When the taxi came, I hugged him and left. So there you have it. My truth.

RAUL

Of course now I know. Facts, facts, theory, research. Is "syndrome". OK. Very good. I am "syndrome". Brothers, sisters, blah blah. Shit. Doctors understand. Me, I don't understand. Why doctors? I was not ill. "Syndrome"? Does "syndrome" mean the world turns over? Everything, the sun, the moon, all change? She was not my sister. She was my reality. My everything. She was me. I don't believe in God. But making love to her was to be with God. It is not possible to call that a sin.

It was illegal.

Yes... The rules are written so. Not by me. I can do nothing about rules. But, Mister Attorney, what happened between us was... pure... I want to say Holy but I don't believe... For both of us.

You speak for her?

No, she must speak. But she will say so. I know. Many women I have been with. I know the sounds of women, the cries. I know the sounds of fuck. This was not fuck. This was...healing. Becoming. Her, me, me, her. A new life. For both of us.

And you think she would say the same?

(Pause)

I hope. I believe.

You don't think... with your history, perhaps...you are romanticising?

(Pause)

I understand... No.... Was real.... So, of course I think we must be together Of course I think we both go to America. So simple. So right.

But not for her.

(Pause)

She did not listen to herself.

Do you think it is possible that part of you, a little part, perhaps, made love to her because you wanted her to take you to America?

(Long pause)

I want to say impossible. She was me. I was her. We had to be together. I want so much to say no. But now ... time has passed. There are things inside us we don't know... Who can say? Who can say what else was in me – beside love? Who can say what made her do what she did? With me – or later?

[FROM RAUL VENTURA'S WITNESS STATEMENT (6)]

Chapter 21

His eyes were closed. Thin, pale leads from the plugs that only partially obscured the sprouting hairs in his ears became temporarily lost in the tangle of his beard before re-emerging as they trailed down to the iPad resting on his chest. His face was at peace, miraculously unlined. For a brief moment I caught a glimpse of the child behind the tired skin. A schoolboy in his Moses make up.

The nurse was not at her desk by the main entrance. Nobody seemed to be watching. Casually, I took the innocent-looking water bottle out of my bag and placed it on his bedside cabinet. I was becoming a seasoned rum smuggler. He did not stir, either asleep or still floating on the swell of the music.

I pulled up the chair quietly and sat watching him, welcoming the stillness, the sense of being a daughter with a father, the appropriateness of it after so much forbidden, inappropriate turmoil. He breathed regularly, easily, his eyeballs occasionally fluttering behind his lids, suggesting he was asleep and dreaming, not listening to music. I remembered watching you, Billy – you seemed to be the dreamer of the two – when you were small and I had got home late. You slept on your back then, your eyeballs working alarmingly sometimes, muttering a bit, but never waking up. You, Tommy, on the other hand slept all scrunched up on your side, tangled in the bedding as though having a fight with it, and I don't think I ever got a look at your eyeballs, fluttering or not. Now all these years later I was sitting watching my father, old, grey haired but somehow at that moment unlined, his eyeballs quivering sporadically under the wafer-thin skin of his eyelids, and I felt myself allowing, quite consciously, a lifetime of anger to drain from me. There was no place for it now.

Suddenly, movement. Clearly, he had been listening, and not asleep. His hand lurched towards the iPod, his fingers scrabbled at the control dial. He opened his eyes irritably to identify the buttons and arrows. And saw me.

"Hello, Dad."

He glared. Reluctantly, laboriously, his hand struggling to get a grip on them he removed the ear-pieces from his ears continuing, as he did so, to stare at me with beady malevolence.

"Oh, don't worry. I won't hang around if you want to go back to your music. Just thought you might like to know I've brought you some more water."

His expression changed instantly, eyes softening, even the beginning of a smile lurking. He turned to look. His hand started to snake towards the bottle.

"Maybe wait a bit?" I suggested. The nurse was back at her desk now, bent over some forms. "Don't want anyone to get suspicious."

A grunt. His hand fell back.

"Thank... you," he managed to get out indistinctly. Glowering again now, not wanting to be caught being too grateful.

"Glad to be of use."

Still the sulky schoolboy, not looking me in the eye. But at least he was talking.

"Movement seems to be getting better," I lied.

He grunted, glancing down at his left arm.

"Are you feeling any better?"

He worked his mouth, gathering saliva.

"Not... going to..."

"Give it time."

"Don't... want time... Had enough."

"Oh, come on, Dad –"

"NO!" Sharp, powerful. "Out... Finish..." Now he was looking at me steadily. "Want... die... You hear me?"

I returned his look. What was coming?

"Yes."

"Up... to... you."

"Sorry?"

"You... heard..."

His face, steady, juddered, the room juddered. A moment of utter, paralysing terror. I was fourteen years old. My father was asking me to kill him. Calm. There's an answer. Always an answer.

"What do you want me to do, Dad?" I had to clear my throat, my voice husky.

"Think... of something... Don't care... Want out..."

And, strangely, following the fear, in the willed, fragile calm, came a gush of pity for my shrunken old father in this grim hospital bed in Havana asking me to kill him. I reached out and took his hand. For a while it lay limp in mine. The knots and warts that I had never noticed before, the distorted, arthritic knuckles, the tired skin, loose and thickly veined, the patches of brown, once freckles now continents spread out like a map. The concert pianist's hands. The hands that had danced with the gods. His fingers tightened on mine. I looked up. He was staring into my eyes with an expression I had never seen before.

My father telling me he needed me. That he loved me?

Now with my other hand I scrabbled for my handkerchief, defences gone, tears flowing. As I dabbed at my eyes, I became aware of movement at the end of the ward. Rebeca was sweeping through the double doors. She stopped when she saw me and waved tentatively, as though disconcerted. I waved back, willing the tears to stop. She turned away to speak to the nurse on the desk.

"Rebeca's here," I said quietly.

Did she know? Had Raul said anything? Rebeca whom I dreaded meeting. Rebeca whose absolution I so desperately needed.

A grunt from the bed. Then fumbling with his ear-pieces he pushed them roughly into his ears, settled back and closed his eyes with mute eloquence.

She was now striding towards us. I smiled as best I could. She touched me briefly on the shoulder by way of greeting – friendly, seemingly no agenda – then leaned over him and removed the ear-pieces, launching straight into a stern tirade in Spanish. He kept his eyes closed.

Then, straightening, she sat on the bed by his knees and turned to me.

"Nurse say he won't eat. He must eat. Silly man."

I looked across at him. His eyes remained resolutely closed. I had no doubt about the message he was beaming to me.

"I think… He was just saying he wanted me to leave. He wants to rest."

She looked at me sternly for a moment. Suspicious?

"Good. Rest. I have said what I must say. Eat, old man."

She bent over him again, this time kissing him. He kept his eyes shut.

"We leave together?"

"Yes."

I got to my feet, hovering, while she marched towards the exit. I quickly unscrewed the bottle, sloshed a little into his mug and put it in his left hand.

He opened his eyes, saw what I had done, glanced up at me and smiled. Twisted, cautious perhaps, even grudging still, but a real smile.

As I hurried past the nurse's desk, she looked up at me and also smiled, a warm approving smile as for a dutiful daughter.

Rebeca was waiting for me by the lifts. She watched me steadily as I approached. Did she know? My stepmother. Mother to my half-brother. With whom I had slept the night before.

For a tiny moment the fever flared again in my memory, making me draw in my breath sharply. More than remembered, it was, briefly, shamefully relit, followed immediately by a spasm of gut-twisting revulsion. Did I actually shudder as I walked towards her?

"He like his iPad, I think." Gently mocking. Did she know he was only pretending to be asleep? Did she know more? About Raul? I could not take it on. I was still trying to deal with my father asking me to kill him.

"Yes. Well done."

And well done Raul for getting it for him. I wanted to say his name, to talk to her about him, but no words came.

"He make me angry, still, the old man. All his life everything must be his way, how he like. Now is impossible, he is ill, he is old. But still he think it must be his way."

The lift doors opened. It was empty. We got in. She pulled the grill doors shut. The lift shuddered into action. It was wide, big enough for two beds side by side. We stood leaning with our backs against opposite walls facing each other.

I would talk to her about Raul. I needed to. But not yet.

"He still wants to die."

"He said that to you?"

Sudden, fierce. I knew she would react badly. But it had to be spoken of.

"Yes."

"Again?"

"Yes."

Her face closed off, telling me there was to be no more conversation about this. Was she angry because he hadn't the courage or the dignity to want to see his life through? Or because he had confided in me and not in her?

Or did she know about Raul and me?

The lift shuddered to a halt on the ground floor. We stepped out past the little knot of people waiting. As we set off down the drab, dun coloured corridor to the main exit she slipped her arm through mine, wrong-footing me as ever.

"What are you doing now?" she asked.

"Back to my hotel. I have to call my office."

"First you come to my apartment. I make you coffee."

Her eyes were locked onto mine, warm again, safe. No secrets, just friendship. And not open to any disagreement.

"All right."

She smiled, squeezed my arm as we stepped out into the sunlight.

"Do you want to call a taxi? Use my cell. Or are we going by bus again?"

She looked me up and down and grinned.

"Is good you are dressed like Cuban."

I smiled back uncertain why I should be earning points for that. The shift dress was cool and freeing in the heat. She beckoned me to follow her behind a wall to the side of the hospital where two enormous waste bins were parked, with a woman's bicycle squeezed between them. She backed it out laughing at my expression. She stood astride it, waiting for me to climb onto the seat at the back.

"I can't!" I was laughing too. "It's indecent!"

"Sideways. So. Cuban dress is perfect. Come."

Cautiously I eased myself up onto the seat. The bike remained reassuringly steady.

"Hold me."

As I put my hands on her waist, she stood on the pedals and the bike rolled forwards – slowly but with confidence.

"All right?" she called over her shoulder.

"So far."

She turned down the street and to my surprise I began to feel safe almost at once.

"Aren't I heavy for you?" I called up to her ear.

"No problem. Cubans good with bicycles."

I let myself become a parcel, enjoying the sun on my face, the breeze, the movement, the closeness to people, bicycles, cars and trucks. As we stopped at lights, Rebeca's leg braced on the ground, me balancing my weight carefully, I remember smiling at passing pedestrians and them smiling encouragingly back. For a while, Raul, my father, belonged to a distant, manageable world.

After about twenty minutes we arrived in an old fashioned, almost small-village area of the city, dusty sidewalks with a narrow metalled strip badly cratered, detached, single storey houses, some timber-clad, some plastered, variously painted, mostly in shades of cream and ochre but a few in pale blue, almost all with low front porches running the width of the house on which cane and plastic chairs were set amidst children's toys and building materials as though waiting for the cool of the evening.

We stopped in front of a house conspicuous not only for being freshly painted but also for its uncluttered, formal front step, trim pot plants and two rocking chairs perfectly positioned, like a stage set.

"*Mi casa,*" she said, stepping off the bicycle and holding it as I climbed down, my backside relieved by now to be no longer bouncing on the metal seat.

The neat, seemingly uninhabited formality of the house felt out of character. Rebeca read my expression and smiled.

"No, no. Here is doctor at the hospital. Big shot. Wife anaesthetist. I live behind."

She pushed the bike ahead of her down an alley by the side of the house until we came to a whitewashed, breeze-block extension built onto the back taking up part of the yard. This felt equally unlived-in with a metal bench neatly placed between two orange trees and an incongruous collection of garden gnomes. Surely no more Rebeca's taste than the theatrically neat front porch?

She caught my eye.

"Not me. Them. No children." The picture became clear. "Only here is me," she said gesturing to the extension.

My life, she was saying. Just as Raul had done, she wanted me to know her life.

She leant the bicycle against the wall, unlocked a door into the side of the building and led me into a small but sunny white walled room with big windows with slatted blinds looking onto her landlord's garden. The space served as a kitchen-dining-living-room. On one side a simple well-equipped kitchen with a table that doubled for working surface and eating, four stools tucked under it, on the other (acting as a room divider) a large expensive looking maroon sofa faced a wide-screen HD television set on a dark wood cabinet. On the walls were a portrait of Fidel and some romantic prints of rural Cuba. There was a small armchair by a side window under an old-fashioned standard lamp. Behind it was a door through which she led me into her dark green bedroom with its dark wooden double bed under a vibrant yellow cover, large hanging cupboard, also in dark wood and what looked like a genuine antique, curved, glass-topped dressing table. On the wall by her bed were small, framed photographs of both Raul and my father. On the side wall there was a large erotic print apparently by the same artist whose work I had seen in my father's apartment and had not at first identified as erotic. The one in Rebeca's bedroom was considerably less ambiguous, the palm tree at its centre unmistakeably a phallus, the leaves, gouts of semen. They enjoyed a shared taste in art? Or just sex? In one corner, taking up part of the room was a frosted glass partition, its open sliding door revealing a shower, lavatory pedestal and basin and a tiled floor on which stood some rudimentary toiletries, a brush, a sponge, a mug, an unlabelled plastic bottle that may have contained shampoo. Along the bedroom wall leading from the partition there was a small row of neatly stacked, well-worn shoes, one pair male, the rest female. A man's pants and shirts hung on the back of the door.

It was cramped and makeshift but not shabby. It felt comfortable and functioning. Like its owner it seemed to be making the most of what was on offer, without pride or – when viewed by this rich American? – shame.

As she made coffee we talked more about you, about her parents, about Obama, Fidel, his brother Raoul, how Cuba had come close to collapse after the break-up of the Soviet Union, how it had survived, more than survived in her opinion and how confident she felt in its future. And as we talked, I began to think, perhaps she does not need to know. What passed between her son and I can recede into history, known only to him and me.

Or did she know? Again. Was this her way of saying I needed no absolution? Bring me into her arena and talk. Just that. So much, was she saying, and no more?

Why, above all, did I ascribe such unlikely conspiracies to her? Constantly feel the need to double-guess her? What was it about this woman that both puzzled and mesmerised me?

Pepe turned up. If he was surprised to see me, he didn't show it. I took his arrival as my cue and rose to go, asking Rebeca if she would call a taxi. Nonsense, she said. There was a perfectly good taxi outside in the street. Poor Pepe, who had barely sat down was put immediately back onto his feet with instructions to take me to my hotel.

She came outside with us and as I went to sit in next to Pepe she took me in her arms and hugged me with a fierceness that seemed to be saying that whatever it was that I had done, whatever I was hiding from her, she forgave me. Or perhaps she was saying nothing of the kind. I was second-guessing her again, wrongly. She was just hugging me because she loved me as, surely, I loved her.

Almost everything she did surprised me. I knew that by now. It was a lesson that I did not take sufficiently to heart.

Chapter 22

Cuba's hall of mirrors, Right and Wrong bobbing and bending, distorted shapes, uncertainty everywhere. But I had no uncertainty about what was the right thing to do for Raul. He had big problems. I had the means to help.

I have always kept an account in a London bank since the days when we made our occasional trips over to see Granny. I knew there was very little in it. I also knew that what I was planning may have been deemed to be illegal in the eyes of the US Government but I decided – and this, I can tell you, was another first – that it was a technicality and trivial in the context of 'family' considerations and my half-brother's needs. I made a cash transfer from my US account to my London bank (thus, hopefully, bypassing Federal legalities) and from there to a dollar account in Havana that Miguel helped me set up. It took time but it happened.

The morning the money came through, Miguel – did he ever get any sleep? – took me to Raul's place. It was late by now and, as I half expected, Raul had already gone out. I felt in limbo. My programme of restitution was put on hold and the day stretched ahead of me.

I didn't want to be parted from Miguel. He had become my rock. He found solutions, he asked no questions. So first he took me to see my father. It was unrewarding. For the most part he had taken to remaining silent and surly, the provision of rum now taken for granted. I lasted barely half an hour. Then, to pass the time Miguel suggested a tourist tour of Museums and Cathedrals and Palaces. I drifted along, grateful for his anaesthetising presence, not taking in a great deal, my bag with the toxic dollars in plastic packets inside, clutched tightly across my chest.

He told me as he drove me back to the hotel that we would have to get to Raul either early or late if we were to find him at home. Both ways, I thought, risked finding him with a woman. I chose early. Miguel agreed to collect me the following morning at 7.30 when he had finished his night shift.

It was close to 8.00 and it was already getting hot when once again I climbed the steps up the side of the building to the rooftop apartment, clutching my bag. We had had no contact since that night. I had no idea how he would receive me. One moment I was calm, confident it was going to be easy, just a question of changing the terms of contract between amicable partners. The next I was bracing myself, fearful of his response. And my weakness.

I knocked on the door. Now that I was – hopefully – so close to seeing him again I felt at peace, sure that what I was about to do would be healing for both of us. There was a long silence. I heard chickens clucking and noticed for the first time a wired run attached to the shed behind his back wall. What if he was away? How impossible life was without cell phones! Another knock. Maybe there *was* a woman there. How would I handle it? I see-sawed back to anxiety, no longer detached and wise.

To hell with him. I turned to go back down the steps.

The door behind me opened.

He stood there in his underpants, eyes unfocussed, blinking at the sun. When he realised who it was, he sighed – it could have been relief, it could have been irritation – and stepped back to allow me in.

I stood my ground.

"Are you…?" I started again. "I mean have you… Are you alone? I want to speak."

He nodded wearily, motioning me in.

I edged past him, his almost naked body a distant thing now. I put my bag down on the table next to the electric oven. He shut the door. It was dark. The place smelt, thankfully, not of sex but of sleep.

"How are you?" It was more than politeness. I wanted to know.

He nodded, indicating that he was fine and that I should say what I had to say. He leant back against the door, beautiful still in his near nakedness, but a stranger, a man with whom almost my only connection was one of obligation.

"I have something for you."

He waited, still impassive.

I removed the plastic packets from my bag and put them on the table. Three of them, thick with dollar bills. Now his eyes registered, shock flitting momentarily across his face before it settled again. Still he said nothing.

"It's just… I am so lucky in my life… And we are… what we are to each other… And I would like you to have… to share a little of my luck with me…"

He was looking not at the money but at the floor, scratching his chin, the early morning stubble rasping quietly in the silent room. Suddenly I felt more than duty. I felt a deep rush of sisterly affection.

"You are… you will always be special in my life, Raul… No, that doesn't begin to say it and… well, I probably can't anyway… probably shouldn't… But I would like to remain something to you… for us to remain in each other's lives if that were possible, somehow… I thought this could perhaps buy you a car, like Miguel and then…"

And then what? Write poetry? Teach again? Go to prison for black market offences, then see out his days here as a cab driver? Suddenly a great hopelessness swept over me. Was this really going to help? Was I thinking sensibly? Or healing myself with my money? He continued to look at the floor.

"Or, I don't know, maybe it could help pay for a good lawyer. Is that how it works…? Have you heard any more about all that?"

Nothing. Then an imperceptible shake of the head. God, I thought, he sulks just like his father.

"Well… There it is…" I had done it now. "I'll let you get on… I don't know when I am leaving. Depends on him, I guess. So I am sure we will see each other…… Oh, Raul please look at me while I am trying to say good-bye!"

He lifted his head, even managing a shadowy smile. I stepped over to him, kissed him on the cheek and let myself out. He had not spoken to me once.

Did I have any suspicion that he might spend the money as he did? I certainly did not admit to it when I first found out what he had done. But even if I had known I think I would have wanted him to have it. What we did was I know, illegal – and no doubt sinful if that is how you see the world. But it was also love.

Your mother is far from being an expert on this subject – as my life so far bears out. But surely love in all its forms, has to be good? The bigger the sum of love we can accumulate in our lives the better. I hope you boys can accept that, whatever you feel about me at the moment. The love we had as you were growing up, however inadequate, however grumpy I was, was at least better than no love. To say nothing of the love we may be able to rediscover now. That I hope, so desperately hope, we will be able to rediscover. Love is love, family love, love of animals, friends, gay love – that may surprise you from me, but yes! – even the 'inappropriate' love I had for Raul. Still have. I shall always love him (or perhaps the memory of him) for the astonishing, transcendental gift of love he gave me, even though it spilled – had to spill – so quickly from my gratefully cupped hands.

I thought as I closed the door to his apartment behind me that I had also closed the door on Raul. But as you both know I have had to pay a price for loving him. And it was only the first crime on my charge sheet.

Chapter 23

His good fingers plucked fretfully at the rumpled bed sheet on his knees, the tempo increasing with every phrase as he forced the words out, each one a struggle.

"My... *fucking*... right... Nobody listening... *My* life... *My* death... Not frightened... do you hear...? Just... want not... to go on... *My* choice... Nobody else's... Somebody... must... listen..."

He was breathing heavily now. It was the most sustained passage of speech I had heard from him since he had been taken into hospital. With each syllable my sense of useless terror in the face of something so final, so impossible increased. My father baying for his own death.

"I'll try to think of something, Dad. I will, honestly. I do understand."

His head sank back, his eyes closed, spent and without hope.

He knew I was just making noises. The insult to his intelligence, the utter impotence was unbearable. Close to panic now, I had to get away.

I stood, leaned over and kissed him.

"I will try, Dad," I whispered, hating myself.

He mumbled something.

"Sorry?" I stood back to see his face.

"Is... difficult... I know... thank you..."

The words seemed to come more easily now. His eyes were open, looking steadily at me, his fragile head straining up from the crumpled pillow. The wise, understanding father that I had always dreamed of.

I fled. As I hurried past the nurse's desk, my hand across my mouth, tears streaming, I saw her blurry face, not smiling this time but following me with wide-eyed concern.

The lift lobby was thankfully empty. I pressed the button and, while I waited, leaned against the wall, breathing deeply.

"*Senora*..." The nurse had followed me.

She beckoned, smiling kindly. Maybe there was something about his treatment that I needed to know. Dabbing urgently at my eyes, I followed through a swing door into a narrow corridor, cleaning equipment stacked along the wall, into a cramped office with one desk, a telephone, a filing cabinet and only a row of nurse's caps on hooks to tell me where we were.

She poured some water out of a bottle standing on the desk into a plastic cup that she took out of a drawer. She passed it to me.

"Not rum," she said, smiling.

I stared at her in disbelief. She knew?

She put her finger to her lips, then exploded with laughter. I started laughing, too, but guiltily, still uncertain.

"You don't mind?"

"Your father, very old. Maybe rum not so bad. But –" She put her finger to her lips again, still smiling. "Sorry. My English not good."

"Better than my Spanish."

I drank the water gratefully, my throat sore with tension. I put the empty glass down.

"My father wants to die. He wants me to arrange it." If she didn't already know, she might as well understand why I had hurried past her, streaming snot and tears.

"Ah," she said as if it was quite normal, even to be expected.

"Is it at all possible that he will get better?" I spoke slowly, clearly. She seemed to understand, nodding. But her only answer was a shrug and a sad smile. Answer enough.

I took the risk.

"What can be done to help him?"

Again that sad smile. We're not here to end life, it said.

"All right. What can *I* do?"

She held my gaze thoughtfully as though making up her mind.

"You American?"

"Yes."

"You have money?"

I hesitated, uncomfortable.

"Yes, I guess I do."

She went to the filing cabinet and scrabbled inside. She came out with a crumpled, glossy one-page leaflet headed 'Clinica Internacional' over a photograph of a crisp, gleaming modern looking building. At the foot was the simple tag line in English, 'Simply the Best in Modern Hospital Care'. Below that a Havana address.

"Is very good. Private rooms. Very good. But I no say so – understand?"

Again the finger to the lips and that melting smile. She reached over and touched my arm, a brief gesture of sisterly understanding. Then she opened the door indicating that the meeting was over. She had to get back to the ward to look after her patients – including my despairing old father.

The 'Clinica Internacional' was set back from the road with a ramped concrete driveway circling a large bed of brilliantly vibrant flowers, glistening with freshly-sprayed water, up to a colonnaded porch large enough for three ambulances. It was a magnificently assertive building faced with blocks of large white stone that looked as if they could have been marble but probably weren't. A row of international flags hung from the leading edge of the roof. Everything proclaimed solemn self-confidence and money.

Inside there were wide, thickly carpeted floors along which gleaming medical trolleys flowed noiselessly, and a vast Reception desk behind which sat equally gleaming men and women with smiles as white as their crisp starched uniforms, all speaking excellent English. At the first sound of my accent coffee appeared as from nowhere, followed almost at once by a grey haired charmer who introduced himself as the Registrar and took me into his enormous office where we sat in armchairs, light as clouds, as he outlined the hospital's history, policies and terms, pressing glossy leaflets (this time the size of magazines) into my hands. On the walls no Fidel, no Che, but prints of catamarans straining magnificently into a stiff breeze as they and their overpoweringly healthy crew skipped nimbly across sun-flecked oceans.

Then the tour. Silent lifts that reached the appropriate floor without any indication they had even set off, gleaming, all-smiling nurses scurrying purposefully and equally soundlessly down the carpeted corridors. Futuristic medical equipment glimpsed through porthole windows set in treatment room doors. Finally, the rooms themselves, spacious, beds curtained in soft muslin, at their head consoles of buttons and dials and switches like an aeroplane cockpit, all geared to regulate temperature, summon assistance, turn on the television, the DVD, the radio. A fridge, ample hanging space for clothes, a large en suite bathroom with a shower that had a variety of nozzles set at different heights and in different parts of the wall ready to aim at any conceivable part of the body, with a well-positioned padded seat for the elderly or lame or lazy to sit while the shower and its robotic attachments worked their magic, cleansing and refreshing the world's wealthy.

By contrast with the dingy Hospital Simon Bolivar where my father was querulously seeing out his time, or the altruism of the Chernobyl project at Tarara this palace of opulence truly merited the word obscene.

And I knew at once that – however unequal, however corrupt this shining monument to capitalism might be to most Cubans – this was what I wanted the old man to have. He could have it because I could pay for it. It wasn't noble. But it was the truth.

I called Pepe to make contact with Rebeca. She joined me at the hotel that evening. We took our *mojitos* – of which I was growing alarmingly fond – out to the cannon in the garden overlooking the Malecon.

I did not expect her to welcome my proposal and I was right.

"He would not want that."

"Are you sure? He is not happy where he is."

"He will not be happy in a capitalist's hospital."

I knew I must not let my irritation show.

"Does it matter that it is capitalist? I mean – really? Who knows how long he has left? Why not the best for him? I am lucky, I can do it and I would like to."

"Thank you but it is impossible."

"Shall we ask him?"

I had kept this as my best card. She said nothing, sipping her drink, looking out to sea.

"You are being kind, I know."

Was she shifting?

"How long will you stay in Cuba?"

No. Stating her primacy. The wife. The one who has been with him all these years. The one who stays, not the fly-by-night.

And it was a good question.

"See how he gets on, I guess. My father asked for me. We haven't done much for each other in our lives. I would like to try and put that right. Maybe for me as much as for him. I would like to honour him. Do you understand?" She nodded thoughtfully. "And I don't have a lot to go back to America for right now. Except making money."

"So you stay?"

"Is that a problem?" Something was going on which I couldn't unpick.

"No problem. You know is hurricane season?"

"Not really. Does that make a difference?"

"No, no. No difference. Is good you know, I think." *Theeeenk.* Raul that first evening!

"Yes."

She said nothing for a while, looking down at the ground.

"Have you seen him?" she asked.

"Who?" I knew, of course.

"Raul."

"Not for a few days." What had he been saying?

"Nor have I."

For a moment I thought she made it sound ominous. Then I thought I must have imagined it.

REBECA

My poor friend Pepe say he know my son do not like him because so many time when Pepe visit me, we are in bed and we are busy we hear – bang, bang, bang! – on door. My son want to speak with me. Poor Pepe. Is not Pepe my son don't like. Only my son want me always to himself.... Yes. Then *he wanted me.*

Not now?

Stupid question.

I'm sorry.

Pepe is a good man. Good to my husband. Good to Maggie. Hurricane Yankee he call her. He like her but he call her Hurricane Yankee.

Is he good to you also?

Of course. Why not? Why would I keep him if he is not good to me? Is not like Cuban men. I am boss but he is happy. You understand? He like to help me. Do things. He is good father to his daughter Gertrudis. No wife. She suicided when Gertrudis was born .... Sad woman. But Pepe, he look after Gertrudis. His mother also look after, but Gertrudis most. Good father. She is now at University... Yes. He is not like Cuban men. He does not say me he loves me, I do not say him also. Is enough. He works, he plays chess, goes to baseball, visit his mother, does not bother me. But if I ask he comes. He is my friend. We make sex. Good sex. Until it is Raul – bang, bang, bang! (She laughs) *Yes .... Only this time was not bang, bang, bang, it was ta-taaa, ta-taaaa, ta-ta-ta-taaaa. Pepe's telephone. And we are busy. Very busy, we do not want to talk. The telephone stops. We do not. But then it starts again. Ta-taaa, ta-taaaa, ta-ta-ta-taaaa. It is on the floor in his pocket. He not want to stop sex to get out of bed and turn it off. He continue to sex with me. But I have stopped. I know who is calling. Always with Raul I know when his life is bad. When she went back to America, Maggie, I knew something he was bad. Maybe to do with her, maybe not. He had secret from me. Oh men always have secrets, but this was ... different. Then when she came back it was worse. Now for three, maybe four days I do not see him, he does not call. I knew there was trouble, big trouble. The sex was finished for me. Pepe knew. He stopped, looked at me. The telephone stopped.*

- I turn it off, he said. Be better.

- No, I say him. It will go again. Answer.

We waited. The telephone goes. Pepe gets out of bed. He picks up, comes back.

- Hello?

150

He listen. I watch his face. I cannot hear what he is hearing. But I knew. He give me the cell.

- Raul, he say. He call you from Mexico. The Island of Women.

[FROM REBECA VENTURA'S WITNESS STATEMENT (6)]

RAUL

Had you thought about it before?

Of course. Many times. I knew the man. I knew the secret place to find him, I knew the price.

Which is?

Also secret, Mr Attorney. (He laughs)

The only reason you hadn't gone before was that you didn't have the money?

I didn't have the money now.

What do you mean?

What she gave me was not enough.

So how did you manage it?

My Fate managed it.

Please explain.

Is difficult. My head was full of so many things.

Such as?

I didn't want the money. I wanted her. To be who I became with her. To feel ... right. Together we were not in one room but a whole house. You may say is romantic. But is how I felt. And she pushed me out of the house to be alone again.

You felt angry?

Not angry. Empty. So much waste. Why push away when is good? Like when Liset marry her big Party boss man. If is good push him out. Yes! Go! You are a lovely boy but I don't want you. Go. Be bad. Be lonely.

But you understood why –

Yes, yes. The law, always the law, fuck the law. I wanted her love. Instead I had her money.

But not enough to pay for your escape.

So many years I had dreamed of going. Cuba my prison. Always impossible. Now I think maybe the man take what I can give, why not, maybe I can pay him when I get to America. If I stay in Cuba do I go to prison? Real prison. Not nice. Then I think of leaving Cuba forever. I think of my mother. My mother. How can I leave her? Then again of her, of Maggie. To get away from her when I want to be near her. But she doesn't want to be near me. Or to go to America, be with her there? One day? Foolishness. So many things in my head. So I say Fate must decide for me. If the man take my money I will go. I will become a "balsero", a raft man with a new life.

And he accepted.

Leaving in three nights. Place for one. I was lucky. Not Miami, not from North. We go West he say. Fishing village on West coast – no, no names Mr Attorney! – we go through Mexico. Longer but better, he say. To Island of Women first, then across Yucatan, up through Mexico to the border. There he has people who know how to get us across the river. Then "Democracy for Cubans" they meet us and look after us. Long journey, trains, buses, expensive but good. I keep a little money, offer him the rest. He say yes. I must not tell anybody else on the journey how much I have paid, he says. OK. Decision made. Thank you Fate.

So it was easy in the end?

To leave my mother? Not easy. I could not tell her. I could not see her to say goodbye.

Why not?

She stop me.

How?

Believe me, Mr Attorney, if my mother want to stop me, she stop me. Strong woman. For her it is better that I am in a prison in Cuba than in America.

OK.

So.... I tell nobody. Nobody. I walk around, see my friends, hello, how are you anything happening, any deals, plans? All normal, normal. Then, when the day comes I take one bag, all my life in Cuba in one bag, Neruda poems. Condoms. Ha. I catch a bus to Pinar. Then another to village-without-name. It is evening when I arrive. I find the house the man-with-no-name told me. I meet the others. Eleven. I am number twelve. The Twelfth Disciple. You see? My grandmother taught me well. Disciples of freedom. Mostly they are my age, men, women, some married, two children, one baby. We don't talk so much. I am shy, maybe they are also shy. Or frightened. Our guide, our "boss" – shall we call him Jorge? – make us a meal. After, I try to sleep on the floor but people are moving, going outside to the toilet, speaking quietly, the baby is crying. When it is dark, the village is going to sleep, 'Jorge' tells us we must go. Outside is a farm truck, big, for animals, pigs, cows, with the back hanging down. We climb in. There are many cans of petrol at the front which smell. The air is still warm but I am cold. I want to jump off, say I am not going. But I stay. 'Jorge' makes us all lie down in the back. I am near the cans of fuel and the smell and the bumps make me feel sick. Then the road becomes quiet and the wheels of the truck now make no sound and we can hear the sea and I know we are on the beach and I lift my head above the side. The beach is big, big, One way, far, there is the sea that is going to take me away. Behind, the other, there is the land getting smaller behind me, becoming not Cuba where I have lived all my life but another country, a foreign country, and I am frightened of America, of which I have dreamed for many years, so full of guns and money and everything big and strange.

Now we are all sitting up, looking. But we can see no boat. Instead near the water is a strange thing, not a raft because there is nowhere to sit or stand, but made of big oil drums and thick plastic bags that are pumped up with air. There is a space in the middle the size of our truck.

The truck stops. 'Jorge' gets out. He comes round the back and climbs up to talk to us. Like our prison guard. People are asking – Where is our boat? What is happening?

He tells us not to make noise, that we are going to make the truck to the drums and things so we float, we make the truck engine to a propellor, we put in the thing to steer, what-you-call –

Rudder?

Rudder, yes. 'Jorge' smiles, he looks very proud. But people are frightened. Some are silent, cannot speak. Others say – no, they want their money back this cannot be safe. One woman is crying.

'Jorge' gets angry. I have done this many times, he tells us. It is safe, very safe. My life, too. I have wife, children, he says. And your money is not here. If you are frightened – go. But no money. Money is gone.

Our prison guard.

We do not speak now. I think maybe I will die, maybe not. But I will go. The decision is made, my Fate is leading me.

For maybe half an hour we sit on the beach. We watch, still not talking as though we are ashamed to know each other, ashamed of what we are doing, while Jorge and his friend and two men from the village make the truck into a boat. They have many tools and what-you-call bolts, and they twist and tighten the iron frame onto the truck in special places. They work like they have done it many times before. When it is finished they all jump on it, pull it, push it. It is strong.

'Jorge' tells us to get back on. I think maybe I am dreaming. Am I truly going to cross the sea in a farm truck? But I follow my Fate. Everybody gets on. I think this is sad. We all want so much to leave our Cuba. But inside every Cuban – "Soy Cubano". I am a Cuban. Proud. Not us. We want to leave. We are the gusanos, the worms.

Jorge get in front to drive. His friend come in the back with us to steer. He smiles a lot, tries to make us happy. But under his shirt I see he has a gun. Jorge starts the engine, but he cannot drive because it is not connected to the wheels so the two men from the village push us across the sand. As the wheels go into the sea I am sure we all think we will sink. I am ready to jump.

But we float. Easy, comfortable. The engine noise changes and slowly, slowly we start to move. Our farm truck is sailing across the sea.

Behind us the land gets darker and smaller until all we can see is a line of white that had been the beach, making a ghost-smile in the darkness, Cuba gone away, the only earth I have ever stood on. Now there is nothing but the sky, the stars, the sea and the sound of the engine dark and deep under our feet. The engine goes on and on, and on, never changing, like the sea and the sky and the stars, and soon it begins to feel safe. And, a little while after, boring.

I talk to 'Jorge's' friend, the man steering. He has a torch and that magnetic thing in his hand, round, a little finger points to North.

Compass.

Compass. He say with the compass and the stars he knows the way. Easy, he say. I think – my Fate. He tell us that in a few hours it may get windy. Hurricane Bess is passing to North. Long way but we may get a little more wind than usual. He laughs like it will be fun. Some people are frightened but he say me to hold the rudder keep the little finger in the compass just so while he get coffee for everybody. Behind the petrol cans is a big pot of coffee, a little cold now but nice. Everyone feels better. I want to sleep but the baby is crying. I wish I could put my arms around it. I would like to put my arms around somebody. I would like to put my arms around her. My Maggie.

When I wake dawn is coming and the wind is getting a little big. Our truck is going up and down – crash! – up and down – crash! Is it strong enough? Fate now, all Fate. Somebody is being sick over the side. Others look frightened. The man with the rudder is smiling. He say everything is OK, normal. I want to believe him.

I see a man, his back to us, pissing over the side into the sea. I also need to piss. I go to the back so the wind take it away from us. Is good, says the man with the rudder, lavatory at back only. And he laugh. For women is not so easy. They must hold their man and sit, bottom out of the truck while we crash up and down. Not nice for them. I look away. I hope everyone look away. Same for men who must shit. Must find a man to hold to. I hope I don't have to shit.

For maybe five hours we crash through the sea. Slow, very slow. Grey sky. I am hungry. We have biscuits but no more coffee. Then the wind becomes quiet and the sun is in the sky and it is very hot. Soon we have finished the water and my tongue is getting thick, my head hurts. There is no shade. I put my head under my bag but it is not good. What if Mexican Sea police find us? A farm truck sailing across the sea. Mad, mad, mad. I shall be sent back to Cuba, to prison. I am getting angry. But I am too tired and my head hurts too much to be angry. The man with the rudder still smiles, tells us all, be patient, soon we will see Isla de Mujeres. The Island of Women. When I first heard of a place called the island of Women I thought – sexy. All those women, no men. Until I arrive. Yes. Now I cannot think of sex.

I think I have slept. I feel a foot pushing me in the back. It is the man with the rudder. He is smiling again, pointing ahead. I stand and look. I can see nothing. Everyone is standing now looking ahead. Silent. Have we done it? Are we free? Do we want to be?

Slowly, slowly we can see something on the horizon, something between the sea and the sky. Slowly, slowly it becomes land. Then trees, houses. The Island of Women.

I tell myself, you should be happy. You chose this. But I am tired and hungry and dirty and there are so many dangers ahead. Where are the Police? Will we be sent back? But nobody cares about this strange boat-truck arriving in the harbour. They have seen it before? I can see few women on the Island of Women. Many men. Boats being painted, fish being sold. They do not look at us as we climb out onto the wooden steps and go up to the harbour road. My first time to stand on earth that is not Cuban. I feel nothing. I am walking but asleep.

We are taken to a hut where there is food. 'Jorge' and his friend say they will stay for a few days because they have heard on the radio that Hurricane Bess has turned and is going towards Cuba so it would not be good to sail back. I give 'Jorge' a dollar to borrow his cell to call Pepe. He is with my mother. I did not expect that. I hoped I would just tell him and he would tell her. I am a coward. I have to speak to her. I do it quickly. I warn about hurricane Bess. When I have finished talking to her I want to cry but I do not. It is the loneliest time of my life.

When we have eaten we are taken across to the other side of the island where a proper boat is waiting which takes us across to Yucatan. We are given papers. Still no Police. Everything seems OK. We go by bus, then train – sitting on the roof, like in films, very dangerous! – to the border where there are people who show us how to get across the river. Then we are met by Cubans and friends of Cuba. Is illegal Mr Attorney, of course, but I think you forgive us because we come from Cuba, no? We are against the Castro devils so we are forgiven, no?

And now – the miracle – I am in New York where you are talking to me. I am staying with my friend Pablo, making the new Raul.

It's been, what, six weeks?
Two months.
How are you doing?
Is strange. But Pablo say I will do fine. And I will.
You have done what you wanted to do.
I have done it.

[FROM RAUL VENTURA'S WITNESS STATEMENT (6)]

Chapter 24

He was breathing heavily by the time he had settled into the chair. He stared ahead, not looking at either of us, as if he knew what was coming.

Rebeca had sounded brisk when she called me. I had been asleep. I jolted awake, adrenaline pumping. I peered at the clock beside my bed. 7.00. She had waited until then to tell me, she said, because she saw no point in me losing sleep as well. She was going in to see Bernard in the hospital to break the news. Did I want to meet her there? Below the shivering, clear-headed layer of wakefulness there was still a thick cloud of sleep. I understood the words, I knew what had happened but the enormity of what she was telling me remained abstract, out of reach. Raul fled. Gone. OK – deal with it. I knew at once – or I assumed – that it was my gift that had done this. But I shut down instinctively, numbing myself. His choice. Entirely his. Let's go.

Still on auto-pilot I showered, dressed and got a cab to the Simon Bolivar. Rebeca, in uniform, was waiting on a bench in Reception, Pepe beside her. Neither of them looked as though they had slept. Pepe said he would wait while we went up.

The ward was busy. Breakfast was being served, cleaners moved between the beds with buckets and mops. The nurse behind the desk was new to me. Rebeca and she spoke in Spanish. The nurse nodded and got to her feet.

The three of us made our way to his bed. He eyed us suspiciously as we approached. Rebeca spoke to him – again in Spanish. After a moment's silence he grunted an assent. The nurse helped him out of the bed and into a gown and sandals. She and Rebeca walked him up the ward as I followed, the cleaners and breakfast servers backing off to let us pass. At the door at the far end we turned into a corridor. A short way down there was a small, empty room. It had a table with some old magazines, a television with the unplugged lead trailing on the floor, and a variety of chairs, mostly plastic and upright but one that was low, padded and had arms. Carefully they lowered him into it. Then the nurse left and Rebeca and I drew up chairs to face him, one on either side, both looking down. The room was hot and airless. I was shivering.

"Bad news, old man." She spoke now in English. "Our boy has gone."

Not a muscle flickered on his face.

"Raul call me last night. From Mexico. He went across to the Island of Women. Two nights ago. He is on his way to New York."

She paused, waited for a reaction. There was none.

"So." She folded her hands on her knees. The end of the story.

He continued to stare ahead. A long silence.

"*Gus.... ano,*" he said at last. I had to strain to hear.

Rebeca nodded, her eyes glistening.

"*Si. Gusano.*"

His arm gave a lurch. His hand wandered across to rest on hers still folded on her knees. He mumbled in Spanish, still not looking at her. Now her hand flew to her mouth as she sobbed, the tears flowing freely now. Then suddenly she lifted her face, laughing and dabbing her eyes. She turned to me, the smile bright.

"He say I was saint mother, he shit father." She turned to him, this time putting her hand on his. "Maybe so, old man, but it was Cuba, Cuba's fault, not us, not you. They don't understand, the young ones. Is sad."

Slowly he nodded.

Not Cuba, I thought. Me.

"I am so sorry, Dad."

It was the first time I had spoken. He did not acknowledge me. Had he guessed what had happened? The neglectful daughter, who was failing to help him die. Who, though he did not know it, had corrupted and stolen his son.

"Want... bed..." His hand jerked irritably in his lap.

Rebeca and I stood either side of his chair. Taking an elbow each, we eased him onto his feet. Slowly we all shuffled back to the ward. Rebeca adjusted his sheets and pillows, removed his gown and lowered him into place. I bent to kiss him on the forehead. He smelled, faintly, of urine.

"Goodbye, Dad. I'll come and see you later."

If he understood my rum-smuggling code he gave no sign of it.

Then, as we turned to go, he muttered something in Spanish. Rebeca went back. She leaned down to him, her ear close to his mouth. He spoke again. She took his hand as she replied, then she too kissed him on the forehead and joined me.

"What was that about?"

"He say – how did he find the money?"

It was unbearable. I had done this to them. I had to tell her.

"What did you say?"

"He buy, he sell behind the law. Sex? Steal? How can I know?"

We went down in the lift in silence. When we came out into Reception Pepe stood. Rebeca took his hand.

"He take me to work, then you to hotel, yes?"

I hesitated. But it had to be done.

"I would like to walk with you to your hospital. Is it far?"

She looked at me curiously.

"You want to walk? It take maybe twenty minutes."

"I'd like to."

She turned to Pepe. They spoke in Spanish.

"Come," she said, taking my arm.

Outside the wind was gusting, leaves and paper scurrying along the pavement.

"Radio this morning say we may get hurricane tonight. Hurricane Bess. Not so strong. But enough. Hurricane make you proper Cuban."

A hurricane felt a distant prospect. I had my own storms to deal with.

We walked in silence while she waited for me.

"I am so sorry, Rebeca," I said at last. "I know how close you and Raul were. Are."

"It must happen one day. We lost him long time ago."

She spoke, it seemed, as though from a script, the words not important, impatient to hear what I had to say.

We were passing a tree-lined grassed area, set back from the road, too small to be called a park, an urban garden with flowerbeds and a dry fountain. There was a small wooden building advertising ice creams and cold drinks. The counter window was shuttered up. A man in an apron was collecting folding chairs – some already sprawling in the wind – and tables to stack in the back of his stall, closing up shop. Otherwise the place was empty.

There was a metal bench near the old fountain, its legs set in concrete, impervious to the wind.

"Can we sit there?"

She nodded.

The man in the apron was standing on one of his folding chairs, dismantling the unruly canvas awning above the counter. My hair flicked across my face. The wind was warm, playful.

She watched me, waiting.

"I gave him money," I said. "I think that was how he paid."

I felt her stiffen. Whatever she had expected it was not that.

"I'm sorry," I went on. "I didn't dream he would use it for that." Which was, at that moment, my absolute truth.

"How much?"

"A lot. Dollars."

"Thousands?"

I nodded. The actual amount seemed not only meaningless now but somehow insulting. She didn't press me.

"Why did you give?" she asked the question gently, almost tenderly.

"My brother… Half-brother… I wanted to share…"

All this was true. But it was not the truth. She knew and waited in silence.

"I loved him."

She nodded, as though she expected this and was still waiting. The wind seemed to hold its breath. I couldn't bring myself to say the words. She said them for me.

"You made sex with him?" Still so gentle.

I started to shake. An avalanche, centuries old, of guilt and disgust overwhelmed me. Incest. The word rose in my gorge like vomit. I could hear myself sobbing.

"I am sorry… so… sorry… it was wrong… I am so ashamed…"

The words struggling to find air between the sobs.

"You loved him?"

Yes. I had loved him. Was she saying that made it all right? I nodded, the sobs subsiding. She put her arms around me and pulled me to her fiercely.

"Sh… Sh… You love him. Is good. Love is good. Is natural –"

"No! No!" I pulled away from her. This could not be right. Over her shoulder I saw the man in the apron look across to us.

She eased me back to her.

"Is not important… Sh… sh… You love him. Is good. He love you. I know he love you. Give love is good. Sex not important… Pffff. Two bodies… Then finish. My son is beautiful. He love you. Of course you want to sex with him."

Suddenly she held me away from her and looked into my eyes as though something had just occurred to her.

"You do this many times? For all these weeks?"

"NO! Once, only once… I was so ashamed."

She pulled me back into her arms and began to rock me like a child. Her head barely reached my shoulder as we sat but I felt small and comforted.

"Come," she said. "The wind will get stronger soon."

When we got back to the road, Pepe was waiting with his taxi. He had been following us. He beckoned impatiently, urging us to get into the shelter of the car. Leaves, even twigs were flying through the air now, flicking at our bodies, faces. But inside my own storm was abating. The hurricane may have been on its way but for me, I was sure, the worst was over.

But, of course, it wasn't.

As the day went on the wind grew stronger. At first it felt playful – unpredictable, sometimes gusting forcefully but not threatening. As Pepe drove me back to the hotel a few shop windows were being boarded up but traffic was still moving, although there were fewer bicycles than usual and the pavements seemed quiet.

"Normal, normal," said Pepe with one of his rare smiles.

As I got out of the car on the Nacional forecourt, just as I had shut the passenger door a sudden gust hit me without warning, toppling me against the body of the car. It was gone almost as fast as it had arrived, hit-and-run. Pepe came hurrying around to me, leaning into the wind. He took my arm and together we made our way carefully up the slope into the hotel lobby, where it felt immediately hushed and safe.

"Will you be all right getting back Pepe?"

"All normal. Two hours I work, then maybe I go home."

Another shy smile and he shambled off as though uncomfortable in such capitalist surroundings.

By the time I got upstairs to my room, the rain had arrived, sudden and fierce. It was drilling viciously against the windows, blocking out the light. Putting on a cardigan for the first time since I had arrived in Cuba, I sat down to my daily chore of emails. Along with the usual contract details to be checked and strategy queries to respond to I had a personal message from Howard, warning me – in case I didn't know – that Hurricane Bess had been downgraded to Category 1, but had changed course and was now in the Straits of Florida heading for Havana and the North Cuba coast line at a reported 12 miles an hour, winds gusting at 70-80, and was expected to reach land by nightfall. I should, said Howard, take every precaution. Well, it was possible I might not have known. I was touched that he had taken the trouble. I was grateful, too, that he was not pressing me for an explanation of my behaviour nor asking when I would be coming back. There was a short email from your father hoping I was OK which was nice. And characteristic. None from either of you!

Later in the morning there was a knock on my door and a Hotel porter, Ruiz, whom I had got to know a little, asked – or, rather signed – if he could secure my shutters. As he set about one at the far end of the room I stood and looked through the window nearer to me at the wind-twisted landscape, sheeting rain and whipped trees wrapped around the stolid buildings of the city like a handsome face pulled out of shape by G-force. Traffic was still moving, Ruiz showed no sign of alarm, there seemed no need to worry. All normal, normal? I could even see a spume of misting sea rising above the roof tops as it crashed onto the unseen wall of the Malecon below the houses. From my safe, dry fortress it looked fine and dramatic. What was it like for the old man in his hospital bed? I shivered and went back to my emails.

When I came downstairs at lunchtime Miguel was sitting on a bench by Reception, listlessly reading a copy of Gramma. He tossed it aside and stood as he saw me approach.

"Is it still possible to use the car Miguel?" I asked.

"No problem."

"I ought to get something to eat, and then could you take me to the Simon Bolivar? I want to visit my father."

"No problem."

That's how I still think of Miguel now. No problem. Never a problem.

He arranged to bring his car into the hotel porch to make it easier for me but even so the wind rocked me as I came out of the door – the porch, unexpectedly, forming a wind tunnel – and both of us had to battle to get into the car.

It felt easier as we pulled away, the wind and rain still jostling and pressing on us but for the time being impotent. Across the howl of the storm I could hear the sirens of emergency vehicles but none came our way. There were other cars on the road, even pedestrians leaning in to the sharply cutting rain and wind. No sense of panic and nobody, least of all Miguel, looked fearful. Normal, normal.

"Have you heard about Raul?" I had to raise my voice.

"Yes."

"What do you think?"

He hesitated. Miguel was not somebody to move incautiously.

"Good for him. But sad for his Mami."

"Were you surprised?"

Again he hesitated. Was I asking him to cross a line? He had helped me collect the money. He had taken me to Raul's to hand it over. The relationship between this quiet, formal man and I had developed into something more intimate than perhaps either of us had intended. Did he know about Raul and I? Had he guessed? I hoped not.

"All right." I tried a change of tack. "Did you think this was something he might do with the money?"

"Maybe."

"Did he say anything to you?"

"Nothing."

And if he had, you would be too loyal to tell me, I thought. But I wanted to trust him. Miguel had been nothing but trustworthy,

Talking about Raul with his friend brought him close to me again. I wondered what he was doing at that moment, where he was. Still in Mexico? If he got to the States where would he head for? I wanted so much to believe he could make a new life for himself. A good life.

What were the chances of us seeing each other again? How would we treat each other? As family? As former lovers? As strangers?

Did I want to see him again? All I knew was that I wanted life to be good for him.

I directed Miguel to the Plaza where I had bought the rum but the grill and shutters were firmly in place. We sat in the car, rocked occasionally by the buffeting wind, while I wondered whether to confess to him about my rum smuggling and enlist his help, in so doing revealing yet more of my secrets. Was it putting him in a difficult situation? He was a Doctor, after all. I decided that as he was a friend of Raul's it was unlikely.

Rum? No problem. He knew a friend. (Of course.) We drove not more than a few blocks. The rain, if anything, seemed to be easing. Had Bess changed course again? We stopped in a narrow street in the Old City parked tight up against a large wooden door. I glimpsed a huge cobbled courtyard as he slipped out of the car and through the door in the wall.

I waited, the windows steaming up. Ahead I could see a cyclist battling towards the car. He struggled past making slow headway looking, from what I could see through the window, as if he had been pulled from the sea. Behind me I heard a siren approaching. It got louder. Had Miguel left enough space for it to pass? Only just. It inched past, the siren howling impatiently, too close for me to see if it was Police or Ambulance. As it disappeared down the street, I sensed a blur out of the corner of my eye and the wooden door was moving and then Miguel was in the driver's seat, the wind blasting momentarily into the car as he opened the driver's door.

Rain was dripping from his nose and chin as he passed a water bottle full of white rum across to me with a smile. I scrabbled for a bill.

"Is OK. You pay when we finish," he said.

"You know so much about me, Miguel. Maybe too much. And I don't even know your surname."

He smiled, reached into the glove compartment and passed me a card. It read *'Miguel Montalvan MD. El medico del pueblo'*. The people's doctor. It gave a cell number and an email address.

"Are you married?"

He nodded.

"Two children."

"Does your wife work?"

"Nurse."

"You sound like a happy man."

"I am happy. Happy Cuban man. Is possible. Understand karma. Be happy."

"Is that how it works?"

"Karma. Accept."

"Unlike my half-brother."

He nodded wryly in acknowledgement.

"Is dreamer. Is hard for dreamer to be happy. Even in America, I think."

He started the engine and we headed for the hospital. I envied Miguel's wife.

My nurse friend, Sandra – we had exchanged names by now – was back at the desk. She gave me a discreet conspiratorial smile as I swept past, hair windswept and dripping, my capacious handbag with its smuggled booty clutched under my arm.

The shutters on the window at the end of the ward were closed against the storm, making it even gloomier than usual. They rattled as the wind soughed and thudded against the walls.

My father was lying back, his eyes closed, listening to his iPad. He stirred, aware of movement, as I put the bottle down on his bedside cabinet.

He looked at me, then the bottle, then fumbled with his iPad to turn it off.

"Thank... you." His voice was high now, the vocal cords stretched.

"I promised, didn't I?"

He looked puzzled. As I suspected, he hadn't read my code. I pulled up a chair.

"I can't stay. I've got a car waiting. Thought you might appreciate this with the storm coming."

"Hurr...i...cane."

"Apparently. Quite exciting. Are you all right?"

His eyes clouded, he looked away. Stupid question. I unscrewed the bottle and handed it to him. He raised it shakily to his lips and swallowed.

"I am sorry about Raul, Dad." It still felt strange to call him that. But also good to use the word.

He took another swallow. He seemed to be gathering himself. I waited.

"What... he... wanted..."

"So I understand."

Another silence. Another swallow.

"Will you... look after him... in America?"

My father being solicitous? Towards the son he despised?

"If I find out where he is living." And as I spoke, I thought, yes, I could do that now. We could meet again. The fever has gone. A memory.

He lifted the bottle towards his mouth again.

"Why don't you save some for later?" I suggested.

He let me take the bottle from his hand.

"I've got to go, Dad. I'm told it is going to get worse. I'll come back as soon as I can."

He was no longer looking at me, his eyes once more dull with despair.

There was a note from the hotel management in my room when I got back. It was in Spanish and English. It confirmed that Bess was now a Category 1 hurricane and was likely to reach Havana that night. It assured guests that the hotel was capable of withstanding any hurricane, that a generator would maintain power in the event of a grid breakdown, that bedding was being made available in the basement for any guests that did not want to stay in their rooms, that meals would continue to be served at the usual times, though menus might be simplified as some staff had not been able to get to work. It was like being in a Second World War film. My chisel-jawed friend the Chief Receptionist (airline pilot *manqué*), Senor Suarez as I now knew him, remained as unflappable as ever, calmly insisting that it was all routine, that they went through this every year. As evening came the thud and piercing roar of the storm reached such a pitch that I thought surely the walls would implode, the roof be torn off and scattered across the city. But inside waiters continued to walk the corridors carrying trays and smiling, as though Armageddon was not, after all, at hand. With all the windows shuttered, the terraces bolted, I could only guess at what the rest of hurricane-tossed Havana might be like. In that hospital. In Rebeca's breeze block extension. Was she in a shelter? With Pepe? Or at work? And Miguel and his nurse wife – comforting their two children? Or also at work? Were the streets impassable, debris hurtling everywhere? Occasionally when the noise dropped a little, I could hear sirens so I knew the emergency vehicles could still move so the roads weren't completely impassable. And the Cuban faces around me – markers for panic, like the faces of the cabin crew when the plane falls through an air pocket – registered continuing calm. The management had piped a Cuban film with English subtitles to every room as no television signal could be received. I lay on my bed and watched it, feeling warm and safe like a child curled up in the back of the car at night driving through the rain.

I wondered if my father had finished his rum. Whether he was able to sleep. I wanted very much to be with him.

My own sleep, such as it was, was threaded through with the almost lulling effect of the hurricane raging impotently outside, punctuated with sharp waking starts of anxiety, even terror at the thought of the old man tossed about in his bleak bed in the savage storm, waiting to die.

I woke finally to fingers of daylight filtering past the shutters. The storm still howled but possibly, I thought, with less violence.

A switch flipped inside me. I knew at once that I had to get to the hospital to be with him. I could not let him be alone.

Senor Suarez was still at his desk, upright but red-eyed for lack of sleep. He confirmed that the hurricane was moving on and had passed its peak but said he had no taxis available and that it would be unwise to try to get across the city for a few hours yet.

I stared at Miguel's card in my hand. Could I call him? Had he been working all night? Was it mad to try? I dialled his number. He could always refuse.

He said he would be with me in twenty minutes.

On the table in Reception as I waited for him was a collection of tourist leaflets carefully laid out in a perfect fan shape showing infuriatingly toned young women in white satin bikinis and feathered head dresses doing a lavish dance routine at a night club. Batista's Cuba still thriving more than half a century after the Revolution, while Raul hustled the streets and my father lay in that grim, dim hospital listening to the howl of the hurricane. Why should I be surprised?

I tossed the leaflet back on the table. Senor Suarez glanced up. Disapproving? Had he heard me call Miguel, ignoring his advice, and ask him to drive me across the city during a Category 1 hurricane? A selfish, irresponsible tourist. And an American. Perhaps he was right. Perhaps Miguel with his belief in his karma was an unreliable judge of danger?

I checked my watch. More than twenty minutes. An accident? Were the roads blocked?

I looked at my cell. No signal. I started editing my Inbox.

"Car is here."

As so often with Miguel he took me by surprise. I stood.

"I feel bad asking you to do this. Are you all right?"

He pulled a so-so smile.

"Is a little bit strong still. But no problem."

"And you've been working all night."

He shook his head.

"My boss live outside the city. Could not get in. So I stay at home too. I sleep well."

"With your lovely wife and children. How nice. Well, I thought I should be with my father."

"Is good. We go?"

I sensed Senor Suarez' disapproving look following me as we walked towards the big heavy wooden doors leading out onto the porch. A hotel porter was standing by them, on guard. Miguel stopped as we reached them.

"Most of time is no problem," he said. Then suddenly, he clicked his fingers dramatically. "Whup! Very, very strong. Like explosion. Car, maybe jump a little." He smiled at my expression. "But mustn't be frightened. You help me, I help you."

"OK."

He had just driven across the city. He must know what it was like. Besides, this was Miguel-the-Rock.

He nodded at the porter. Together they carefully opened the door. The wind flooded past, screaming, as though it had been knocking and was desperate to be let in, fleeing from some even mightier force. Surprisingly, after the first blast it turned out to be manageable. We pushed our way out and heard the door behind us close above the constant howl. Miguel pulled open the passenger door, holding it with both hands as I scrambled in. I watched as he struggled around the front of the car, holding onto the hood and thought, this is madness, this is death. He opened the driver's door letting in a blast of sound and wind, flung himself in beside me and slammed it, shutting the furies out.

The car wrapped itself around us, a sanctuary.

He started the engine and we edged slowly down the slope to the hotel entrance. We were rocking a little but it still felt reassuringly solid, though through the windscreen, glimpsed as the wipers momentarily cleared it, the tree-tops twisted, buckled and danced like souls in hell.

At the edge of the road we could see across to the Malecon. A heart stopping, wholly impossible, wall of water climbed high into the dark grey sky where it seemed to vanish as the wind snatched at it furiously, and pulverised it into tiny invisible drops.

Miguel waited, chose his moment and then accelerated as fast as he dared up the road away from the sea front. Flanked as we now were by high buildings and travelling at a careful, steady pace the wind felt less threatening. A handful of other cars and vans also crawled along. No sign of pedestrians. Windows that had not been shuttered or boarded were broken. As we turned one corner, we found a high-sided truck lying on its side, hood on the pavement, chassis skewed across the road. As we edged around it and saw its empty interior Miguel tutted at the stupidity of its driver. Going out in an empty high-sided truck in these conditions! *Marecon!*

At one point a bicycle that had been lying on the side of the road came skittering across in front of us, spinning on its pedals and then suddenly flipped upright onto its wheels and for a few crazy yards bicycled itself until the wind seemed to get bored and swung the front wheel around so the bicycle pitched forward then somersaulted across the roof of a parked car and landed incongruously on the broad steps of some graceful important-looking building over which the tattered remnants of a Cuban flag jerked crazily from a flagpole.

The car remained our fortress and the longer we drove the more inviolable I felt. Until we came to a junction with a broad tree lined avenue. Here uprooted trees were lying across the road. The tops of those still standing streamed, long-haired, demented, in one direction one moment, then the next jerked upright as though shot and immediately streamed just as frantically in the other direction. In the midst of the whirling chaos the traffic lights went calmly through their sequences as though confident they would be obeyed. Miguel edged forward warily. As he reached the middle there was what sounded above the roar of the wind like an explosion. The car was pushed violently to one side. Miguel wrestled with the steering wheel. I could hear the engine note rise as he tried to accelerate out of danger and get into the lee of the buildings in the avenue ahead of us, but we seemed to make little headway.

I glanced to my right. Everything went into slow motion. A sheet of corrugated iron was dancing down the street towards us. It lifted gracefully into the air, turned slowly on its axis before dropping back down to the road where it seemed to pick up speed aiming directly at us, perfectly aligned to slice the car in two.

"Miguel!" I screamed.

Now the engine was straining even more but still we hardly moved, a nightmare, legs pumping leadenly in deep, soft sand. Then, suddenly, as the sheet hopped and skipped its macabre dance towards us, just as it got beyond the central line of trees, it slapped into a cross wind, turned an abrupt right angle and – as the car lurched forward at last – sailed, vast now and utterly terrifying, a few feet behind us, its murderous clatter on the road now briefly audible above the soaring, howling wind.

As we got across into the relative safety of the avenue ahead, partly sheltered by buildings on each side, the noise abated. For a while I thought I could hear my own heart beating. Neither of us could speak.

A Police car was coming slowly towards us. It flashed its lights and moved to the crown of the road. The driver stopped, wound down his window. Miguel did the same. What had we done wrong? Was I going to be the cause of him being arrested? They called to each other across the wind. Then the policeman waved and drove on.

Miguel wound his window back up.

"Just – are you OK? Being nice. This time." He smiled at me, reassuringly. We might not have just come within feet of being sliced in half. His karma still holding up.

We rounded a now familiar corner. An ambulance was parked in front of the entrance to the Simon Bolivar. As we got closer, I could see its heavy, lumbering chassis rocking sporadically in the wind.

Miguel parked behind it. He pulled on the brake and turned to look at me.

Maybe he had the right to look proud, I thought. He had got me here, as promised. He had taken me – both of us – through a kind of hell to reach my sick, old father. The journey made, a promise fulfilled. But it barely registered. All I could think of, replaying itself over and over again, was the image of that careering sheet of iron guillotining its way towards us. I reached for a clutch of dollar bills and, without counting, passed them to Miguel who put them wordlessly in his shirt pocket, also without counting.

"Thank you. That was… something. You go home now. Be safe. I don't know how long I shall stay here."

As I went to open my door he hurriedly got out, scrabbled around the front of the car and came to help me. He took my arm and we made our way, lurching unsteadily as the wind buffeted and bullied us, into the hospital.

There was nobody in reception, no nurse, no porter, no patient.

"Go home now."

He looked uncertain.

"Go on. Say hello to your wife and children from me."

"Say hello to your papi."

"I will."

He left. My Rock.

I went towards the lifts in what felt – despite the now distant howl of the hurricane – an uncanny silence. Had the place been evacuated? I was startled by the sound of a door opening. A nurse came out into the corridor. She was pushing a trolley of medication and clip-boards. I smiled at her. She acknowledged me, red-eyed. As I turned towards the lifts, she said something and beckoned me to go with her. I understood. The lifts weren't working. She led me to the foot of the stairs. As she prepared to try to manoeuvre the trolley up, I took one side and together we carried it up two flights where she thanked me dully and disappeared into a ward.

I continued up one flight. As I came into the old man's ward and looked towards his bed I stopped.

The bed was stripped. And empty.

I swung around to the nurse's desk, icing up. There was a male nurse on duty whom I had not seen before. I pointed up the ward.

"What's happened…? Is my father…?" He looked up at me blankly. "Do you speak English?" His eyes dull with tiredness. He shook his head. "*Mi padre… Donde?*"

Now he got to his feet, indicating that I should follow him. He looked suddenly alert, grim. Through the swing door, down the same corridor, to the same office. Knees weak, breathing difficult. My father dead, my father dead.

Sandra, was asleep at the desk, her head on her hands. The male nurse had to shake her gently to wake her. She looked up groggily, saw me and jolted unsteadily to her feet.

"Senora Maggie…" her voice furred.

"Has he died?" Like a gun shot.

Now her eyes sharpened. She put out her hand to me, still blinking.

"No… No… Not dead… Stroke. Small stroke… Please…"

She positioned the chair. I slumped into it. The male nurse backed out closing the door.

"Another one? Does that mean…?" I was shivering, finding it hard to form words.

"Small… small… Sometimes happens, is all. During night. No telephones, we send Ambulance for Doctor. He come quickly. Your father with Doctor now. Sleeping."

"Will he live?"

"Of course!" Then, a change of tone – "We must see how bad."

"What do you mean?"

"Which part of brain. Soon we know. Today, later, he come back to ward. You will stay? You must not travel again in hurricane."

I took a moment to recover.

"Sorry I woke you. You must all be exhausted."

"No problem."

Everyone, no problem.

"Yes, I'll stay. Does his wife, does Rebeca know?"

She shrugged.

"No telephones. Also, no power. We work from generator."

She smiled cheerfully, reached across and gave my hand a squeeze as though it was me at the battle front not her.

"You want coffee? Eat?"

"Coffee would be nice."

The same waiting room. Nobody but me. As well as coffee she found me a book in English – Gabriel Garcia Marquez' *No One Writes to the Colonel*. I didn't get very far.

I wanted very much to call you. I wanted you to know about your grandfather before he died. I wanted to speak to somebody I was close to. But there was no signal. And the truth is part of me felt relieved. I realised that this wasn't a conversation we were ready to have.

And it was at that moment, sitting in that empty hospital waiting room, my father sedated, possibly close to death, a hurricane howling outside, that I realised how far away from you I had grown. It was the first time I had properly faced up to it before. And worse than that. I realised I wasn't really close to anybody. And that was what had made Raul – the illusion of Raul? – so miraculous for me. My tram-line life. It had to change. And the change had to start with you, my two children whom I desperately longed, as I sat there, to hug and hold.

Around mid-day the trolley arrived with a pre-packaged meal of rice and beans from the hospital's emergency stock. Sandra allowed me to help serve. She insisted I eat my father's portion. I tried but wasn't hungry. The rattling of the shutters, the constant scream of the wind became wallpaper, like a television in the corner of the room that nobody is watching.

I was asleep in the armchair in the waiting room when the male nurse shook my shoulder and beckoned me to follow him. I looked at my watch. Half past four. I had been asleep for two hours.

They were lifting him from the gurney onto his bed when we came into the ward. I held back until they cleared, then found a chair and went to sit by the bed.

Laid out, arms by his side, his slight frame barely registering under the cover. Utter stillness. Outside, vaguely, the hurricane.

"He sleep for maybe long time." Sandra was standing beside me.

"Sedatives?"

She nodded.

"What do we know?"

"Blood pressure, heart, pulse, kidneys all good. We learn more when he wake up."

She touched my shoulder and moved away.

It was hard to be sure he was breathing. That clear, unlined boy's face again, nestling in the old man's white hair.

What would a different life have been like? For me, as well as for him? If he had not (as, in my anger, I always liked to think of it) defected to Cuba? What kind of ragged, tempestuous life would we have had as a family? Years of attrition, leading to my parents' inevitable, bitter divorce? How would I now be looking on his frail, aging body, inert in its hospital bed? With tenderness? Or merely a ravaged, worn out sense of duty? What was certain was that as I sat in that hard, plastic chair watching him now, so peaceful, I was filled with an aching tenderness for the skeletal figure in front of me. My father. The monstrous, selfish bully my father. Why? A lifetime of love displaced? Locked away, dispersed in the vapour trail of that aeroplane taking him to Havana? Some childhood, atavistic need for a father now resurfacing, blindly, irrationally? Need, not love? An egotistical, ill-tempered tyrant. A fearful, trapped idealist.

My father. Whom I loved.

Later I helped with the evening meal, poured glasses of water. Cleared away. I escorted a couple of patients to the lavatory, waited outside and escorted them back to their beds. When the doctor came around, I asked him about my father but learned nothing more than Sandra had already told me.

I sat by his bedside. Still no sign of movement.

Sandra asked me if I was going to try to get back to my hotel. I told her I would prefer to stay in case he woke up. Not long after, two porters arrived. They lifted a mattress from an empty bed and placed it on the floor next to him. Sandra gave me a pillow and a blanket.

When the lights on the ward were turned out I took off my shoes and lay down on the mattress. For a long time, I listened for any movement from his bed above me. Finally, I slept. I remember thinking that the wind was lessening, the shutters creaking now, more than rattling.

I sat up, galvanised, heart beating, still clogged by sleep. The wind was howling, moaning, and no longer outside but right here in the semi-darkness of this strange room, this... what? Where was I? And then sleep cleared and I knew that it was not the sound of the wind I was hearing but a patient in a bed across the aisle, groaning, a high-pitched murmuring wail, rising and falling, in pain or in the throes of a nightmare. Now I could make out a nurse bending over his bed, talking to him quietly, soothingly. Gradually he settled. As did my heart beat.

I looked at my father on his back, in profile to me, as still as ever, the stone figure of a Mediaeval knight resting on his tomb. I could just detect the sound, if not the movement of breathing. As I watched him, I vowed that I would do everything in my power to get him out of this place. I settled back to try to sleep again.

I woke to daylight spreading through the ward and the sound of the shutters being opened. Watery sunshine. No sound of wind.

My bladder was full. I contemplated the journey to the bathroom.

Movement from his bed. I sat up fast. His eyelids were flickering. His left arm stirred, fingers feebly clutching at the sheet.

I got to my feet, kicking the mattress under the bed. His eyes opened, briefly, then shut again as though the light was too much. He made a noise. Indecipherable.

"Dad?" I bent to him, speaking quietly. "Are you awake?"

Nothing. I waited a moment. Nothing. Dreaming? I bent to pick up the blanket off the floor, fold it. My bladder was making more urgent signals to me. I should be getting to the bathroom before the morning rush started.

Then I heard the noise again. Not a clearing of the throat, not a cough, a definite signal, a grunt. An intention.

"Dad? It's Maggie. Are you awake?"

Grunt.

I took his left hand. It closed on mine.

"Can you hear me?"

Again the grunt. He had lost all power of speech? Fear chilled through me. Maybe it was just temporary?

"All right, don't try to speak now. I just want you to... Can we do a test? If you can hear me just squeeze my hand."

His hand gripped mine.

"Great. Just to be sure, will you do it again? *Now.*"

Again.

"OK... Excellent." Seize the moment. "Now – you've had another stroke. A small one. You mustn't worry about it. You're in excellent hands here but I've got an idea to make it all even better for you. There's a hospital I've been to see not far from here. It's called the Clinica Internacional. It is absolutely wonderful. Fantastic equipment, excellent staffing, your own room with your own bathroom. They are lovely, I've seen them. Everything the best. I would like to get you there. I think they will be able to give you more personal treatment than the terrific nurses and doctors here have time for. It will make everything so much better for you. Would you like me to arrange that? Squeeze my hand if the answer is yes."

Nothing. For a long time. His face remained utterly still. I knew the battle that was raging. Betrayal of everything he had spent his life working for.

My need for the bathroom was getting more acute by the minute.

Then he squeezed.

"OK. Just to be sure, let's do it one more time. If you want me to get you moved to the Clinica Internacional squeeze my hand... now."

He squeezed. Hard.

This time my knees buckled. My father and I. A team.

"OK, Dad. Leave it to me. Now – I've got to go to the bathroom. When I come back, we'll work out how to organise it. Yes?"

Another squeeze. The eyes remained closed.

I hurried off hoping desperately the bathroom was not in use.

When I came back onto the ward. Rebeca was sitting on the edge of the bed, holding his hand. I paused momentarily. She had not seen me. There was going to be resistance, I knew.

171

She looked up as I approached, her eyes rimmed with tiredness.

"They told me. Another stroke. You slept here?"

"He's only just woken up. They tried to get hold of you. The lines were down. You look like you haven't slept much."

She nodded.

"They say his speech, maybe… Need therapy. And time."

I hesitated. Then – why wait?

"Rebeca… He understands – don't you, Dad?" A grunt. "I've talked it over with him. I want to put him in the Clinica Internacional. I have been to see it." She nodded, staring at me, wide eyed. "I've asked him if that is what he would like and he said yes. We've agreed that to find out what he wants you hold his left hand and if the answer to a question is 'yes' he squeezes. Would you like to try?"

She stared at me. More surprise than hostility. Defeat? I didn't want to displace her. But I did want the old man to have the best. She turned back to him, taking his left hand in hers.

She spoke quietly in Spanish. I watched their hands carefully. Would he change his mind faced with the woman, his wife, who had been his moral and political compass for so many years?

When she had finished speaking his hand closed firmly around hers.

Gently she disengaged, looked up at me, tears in her eyes, and nodded.

Chapter 25

I screwed up my eyes. The room was so much brighter, dazzlingly so, than I remembered. No trace of colour, everything bleached, pulsing in its brightness, a pearly-gated, scouringly sanitised ante-room to the afterlife. His tangled hair so white, bloodless skin, eyelids closed, white on white pillows, white walls, floating on a shiny white floor, hovering, it felt, on some ethereal cumulus. The nurse, pale skinned, Chinese looking, all in white, Rebeca also in uniform, all in white. No sound. A terminus. Only Rebeca's fiercely troubled eyes anchoring the moment in reality.

He had slept – or appeared to – throughout the process from the moment the gleaming, softly padded wheeled stretcher slid soundlessly up the aisle between the rows of beds, the aristocratic interloper, warily eyed by the local peasants. Its immaculately liveried porters lifted him gently from his ancient, creaking hospital bed into its safe, welcoming arms then wheeled him, equally soundlessly, in apparent icy disdain, away from the squalor of the public ward, archangels rescuing a soul from purgatory. Rebeca kept her eyes firmly on the ground, unable to watch the whole humiliating pageant. Still resolute, but also feeling uncomfortable, I nodded good-byes to the remaining patients with some of whom I felt I had bonded, even if only slightly, over meals served or trips to the bathroom that I had accompanied them on. They acknowledged me with what in my guilt I hoped were forgiving nods and smiles. Nurse Sandra got up from behind her desk as our procession passed and came to shake my hand to say good-bye. With her other hand she squeezed my elbow. Her complicity still a secret but wanting, I felt, to reassure me that I was doing the right thing. Grateful, I bent to kiss her on the cheek, our alliance sealed.

Now in this cold, sanitised tomb I felt less resolute. Was all this an exercise in self-indulgence on my part? How absurd, how grandiose that I should seek to mend what life had broken. Was this for me or for him? And if it was for him, was it enough? I looked across at him again. He seemed to me much as he had on the public ward, a listless shell. Was this place really going to make his life better? Or his death?

The nurse watched me as I rotated on my heel taking in once again the cold, antiseptic panorama of white walls, white curtains and emptiness.

"You want bring his things from home is good. Welcome," she said, smiling with well-practiced warmth.

What things? That bleak, bare apartment. How could the life of a man so rich in passion and energy end in such emptiness? What things? The used takeaway cartons of food? The bottle of vodka? The upright piano?

Then I thought of the paintings on the walls.

I turned to Rebeca.

She shrugged as though reading my mind.

Christobal, my father's normally voluble neighbour, pressed the key solemnly into Rebeca's hand for safe keeping, gave me a sympathetic pursed-lip smile of condolence and left in tiptoeing reverence as though the old man was already dead and we were in mourning.

Rebeca wandered off through the arch into the rest of the little apartment, still clearly not reconciled to the whole process, leaving Pepe and me with the pictures. Although it had taken me some time, I had come to realise that they were of female genitalia. What I had not seen until now was that they were also Cuban landscapes, sea breaking on rocks, palm trees, mountains. Cuba as vagina. Did that have some kind of meaning for him? Or was he just another male drooling over any image of female sexuality? If he was to die in that room would the sight of vaginas on the walls bring good memories, stir the embers as he floated off? Well, why not? Better than white walls. I nodded to Pepe who lifted them down and stacked them by the door.

Rebeca re-emerged carrying an old-fashioned Dictaphone. She put it on the table as though it was a discovery of some importance. I waited for her to explain.

"Always he keep a diary. Every day he would write. It was nothing, he said. Just to remember. He told me I could read. Why? I said. To read about your girl friends? Today I fuck Maria, I fuck Zully, I fuck Liset… Thank you, no." She trailed her hand over the Dictaphone, the anger still visible. I waited. "The first time in hospital, the first stroke, he asked me to buy for him. I think is now his diary."

It hung in the air. Could we? Neither of us spoke. Then Rebeca pressed the button.

The cassette turned noiselessly. Nothing. She stopped it, still not looking at me. But there was no going back now. She pressed rewind. Then play.

Had the machine been empty or the battery flat I don't think either of us would have taken it any further. To find a battery, locate a missing cassette disassemble the machine would have felt a violation. But to press a button was almost nothing, something that had just happened while neither of us was looking.

That's how I heard my father not only call me a sanctimonious cunt (which did not surprise me) but also to speculate that he might never see me again. He sounded regretful, even frightened. It felt as close as he had ever got to telling me he loved me.

What had been broken *had* to be mended. Somehow. And so little time.

Rebeca came across to me, dabbed at my tears with a tissue. She put her arms around me, her head resting on my shoulder. I seized on it gratefully as forgiveness. Another reunion.

The only sound was the almost inaudible hum of the air conditioning. Then the consultant, Doctor Fernandez – straight out of Central Casting, shirt-sleeved, prematurely grey, good looking – turned over the page in your grandfather's file laid out symmetrically in front of him on his uncluttered glass topped desk, the crisp rustle cutting across the murmur of the air conditioning.

"All the indications are good," he said finally. He spoke with clipped calm, a soft, to me slightly irritating purr. "Blood pressure, heart, urine output, liver, kidneys, all very sound. No trace of diabetes. Aside from the damage associated with the strokes he is a very healthy man."

I glanced across at Rebeca sitting on the chair next to mine, both of us facing him across his desk. She was looking resolutely at the floor. Anywhere but at him.

"Will he... Could he recover his power of speech?" I asked.

The blue eyes stared levelly at me. He was so professional, so polished I wanted to shake him.

"It is very unlikely. I would say impossible."

"So... what? You are saying he could live like this, in this state, for... Well, quite a long time?"

"I am."

The walls, my chair, my body lurched. I realised that without acknowledging it to myself I had assumed he could not now live for very long.

"For months?"

An arching of the eyebrows, a discreet tilt of the head.

"Another stroke might of course prove fatal. But otherwise your father could live for years."

"Years? You do mean years?"

"I do."

"But he does not want to live! My father wants to die!"

Fernandez stared back at me. Expressionless, but not unkind.

Rebeca's eyes still on the floor.

Looking back, I think I knew in that moment what I would have to do to mend what life had broken.

Setting about it was another matter. I couldn't – or, at least, I didn't – directly confront it, pick the word up (you see? I still find it hard to say) and stare at it saying this was what I was going to do. I focussed on the peripheries, the details, the execution. What had to be done before I could do it.

Which takes us to the heart of why all those weeks ago I began to write this account for you. (I have been writing it for myself as well, of course, but primarily it has been for you.) It certainly takes us to the hardest part. Harder than the stuff about Raul. By far. Harder for me, not so much to understand as, quite simply, to accept that I did it. It remains somewhere outside all terms of reference I have ever known. It happened, I know, I did it, but it involved quite another me. Which I think is how I operated.

Okay, this is how it was.

The first thing I had to do was be sure that he still wanted to die. When I was next on my own with him, I turned the volume down on the iPad and removed the plugs from his ears. His eyes opened irritably. I took his hand.

"I'd like to talk to you."

Still apparently truculent he stared ahead, not looking at me.

The three paintings were on the walls in front and to the side of him. Perhaps they could be a way in.

"Is it nice having them here?"

No response.

"I just thought you had taken the trouble to bring them from your house to the apartment, maybe they were important to you. Are you pleased?"

Again no response. For a long time. Then a gentle squeeze of my hand. Softening. Not wanting to hurt me?

"I'll take that as a yes, then, shall I? You like having some vaginas to look at?"

I caught myself by surprise. The wrong note? We hadn't had much practice being father and daughter. I watched him carefully. A grunt. Not angry. And was that a glint of a smile in his eyes? Seize it.

"I want to ask you something, Dad. I want you to tell me the truth. Is it better for you here than in the other place? Are you glad I brought you here?"

No response. Anger quickly displaced disappointment.

"Do you mean you would rather be back there? I am sure it could be arranged." I knew I was being childish.

Slowly, light dawned.

"Okay… Do you mean it is no better here than anywhere? That everywhere would be the same?"

Now a firm squeeze.

"Right. I think I understand. It is all terrible. Is that right?"

Squeeze.

I hesitated. Framed the question.

"Now answer this. You told me before that you had had enough and that you wanted to die. Is that still true?"

Instant squeeze.

"You're sure?"

Another.

"How about… It is just possible that you will regain your power of speech. If that happened would you still want to die?"

Now he hesitated. Then squeezed.

"I want that again, please, Dad. I want to be sure you are sure."

He squeezed my hand again. Even more firmly. At the same time his head turned to me, his eyes open. Clear, forceful, commanding. A look that will remain with me forever.

I stumbled a bit, had to clear my throat.

"Let's be sure again, shall we? You want to die as soon as possible?"

A squeeze. Followed by another. Getting irritated. Then his head flopped back on the pillow. Exhausted myself, I stood, kissed him on the forehead.

"I'll do what I can."

He had been in the clinic only two, maybe three days but it felt longer. Rebeca and I had organised ourselves on a rough shift system to be with him – not that he appeared to be very aware of us, whether lying in bed (usually with his iPad listening to music) or sitting in his armchair where the nurses often placed him after one of his therapy walkabouts. The major part fell reasonably enough to me as Rebeca had her own hospital shifts to do and I could bring my laptop into the Clinic, which had broadband access. We were both becoming familiar figures to the staff, Rebeca even helping with some of the nursing duties. It wasn't possible to talk very much when we did cross over. We were friendly enough but there was still a constraint, and the Clinic was the wrong place.

Which was why I invited her to breakfast at the hotel. She had been on night shift. I had stayed with him until maybe half past one when his breathing was steady and I was sure the sedatives had kicked in. Back at the hotel I didn't sleep much. Over breakfast in the dining room Rebeca and I talked generally – and still warily – about how he was doing. Then I suggested we took our coffee out onto one of the terraces. We found an empty one. It was still blessedly cool.

I lay back in the planter's chair, my coffee cup balanced on the broad wooden arm. I was very conscious of my sleepless night. Rebeca sat forward on the edge of her chair, hunched, her coffee cup held on her knees. I don't think she wanted the conversation any more than I did.

"Do you agree that he might live for a long time?"

She took her time.

"Is possible."

"The way he is now? Comatose, barely eating, not responding –"

"Because he does not *try*!" Cutting fiercely across the stillness of the terrace. Then she took a sip of her coffee to soften the moment.

"Isn't that the point?" I said, finding my footing again. "He's given up. He wants to die."

Again a silence. Then she shrugged. No point in disagreeing.

"And you still think he could live for years?"

"Yes. Very expensive for you. Thousands of dollars for many years."

She looked angry. Even mean. It was an expression I had not seen before.

I sat forward, craning across, trying to look her in the eye.

"It has nothing to do with that! Money isn't the issue! It's *wrong*, Rebeca! It isn't fair. He should not have to go through that!"

"What is fair?"

She still would not look at me but her face was softening. Regretful? I sensed withdrawal, even agreement.

"We could try and make it fair. We could do something. Couldn't we?"

She sat in rigid silence. I braced myself.

"Is there something you could give him? As a nurse you must have access to… something… that would help him on his way… peacefully… help him go… as he wants. His life is not a life, this so cruel! Please…"

"Nothing. I can do nothing."

I had hit rock. Solid Hippocratic rock. I reached out to touch her arm by way of acknowledgement.

"But you understand, don't you why I think It should happen? Even if you can't help? Why I think it is our – my – duty?"

She nodded. Barely perceptible.

"I am going to have to do it," I heard myself saying. "And now I am going to tell you what I have in mind so you will be able to warn the Clinic and they can call in the police and have me deported before I do. Is that fair enough?"

I had not planned this. It came from nowhere. But as I said it a wild hope flared that she would report me and that I would not have to go through with it. I would not have to kill my own father. I could go back to my fatherless life.

I waited. Finally, she spoke.

"Is what you always wanted."

I didn't understand.

"What?"

"To kill him. You say me you always want to kill him. Since you were a child."

It may seem odd but I had not made the connection. For a moment it left me winded.

"Yes, but… not… Now he wants to die. I want to help him. We call it mercy killing."

"You sure?"

"About what?"

"That is reason?"

I was so shocked I could not speak. Her face crumpled, she shook her head as though angry with herself.

"I don't mean, I don't mean…" She put her hand out, touched me. "Now is love. I know now is love."

"Then why –"

"Sorry. I am sorry."

She got up, knelt by my chair and put her arms around me. "You are right. You are brave. I am frightened, is all."

I was still angry. She went to sit down again. She looked so lost, so confused. So unlike her.

"All right," I said. I tried to keep my voice level. "I intend to smother him with a pillow. I shall suffocate him to death." My throat dried up. I had to swallow several times. "But I need you to tell me something. How will I know when he is dead? How long does it take? Do you know?"

Another perilous silence. She ran her tongue over her lips. She put her coffee cup down on the table in front of her. I thought she was going to get up and leave.

"Long time... Maybe four, five minutes..."

"Jesus..." I had no idea. I can't do it, I thought. I can't do that.

Rebeca was saying something.

"They will know. You call it mercy killing. We call it murder. You will be arrested."

I batted the word away, switched back to practicalities. I had been busy.

"On Thursdays there is an early flight to Mexico City. 6.45. If we both sit with him that night, they won't come near him – especially if you are there. Around 4.00 you can go outside and sleep – or pretend to sleep – on the sofa in the corridor outside his room. I will have checked out of my hotel, will have all my luggage in Reception. They will know that I am leaving and have decided to spend my last night with him. If Pepe is waiting for me at 5.00 then he can take me to the airport. When they come around at 7.00, they will find you asleep on the sofa and by the time they go in to him I will be in the air and beyond anybody's reach. Besides... won't they need to do a post mortem before they know?"

"May be. Maybe not. Maybe they know at once."

I hesitated. Then shook my head pushing the possibility away. I had cast myself and had to see the play out.

She got to her feet.

"I must sleep," she said. She bent down and kissed me. She seemed about to say something. Then stopped and walked away.

The unbearable silence in that white room. Just the two of us. I had turned off and removed the iPad. He hadn't appeared to notice.

"Please, Dad, open your eyes to show me you are listening..."

After a moment – truculently as ever – the lids flickered open staring implacably ahead. I took the hand that was resting on top of the sheet.

"I am going to do it. You know what I am talking about? But I want to be sure, absolutely sure this is what you want. Is it?"

Now his eyes softened, flicked across at me. He squeezed my hand.

"OK." I breathed carefully two or three times, preparing myself. "I am going to suffocate you with a pillow. You need to know it won't be very quick. It may take five minutes before you are completely gone though you will lose consciousness sooner than that. You may instinctively panic and fight me. I shall have to fight you back. I am telling you this in case you want to change your mind. Do you still want me to go ahead?"

No movement. He had changed his mind? Panic fought relief. Panic that it was going wrong. Relief that I would be spared.

"Does that mean you don't want to die?" my voice husky.

Now he shifted on the pillow trying to lift his head. He seemed distressed, making little moaning sounds. Suddenly I thought I understood.

"Is it because you are worried about me? That I will be arrested?"

The flailing stopped, his head relaxed. He squeezed my hand. I flooded with love, closer to him then than I could ever have imagined possible.

"It's all right. I have planned it. By the time anyone finds you I will be out of the country. There is no need to worry about me. Do you understand?"

He was still breathing heavily. A slight squeeze.

"OK. I'll ask you again before I do it but I want to be sure that at the moment you still are certain that you want to die. Is that the truth?"

A squeeze.

"Again, please, Dad. Do you want me to help you die?"

He did. Without any doubt at all.

My last escape route closed. Now there was nothing to stop me killing my father. Our pact. Before me a grey, granite wall of dread and fear. But also calm. I felt in that moment both loved and loving.

Chapter 26

Senor Suarez gave a little bow as he handed me back my credit card, folded into the hotel receipt. I fancied there may also have been a little click of the heels – I had been a pretty good customer, as the size of the bill attested – but that could have been my imagination. I reached out to shake his hand. I had long stopped thinking of him as a spy.

"Thank you for looking after me so nicely."

A rare smile – well, more half smile – as he took my hand.

"Please come back Senora. And I hope good recovery for your father."

That stopped me. But only briefly.

"I am sure he is in a very good place. I'll be back to see him when he is stronger. Hope you will be able to give me the same room."

My turn to smile charmingly. It was horribly easy. Maybe I should have been an actress.

As I turned to leave, I was aware that the hotel had become a place of safety. Home. I hesitated. But Miguel, beside me, bent to pick up my two suitcases and I followed him through the lobby for the last time heading for the familiar Datsun with the still dodgy passenger door.

I had particularly wanted Miguel to take me to the Clinic so I could say good-bye to him. He had assured me when I called that it was "no problem" to change his evening schedule so that he could do so. I wasn't convinced. I feared it may have given him some difficulties with his boss. But I was grateful. He understood – as did senor Suarez – that it was my plan to spend my last night with my father in the clinic before catching the early morning flight. Indeed, Miguel offered to come back at dawn and take me to Jose Marti Airport but I was able to explain how Rebeca's partner Pepe was already scheduled.

The offer was typical of Miguel. Nothing was a problem. He had been my companion on many, for me, momentous journeys. It seemed as though we knew each other well – perhaps better than in truth we did. I certainly felt a great tenderness for him as we drove the now familiar journey – for his tact, his silence, his love for his family, his belief in karma. Raul and Miguel. Both young Cuban men. From two different Cubas.

As we reached the Clinic and parked, he looked, I wanted to believe, a little sad. I gave him a bundle of dollars as usual, and he tucked them away without counting them. As usual. Maybe that was all it was, I thought. A dollar relationship. Perhaps that was all it could be between an American and a Cuban.

My need for friendship, his for dollars. But then I looked again at his face. Definitely sad.

I leaned across and kissed him on the cheek.

"Goodbye Miguel. And thank you again."

He said nothing for a moment, his body stiff. Embarrassment? Disapproval? Had the kiss crossed a boundary?

Then he turned to look at me.

"I have liked very much to drive with you. I hope all good for you. And for your papi."

This time I had no defence. Terror at what lay ahead of me suddenly overwhelmed me, blotting out the sky. Miguel was as near to a friend as I had. I didn't want to lie to him. For a moment I wanted to tell him that I planned to suffocate my father to death in a few hours, I wanted to share the burden, to hear him tell me it was all right. Instead I struggled with the passenger door, unable to trust myself to speak.

He got out of the car and hurried around the front to ease it open. He took my hand and helped me out. I kept my eyes on the ground in case a tear betrayed me.

He insisted on carrying my suitcases to Reception. Although the Clerk spoke good English Miguel gallantly took over the conversation ensuring that my luggage would be kept safely so I could collect it at 5.00 in the morning to go to the Airport. He knew I was distressed for some reason – maybe because I was saying goodbye to my sick father, which was indeed the truth, or part of it – and he wanted to help me. I liked feeling protected by him. I didn't want him to go. But with a gentle squeeze on my elbow he was gone down the wide elegant lobby out through the automatic doors and out of my life.

To my surprise I felt better. Alone I was tall again and strong. Smiling brightly, I paid the accumulated fees for the Clinic and – once again, effortlessly devious – added enough for a month in advance. Foxy, I thought.

Yes, keep thinking of it like that. A game.

It was after ten when I got to his room. Rebeca was already there, dozing in the armchair. She stirred. A sleepy, awkward smile. Your grandfather had his iPad in his ears, but looked as if he was asleep. I didn't want to get too close to him. I didn't really want to even look at him.

Rebeca and I stumbled our way around a few pleasantries. We didn't find a lot to talk about.

"Has he used the bathroom?"

"An hour ago, maybe."

"That's good. I'll try and get some sleep on the sofa in the corridor then, shall I?" I said. "You have an alarm? In case you sleep too?"

She briefly lifted an old-fashioned watch from the breast pocket of her uniform. It was on a chain safety-pinned just above the pocket. She tapped it.

"My old friend," she said.

"OK…" I smiled, trying to find a handrail for myself. I had the sensation of having moved outside my body. I began to feel a little giddy. The silence piled up. But there really was nothing that could be said. "Four o'clock then?"

She nodded, settling back in the armchair.

I glanced quickly at him. No movement. As though already dead. I tip-toed out.

As I settled on the sofa a Clinic nurse came down the corridor. She smiled, clearly expecting me. Rebeca had told me that she had explained our plan, that we would take it in turns to sit with the old man during the night and that they had agreed to leave us alone as it was my last chance to be with him for a while.

"Nurse Rebeca?" she asked, gesturing towards his door.

I nodded.

"My turn next," I said.

She smiled again, moved on.

To my relief I found myself plunging almost at once into a deep, untroubled sleep.

On the first bleep of the alarm on my cell phone I woke instantly, fresh and full of energy. Then, a moment later, a second, maybe half a second, as I focussed, a tsunami of horror flooded through me. What I was contemplating was completely beyond me.

Then I forced myself to sit up, tried to breathe deeply. It has to be done. The nightmare has to be lived out. Our pact. Something that at last I can do for him.

I heaved myself up on my feet, shook my head. I needed the bathroom. I made my way – each footstep an act of will – as quietly as possible to the visitor's lavatory along the corridor.

When I returned along the dim silent corridor, feeling thankfully calmer now, wanting to get on with it, or at least get it over, I opened his door quietly and went in.

Rebeca was already awake. She got to her feet at once.

"Is he still sleeping?" I whispered.

She nodded.

"OK. I'll take over, shall I? You get some sleep."

And that was that. She left me alone with him.

4.05. Pepe would not be there for nearly another hour. Mustn't do it too soon. If it takes five minutes, best to allow, say quarter of an hour. That means starting at 4.45. Oh, God. I hadn't thought it through clearly enough. I was going to have to spend nearly three-quarters of an hour here alone with him. The last three quarters of an hour of his life.

Has to be done. Simple as that. What he wants. Just a question of passing time. Time always does pass. Every second carries us on. Him. Me. Three quarters of an hour closer to my own death. Everyone's destination. He wants to go there now. Quite simple. Our pact. Mending what life broke.

Just do it.

Time to be passed first. Passing time before putting an end to time.

Movement in the bed. I turned, my heart jack-hammering. The dead stirring in their graves? The old man turning in his sleep. The not-quite-yet-dead.

Thirty-five more minutes to fill. Fast-forward. Imagine time slide by. Think the minutes gone. Pass. Pass. Pass. One, two, three, four, five, six, seven... Don't look at the watch. Not yet. It will pass. It is passing... Memories. Childhood with him? Dangerous? Through the study window with Mum, watching him leap out of the Land Rover, bound up the steps into the house, then his footsteps ringing on the tiled hall floor... One hand on the piano, face glistening with sweat, glaring at the applause... Why did he glare so? And where was it? Wigmore Hall? Queen Elizabeth? That half bow, grudging, impatient to be... where? Somewhere else, certainly. Cuba, perhaps. In bed with a woman other than my mother. My father. Yes. Not this shrivelled, inert sad, angry... body. It is time. He has already gone. Grey faced, barely breathing. Such a fragile line. Our pact. Our pact of love. One, two, three four five, six...

Twenty-five minutes. There – I have looked. It *is* passing. But slowly. And so long still to go. Jesus, I want it to be over. I want it so very, very much to be over. I am more frightened than I can ever remember being. This room is airless, like a coffin. I want to get out of here.

His paintings. The curling tree bark as labia. The tunnelled wave, the white crest a pearly clitoris. Why do men hunger for this sometimes inconvenient... body part? Where we menstruate, urinate? I've never hungered for the penis. Not just to look at it. But for him, for my father – for all men? most men? – a lifetime of hunger. Frequently fed, never satisfied? Now? Surely not. *"Today I fuck Maria, I fuck Liset, I fuck Zully..."* Peace now for him? Or just a void?

That little wizened face with its paper-thin eyelids. So still. Almost there.

Time. Yes.

If I stick my head through the curtain and use it to mask out the reflection of the light above his bed on the glass in the window, I can see Havana by night. Or, rather, early morning. A nightscape? Is that the right word? Although the air conditioning makes the room quite cool you can feel it is hot out there, even now. Or do I just know it is hot? The light itself is warm, mainly amber, and spread haphazardly across the city, with large patches – as seen from up here – apparently in darkness, A low roof line for the most part so you can see a long way. Streets visible in the gaps, the only movement the headlights of a few early-rising, late-sleeping vehicles, mostly trucks and buses. Restful, unthreatening, from up here silent. Not like New York. The white-hot furnace of the Manhattan night sky line, strobing, insomniac, beating to the inescapable, screaming match of car horns and sirens. One my father's world, the other mine.

No sound from outside. Nor from inside. I rested my cheek against the glass. Rest on his world, I told myself. Float on the amber. Think of nothing. Time will pass.

When I next looked at my watch I went cold, momentarily disbelieving. Only five minutes. How did that happen? Time *has* gone.

And the time has come.

I started to shake.

Was I actually going to be able to do it? Could I take life – with my hands, flesh on flesh, family flesh on family flesh – from the man who gave me mine? It would be so easy, such an immeasurable relief to walk away now, to leave it undone. Just go. Now. Wait for Pepe. Catch the flight. Let him go. What pact?

Then suddenly I went cold. I had overlooked something. Something so obvious. And if I, a lawyer, could make such a stupid, elementary mistake what else might I have forgotten?

Quietly I opened the door into the corridor. Rebeca was lying on the sofa. She sat up fast when she heard the door and looked around her eyes wide with fright, as though startled by a ghost.

"I need you," I whispered.

She shrank back, shook her head.

"It's all right – not to do anything," I said. "Nothing has happened yet. I need you to witness his decision."

She shook her head again, turned away. I reached for her.

"Please Rebeca. You've got to do this."

I took her hand. Not resisting now, she got to her feet and followed me. I closed the door behind us and went over to sit by his bedside. Feeling braver now that I was not alone, I took his shoulder and gently shook it. It was the first time that I had touched him that night. *Flesh on flesh.* His skin was shockingly warm, shockingly alive through the material of his pyjama top.

"Dad… I want you to wake up… Dad!"

His eyes opened. Perhaps he had not been asleep at all? If so where had he been? Where did he ever go in those long wakeful silences? Drifting through his life? Floating? Willing himself to die? He turned to look at me. I may have imagined it but he seemed to stare deep into me as though he knew what was happening. I took his hand.

"It's time, Dad." And I thought – how banal, how inadequate. What does 'time' mean to him? He is lying there – enduring. Waiting to go. 'Time' is for me. The threads of our lives have come together at this point for ME to act. It is me that shall have to live with this. It is my time that has come. For him time is – almost – over. "If you still want me to, I am going to do it now – just as we discussed. But I have to be sure. So please, just once more – if you want me to help you die now squeeze my hand."

He looked at me steadily as his hand closed firmly around my fingers.

I heard a sound behind me and turned to see Rebeca leaving the room. She closed the door.

And now the door was closed on me. I took myself somewhere. I don't know exactly where. I was on the stage. I knew my lines.

"OK. You know what is going to happen. I am going to put a pillow over your face so it will be impossible for you to breathe. You'll probably get a bit panicky but you will lose consciousness before very long and it won't be painful. Before I do it, I want to say something to you. You are an extraordinary man who has lived an extraordinary life and have given a great deal to very many people and although you have been a lousy father, I have learned to love you and I am doing this because I love you. Do you understand?"

I had removed my hand from his. Now I saw his fingers clutching at air. I put my hand back. He squeezed. I think – though I can't be sure – he smiled at me. I know my eyes filled – his face became blurry – but I managed to blink them away quickly. I had a job to do.

"Now – I've got to take one pillow from behind you."

I stood, lifted his head carefully, eased out the top pillow, then laid him back down.

Then suddenly I thought of something else I had not planned for. But this time it was a good thought.

His I-Pad was on his bedside cabinet. I picked it up, fiddled with the dial control until I found his playlist. Raul had downloaded three Beethoven tracks. I chose the Eroica. I put the plugs in his ears and settled the console on his chest.

"Your man," I told him. "Ludwig. A good companion."

I felt light and clear headed as I climbed onto the bed, the pillow in my hand. I straddled his chest trying not to put weight on him. He kept his eyes closed. I was grateful.

"I love you, Dad. Find peace."

With one hand I clutched the pillow across my chest, with the other I pressed 'play'. I was utterly calm. Something – adrenaline? – making me light headed. I waited until I felt sure the music had kicked in. Again it may have been my imagination but I thought I saw it in his face, a little tremble of the eyelids, a slackening of the jaw. I even fancied I heard those two big percussive notes, tinny, fluttering like two little midges escaping from his ears. Then, holding the pillow in both hands, I placed it over his face and pressed.

At first stillness. Which went on. I began to panic. Maybe there is a technique, I don't know how to do it. I pressed harder, making sure my weight fell either side of his face so I did not hurt him. I found I was breathing heavily with the exertion. I wasn't sure I would be able to keep it up for five minutes. One, two, three, four, five, six... I couldn't do it! I forced my arms down. I could hear myself starting to whimper. Go, Dad, just go. I love you but go, go, go –

And then he started to fight, and I was fighting back. I felt his frail torso lift in spasm under my thighs, his head flailing – or trying to – under the pillow. I pushed down even more with my arms, clamped his chest with my thighs and knees. We bucked grotesquely on that bed, the act of killing obscenely miming love, father and daughter, as I tried to force death down his face, my breath coming in gasps, tears pouring down my cheeks.

I have no idea how long the battle lasted. Minutes? Seconds? I just became aware that he was thrashing less and with less strength, though occasionally there was another whole-body spasm as the man who longed to die could not stop himself fighting for life. Finally, all movement stopped and his body became not limp but rigid, or so it felt under the bed sheets. I continued – still panting – to press down because I had no idea how long it had gone on whether we were anywhere near Rebeca's five minutes and I could not stop, I had to see it through

186

to the end. I felt nothing from him now, just total inertia but I continued to lean forward pressing my weight down on the pillow, tears blurring my vision. In the still silence of the room nothing but my shivering, panting breath.

Total stillness now. He must have gone. How long had it been? Leaning an elbow across the centre of the pillow I looked at my wrist watch. I would stay in place for two more minutes.

Surely gone now. Father no more. Nothing between me and the sky. My young father – keep pressing down, can't make a mistake – leaping out of Land Rovers, taking bows. Full of life. Now no life at all. – Stay… Stay… Oh God I can't do this – One, two, three, four five… A glance at the watch. Ten seconds short of two minutes. I counted them out.

I sat up, the pillow still over his face.

I couldn't bring myself to remove it. I was still panting. Now I started to tremble. To shake. What if he was still alive? When I took the pillow off would he be staring at me, his eyes popping, a body coming to life in its coffin? Murderer. I had murdered my father.

My arms leaden, I forced myself to lift the pillow.

He wasn't there. The relief. My stomach sagged, winded. His dear, fragile, tired face, sideways on the pillow. But not him. I stopped trembling. Tears – of sadness, certainly, but also a kind of peace, flowed down my cheeks, unchecked.

I climbed carefully off the bed. Then, raising his limp head put the pillow under it. I took the plugs out of his ears, turned the machine off and returned it to his bedside cabinet. I adjusted the position of his head, I was aware as I did so how calm I felt, how easy it was to do now and how strange it was. Then I tidied his hair, which had become badly mussed – more than usual – and finally straightened the sheets.

I had done it. He was gone, completely gone. Where he wanted to be. Enduring no more.

4.55. Pepe should be waiting. Everything going well. I went into the bathroom, leaned over the basin, splashing water over my face and ran a comb through my hair. I looked just the same in the mirror. A little tired maybe but the same gawky, square jawed self I had contemplated – reluctantly – in mirrors for very many years. But of course I was not the same and never would be again.

Despite feeling so calm I realised I had started to tremble again. I went back into the room, collected my hand bag from the armchair, checked automatically that my ticket and passport were in place. I gave him a last look – a brief one, he was gone, it was done – and let myself out into the corridor.

The light was dim. Rebeca was asleep on the sofa – or appeared to be. Something made me decide not to wake her. For what, I asked myself? I tip-toed to the head of the stairs and went quietly down them.

The desk in Reception was unmanned. For a moment panic flared again. This had not been in the plan. Had there been some alarm? Christ, was there CCTV in every room? Were they up there resuscitating him? Had the Police been called?

I saw my two suitcases against the wall behind the desk. Telling myself off for being melodramatic I picked them up and wheeled them to the exit. The sliding doors were closed. I pressed the button on the wall. They opened silently, letting in a waft of warm air and I stepped out into the dark. The doors slid closed, equally silently, behind me.

Safe?

But there was no sign of Pepe. I peered into the darkness. Nothing. Once again panic began to simmer. The doors behind me would open, hands would reach out and seize me, dragging me away. *"My Eumenides…"* I remembered his voice on the tape. That voice no more. And the Eumenides mine. I would not be safe until I was on that aeroplane. Behind me my dead father's spirit, and the demons of retribution. Ahead, no sanctuary but the alien Cuban night. A fatherless child alone in the dark.

Then out of that same warm Cuban night came Pepe. He smiled – and you cannot imagine how comforting that smile was – then silently collected my suitcases. I followed him down the ramp to his car parked in the shadows by the curb.

Surely safe now? The old man was where he needed to be. I had mended what life had broken. Leave it all behind. It was done. And it was good that it had been done.

I got into the back of the car. Pepe's English was little better than my Spanish and I didn't want to talk. I sunk into the seat letting the amber shadows of the Havana night flicker past numbingly. I realised I was shivering. Pepe must have realised it too.

"Is OK?" he said over his shoulder.

I nodded.

His white face on the pillow, still and empty.

You always want to kill him. Since you were a child.

Rebeca on the terrace, staring out at the neatly patterned paths and wiry grass of the Nacional gardens. *The Clinic will cost you many thousands of dollars, maybe for many years… You always want to kill him. And you save money.* The mariposa in the morning sun. Her voice without expression.

The vomit rose, sluicing into my throat. I grappled for the door handle, my hand over my mouth. Pepe was braking. We were still moving, just, as I retched clear bile onto the road, my head hanging out of the door, leaving a sticky, patchy trail as the car came to a halt.

In the stillness my stomach heaved again. I croaked noisily but could fetch nothing up. I was panting. My mouth tasted foul. Still shivering I sat up, aware that Pepe was watching me anxiously from the front seat.

"Sorry…" I swallowed, gathering saliva. "OK now… Please, airport…"

Still looking understandably doubtful, but with that wary acceptance of a man who knows that women sometimes have problems that it is not for men to enquire into he put the car into gear and we moved on.

Exhausted, I sat back, closed my eyes and tried to sleep. The engine droned, time passed. Possibly only minutes. It is possible I had not properly closed my eyes, only half closed. Or the change of rhythm as Pepe slowed down made me open them. Or it was the screeching sound of brakes from the blue truck approaching on the other side of the road that alerted me. The screech was followed immediately by a bang, a metallic thud louder, it seemed, than the brakes (or that is how I remember it) as fender hit body and the boy, vest and shorts, legs and arms flailing, made a slow parabola through the air as the other boy, the one who I knew at once had been chasing the flying boy – now, I remember thinking, almost certainly the dead boy – was turning away and running back up the side street from which they had been sprinting – in anger? competition? fear? at any rate very fast – slap into the path of the blue truck doing probably thirty miles an hour and weighing I would guess several hundred times that of the boy whose arms and legs seemed to stop flailing as he reached the top of his arc and dropped fast, an inanimate, discarded item, onto the tarmac of the empty, now still and silent street. The truck was still. Our car was still. The boy was still. Even the escaping boy had disappeared into the shadows of the side street. For a moment, a tableau.

Now Pepe was scrambling out of his car as the truck driver, too, climbed down. Both men ran – pointlessly I was sure, and I think they must have been as well, but you do, you have to – towards the bundle on the street. They reached it together and bent over. Now it was the truck driver's turn to vomit, turning away on all fours. Pepe stood, took out his cell and dialled.

I sat, frozen. What was happening – *if* it was happening – had no frame. My father's dead, white face on the dead, white pillow. An old man. Twenty minutes ago? And now a dead boy falling from the sky. A young boy. How could it be? One death sought, the other random. A dream? If so, my father's death, or the boy's? It was celluloid, a performance, but this one not involving me, a passage of incomprehensible chaos, lives ending, destinies concluded. Was there a connection? Meaning? Would their two spirits released within minutes, a few blocks from each other, in some mystical way comingle? What was happening?

Nothing. Not madness, no connection, no meaning. Twenty minutes ago, I killed my father. Now a boy I had never seen had been killed in a road accident. There was no frame. It had happened, no more than that.

I needed to get to the airport. Very urgently.

Pepe was walking back to the car.

"I call Police," he said, leaning down to my window. "And Ambulance. I must wait."

Panic flared.

"I've got to catch that flight Pepe! I must!"

Of course he had to wait, I knew that. But I had to be at the airport.

"Can you call me another taxi on your cell?"

"They come quickly. I must wait."

He stood and walked back to join the truck driver now smoking by the shrunken bundle on the tarmac, resolutely not looking at it. A few early morning cars and cyclists slowed down as they passed. One driver crossed himself.

189

If I missed that flight I would be arrested. I was shivering in the warm early morning air, breath coming in short stabs. This isn't me, I told myself. I don't panic. But none of this was me, I had not been me for so long. A rivulet of sweat trickled down between my breasts. I had to get on that flight. I would not be safe until I was on that aeroplane.

I urgently needed to urinate. I looked around for a tree, a low wall, small garden, any piece of privacy. None.

I got out of the car and called across to Pepe. He came warily towards me.

"Toilet… I need toilet. Can we go somewhere, a public toilet or something, and then, maybe, come back?"

His mouth tightened. He looked around. Then he took my arm and led me to the kerb side of the car. The placid Pepe now firmly in charge. He opened the front and rear doors. Looking a little embarrassed he indicated the space between them, which I could see – below window level – offered privacy of a kind on three sides; the fourth being the pavement on which he positioned himself, his back to me, a discreet distance away to keep guard and divert any pedestrians. A trick of Rebeca's? I started to laugh. Another first. In this surreal, nightmarish night of firsts. I squatted against the sill of the door adding embarrassing and surprisingly copious quantities of pee to the vomit I had already deposited further back on the streets of Havana.

I hadn't finished when I heard the sirens. Everything contracted. Now this American lawyer, mother of two, was going to be arrested for urinating in the streets. Still laughing – but now not out loud – I pelvic floored my way to an uncomfortable, premature finish and struggled into my knickers, trying to keep my head down while the all-invasive blue light was flickering on me accusingly, lighting up my hiding place. I ducked into the car, and shut the doors.

I watched the Police and Ambulance pull up either side of the boy's body. I had just brought my father's life to an end. Those people out there would no doubt say I had murdered him. And I was worrying about peeing in the streets? I started to laugh again.

Pepe had gone across the still quiet street and was talking to them. I watched from the car, shivering. I closed my eyes. I was going to miss the flight. What then? It was out of my hands. I cut off.

Then suddenly Pepe was leaning into my window and a policeman was in front of the car by the hood looking at me. I pushed open the door and hurried past Pepe to the policeman, driven I realised by a need to keep him away from the drying remnants – possibly even the smell – of my urine in the gutter.

"Hola!" I said. He didn't reply. I wished I hadn't spoken. Why was I so at ease in a courtroom but abject in front of a policeman on the street? Pepe materialised at my side.

"I say him what I see," he said. "I say him you American woman, must go to Jose Marti now. He want see passport."

Oscillating, as I had been doing all night, between fear and calm I went – calm now – to collect my hand bag off the floor of the car taking from it my passport and ticket.

I was silent as I passed them to him. I felt strong in the shield of my American citizenship, not a killer at his mercy. He glanced at my photograph, flicked his torch in my face. Then he handed them both back. Muttering something to Pepe he turned and retraced his steps to where the Ambulance men were lifting the boy's bagged body into the back of their vehicle.

"We go," said Pepe, climbing quickly into the driver's seat as though anxious that the Police would not change their minds. I followed, stepping carefully over the now almost invisible evidence. The car was already moving before I shut my door. I looked at my watch. 5.45. One hour.

"How long to Jose Marti?" I asked.

"No problem," he said. But he was driving fast, looking all the time in his rear-view mirror for more police.

It was 6.10 as we pulled into the drop zone. It was quiet at that time of the morning. Pepe jumped out and grabbed my two suitcases from the trunk. I followed. We ran into the building. He knew exactly which desk to head for. There was a small line. The gate was still open?

"You see?" panted Pepe over his shoulder, smiling now as he ran. "I tell you – no problem."

There were two couples in front of us. Pepe spoke to the nearest. They smiled calmly as they replied. He turned to me.

"Is OK. They say Mexico City also."

I was still breathing heavily but less so. Maybe I was safe. I would get the flight and be gone leaving everything behind. Erased. 6.15. Half an hour. Why was that clumsy woman on her knees taking so long to repack her suitcase?

Pepe's cell went off noisily, startling me. He glanced at the window, looking briefly puzzled.

"Rebeca," he said, as he put it to his ear. I watched, mildly anxious. Why had she called him? He looked up at me, then moved away. Why? I could not understand anything even if I could hear.

There was only one couple to go.

I was at the head of the line when he returned. He was not looking at me as he put the cell in his pocket.

"I must take her to Hospital. She work. I say goodbye now."

He turned away and scuttled off. I watched in bewilderment.

"Senora!"

The woman behind the check-in desk was beckoning to me. I stepped forward gratefully, letting Pepe's, at that moment only mildly puzzling behaviour disappear with him.

The woman spoke good English. She even smiled as she took my luggage, checked me in and printed out my pass. 6.20.

"No problem," she assured me.

I hurried to security, passport and boarding pass in my hand, feeling light headed. It was going to work.

The uniform in the booth – a middle-aged woman, bespectacled, black – made no effort to return my smile. She stared at my passport as though studying for an exam. She called another uniform over – a man. I started to simmer uneasily. Had there been a phone call from the hospital? The man studied my passport equally grimly, then placed it under the counter. His hands glowed with the reflected light of the machine reading my passport number. I struggled to keep calm. Then he handed it briskly back, without looking at me and stepped away. The woman nodded cursorily over my shoulder to the next in the line behind me. I moved on to the screening area trying desperately not to look as relieved as I felt.

Fifteen minutes before the scheduled take off. There was a substantial line of people waiting, coats and shoes off, belts in hand. No time for punctiliousness. I pushed past them, scattering apologies and showed the first uniform I could find my boarding pass. I feared another grim-faced official who would tell me to get back in line.

"No problem," he said with a smile, and took me to the conveyor belt, gesturing for my hand bag (cell, jewellery and coins hastily pushed inside) and shoes. As they trundled along the rollers, he took me to the to the metal detection screen – politely displacing the man waiting. For once I passed through without a bleep. As I collected my handbag and hopped one-legged into my shoes, he waved me on my way gesturing at the right direction for my gate. I waved back warmly, my faith in Cuban humanity rollercoastering back.

Seven minutes to go. So nearly there. But then as I rounded a corner with one other scurrying passenger, there at the top of a ramp was another clutch of grim-faced uniforms at a desk. For some reason I knew – I absolutely knew – that this was where I was going to be stopped and taken away. I approached with dread. Again my passport required intensive scrutiny. Again it was fed into the machine under the counter. Now there was a muttered conference. I settled myself to wait for the inevitable. Consequences had to be faced. I had always known that. I felt resigned, sad, like losing a case. The plan had been so solid. The breakfast round was at 7.00. Still twenty minutes to go. And then their first assumption would be that he died naturally. Why not? What had gone wrong?

My Eumenides. Consequences had to be faced.

Then my passport was handed back to me and I was gestured in to the now deserted seating area at the gate. Dazed, I walked across it, along the corridor, down steps and through the hooded cowl into the aeroplane.

A friendly stewardess showed me to my seat, fetched me a glass of water – I realised I had eaten nothing – and I settled back, calm seeping into me. It was over. I had done what needed to be done, had mended, as best I could, what life had broken. I had returned my father to me and me to my father. I closed my eyes.

The cabin doors shut, the engines started up. I think I might have dozed.

I was vaguely aware that the doors had opened again. A passenger even later than me?

But it was policemen.

And I knew – of course – that they had come for me.

Consequences had to be faced after all.

Were always going to have to be faced.

I watched, floating calmly, as they talked to the stewardess. She took a clipboard out of a plastic pocket hanging on the bulkhead and consulted it. Then she put it back, walked down the aisle followed by the two policemen and stopped beside me. I didn't wait for them to say anything. I undid my safety belt and got to my feet.

I knew in that moment what I think I had been fearing, even expecting, but did not want to believe. I knew why Rebeca had called Pepe at the airport.

Chapter 27

And that is about it.

I gather my story has caused quite the splash not just in the States but in many parts of the world. I know it must have been, to say the least, tough for you both. That is why I have written this. My side. To explain why your mother is in a Cuban jail, without at present any prospect of release, on charges of incest and patricide.

There. I have written it down.

I hope – if this ever reaches you and you want to read it – you may see it how I see it. A story of love. And that you may think kindly of me. Though of course I realise that may be asking too much of you.

I do know – it is a deep, cold terror that keeps me awake at night – that I may have lost you forever.

There is not much else I can say and very little else to tell you. The mystery remains and may never be solved. Who told the police? I do not know for certain that it was Rebeca. We were friends, more than friends. She knew what I was doing, she did not try to stop me. So why? But who else?

What I believe happened, my imagined scenario, is that she was awake when I left. She waited until she could take it no longer, went in to see him and just snapped. Why not? She had so many reasons. She called a nurse. Maybe Rebeca didn't say anything. Just a look. *The Senora has gone to the airport.* A look. Enough. I think that's what happened. But one way or another it had to be her. How else would the police have known about Raul? She was the only one who knew.

I don't blame her, really I don't. I am a rich American and she hates America. I betrayed her Revolution by putting the old man in a private Clinic. And most important of all I took both her husband and her son from her. Not that I saw it like that at the time. The thought of Raul going to prison was unbearable. And my father wanted his *quietus.* I did what I thought was best. But I should have known that might be how she would think of it. Poor Rebeca.

She has not been to see me. I've tried getting messages to her but no response. One of the wardresses showed me the newspaper photograph of her and Fidel's successor, his brother at your grandfather's funeral. That was quite something. A Castro coming out to honour the old man. A wonderful slap in the face for his enemies. Rebeca, Fidel, his brother, my father, revolutionaries, '*Historicos*' to the end.

I would so like her to come and see me. She helped me learn to love. And for that – and many reasons – I loved her.

So. Life here is what it is. We're in the Immigration Wing in the Castillo del Morro. All foreign prisoners are sent here, apparently. Gloria is a democracy activist and has been involved in linking Venezuelan cells with Cuban ones. She thinks she may be in for some time. Her resilience is remarkable. And her affection, which is a great strength to me. Although I realise in the world's eyes I am an Outcast and Evil, she is helping me think there may be advantages in being the new me. She insists that I only discovered love in Cuba, that I had buried it as a child when my father left us. I think she is probably right.

That means that I know now how much I love you both, however inadequately I showed it when you were growing up and that one day you may learn to love me as out here I learned to love my monstrous father, my wholly unreliable half-brother and the stepmother who in the end betrayed me.

With love from your mother.

Editorial Post Script

Following the historic resumption of diplomatic relations between Cuba and the United States brokered by Pope Francis and signed off by President Obama and Raul Castro a prisoner release programme was agreed and in time Maggie Barrington was returned to the States. As no offence had been committed in her native jurisdiction she faces no charges.

Mrs Barrington has sold her house in Montclair and now lives in an apartment in Hoboken. She has resigned from her legal practice and is taking on projects in the not-for-profit sector.

She reports that she and her sons are working on rebuilding their relationship.

END